# A TRAIL OF DESTRUCTION

## DEBRA ISON

# ACKNOWLEDGMENTS

This book would not have come into being without the ongoing support of my faithful readers. I am humbled by their kind appreciation of my work. Sarah, Sam, and Mac have become almost as real to them as to me.

My faithful friend and editor Carolyn Nemeth has, as usual, been a source of encouragement and inspiration. As we discuss the characters and the plot, we have discovered an endless list of ways to get our protagonists in (and out) of trouble. Carolyn's only complaint when I send her pages to read and edit, is that I seem to stop writing right in the middle of a crisis!

The issue of human trafficking is all too common in most of our communities. I hope that in some small way this book will raise awareness of the challenge we all face in eradicating this problem. Those in my community who work tirelessly to help women and girls trapped in this lifestyle were an inspiration to me in writing this book.

Finally, I want to thank my very patient husband for his encouragement and support. He keeps me focused when I am tempted to set my writing aside. Thank you, Ken, for always being there for me. You are my rock.

I would be remiss if I didn't acknowledge the law enforcement agencies that face terrible situations every day and keep us safe. Thank you for your faithful service.

The characters and events portrayed in this book are fictitious. Any similarity to persons, living or dead, is coincidental and not intended by the author.

Cover:  Todd Thurman

# Table of Contents

# One

Rebecca Dorland put the finishing touches on her makeup, turned out the bathroom light, and walked down the hallway to her kitchen. A glance at the clock on the wall assured her that she had time to eat a piece of toast with her morning coffee.

In her role as Chief Nursing Officer of the local hospital, her day would be busy, with two morning meetings and an afternoon dedicated to reviewing applications and conducting interviews. The position of Director of Nursing had been open for a month and needed to be filled soon. None of the candidates interviewed so far had been a good fit, but Becca was confident the right person would be found eventually.

With a final gulp of coffee, Becca stacked her dirty dishes in the sink, grabbed her purse and portfolio, and headed out the front door. Her apartment did not include off street parking, but she had been lucky the evening before and had found a parking spot under a tree near her building. As she approached her car, she passed her neighbor, Mrs. Crawford, and her dog Benny. Becca exchanged greetings with them as she passed. She pulled car keys from her purse but was surprised to find the car unlocked. She lifted the handle of the passenger side door, intending to drop her belongings on the seat. Once unlatched, however, the door pushed open and a woman's body fell onto the sidewalk. Becca's gasp caused Mrs. Crawford to turn around and, upon seeing the dead body; she pierced the cool autumn air with her screams.

Becca stood motionless as she stared at the body lying at her feet. The woman's eyes were open and seemed to return her gaze. With a shudder, she turned away. As a nurse, she had seen many dead bodies, but having one fall out of her car was definitely a new experience! With trembling hands, she reached into her purse for her cell phone and dialed 911.

The local police department received the call at 7:40 A.M. The responding patrolman was on the scene very quickly and managed the situation until the homicide detectives arrived twenty minutes later. The two men pushed their way through the crowd that had gathered to join the patrolman standing guard over the dead body. Officer Meeks was trying to shield the view of the dead woman as best he could, but the shocked responses of onlookers indicated his efforts had not been successful.

Detectives Tom Warfel and Drew Samuels approached the patrolman. Detective Warfel, a tall man with graying hair, took the lead. "Good morning, officer; what do we know so far?"

The patrolman consulted a small notepad before responding. "According to the owner of the car, Ms. Rebecca Dorland, the body fell out of the passenger side of the vehicle when she opened the door. Ms. Dorland states she has no idea as to the identity of the deceased. The call came in at approximately 7:40 A.M."

Detective Warfel absorbed the information before asking, "Is there any obvious cause of death?"

The patrolman was quick to answer. "No sir; There is a small amount of blood on the passenger door, but I'm not sure of the source. I've not touched the body since I arrived. Ms. Dorland claims she doesn't know the deceased and she hasn't touched the body."

Detective Warfel asked, "Where is Ms. Dorland? Maybe she now remembers something that might help us."

10

"She went back to her apartment to make some phone calls. She said she had to cancel some meetings at work."

"Okay, thanks. Drew will you stay here with the body until the medical examiner comes?" Drew nodded. As the junior partner, Drew Samuels deferred to Warfel's seniority. "I'll find Ms. Dorland and see what she has to say."

Detective Warfel found Becca's apartment quickly on the first floor of the four-plex. He pressed the doorbell and heard a weak "come in." He turned the knob and stepped into a small foyer. The apartment was tastefully decorated, with thick brocade curtains, custom made for the windows. Coverings from the same brocade material adorned the pillows on the light gray couch. Several good antique pieces were placed artfully around the room as if they had been made for their locations. Ms. Dorland was sitting on the couch clutching a cup of coffee in her trembling hands. She looked up as Warfel entered, but didn't speak. The detective used the silent moments to size up Rebecca Dorland. She was an attractive brunette with a trim figure that she showcased in designer clothing. Her eyes still held the terror of seeing a dead woman fall out of her car.

"Ms. Dorland, I'm Detective Warfel from the Braxton Police Department. I'd like to ask you a few questions; may I come in?"

Becca's brain was slow to translate the request, but she finally nodded in response. "Detective, please sit down. I'm sorry to seem rude, but I'm quite shaken at the moment."

Warfel entered the comfortable living room and took a chair near Becca. "I understand, ma'am; anyone would be upset under the circumstances." The detective gave the upset woman a few more moments to compose herself.

Becca attempted a smile, but it lasted only a brief moment before being reclaimed by the shock still surging through her body. "Would you care for a cup of coffee? I just made a fresh pot. I needed it to get warm again; I feel cold all over."

"Coffee would be most welcome at this early hour, thank you. I can get it myself if that would be of any help."

"If you like. The cups are in the cabinet over the sink."

Tom Warfel entered the nearly pristine kitchen. The granite countertops were wiped clean except for the area surrounding the coffee pot. Ground coffee had been spilled on its way to the coffeemaker. The bag of coffee was still open and lying on its side, an indication of Ms. Dorland's agitation when she made the fresh pot. He retrieved a cup and poured coffee for himself and rejoined Becca in the living room. She was still holding her coffee but was not drinking it. Instead, she was staring into the brown liquid as if she would discover in its depths that this was all a dream from which she would soon awake.

Warfel resumed his seat and took a sip of his coffee while studying the woman sitting across from him. Becca Dorland was staring at the floor and seemed to be unaware of his presence. He waited to speak until she looked up at him. "Ms. Dorland, I'm sure this has been a terrible shock, but I need to ask you a few questions. Are you up to it?"

Becca placed her hardly touched coffee on the table in front of her and looked up at the detective. She answered with an unsteady voice. "Yes, I understand. Ask me anything you want." With an effort, Becca sat up straighter and took a deep breath. She knew she must face this sooner or later.

"Thank you; now the patrolman outside tells me you didn't know the deceased?"

"That's correct; I've never seen her before—at least I don't think so. People can look so different once they die, but I don't believe I know her."

"A very thoughtful answer. Have you seen many dead bodies then?"

Becca gave a small laugh, "I guess I should have told you that I am a nurse. Yes, I have seen my share of death in my eighteen-year career."

"I see. I know you gave a statement to the patrolman outside, but I would like to go over that again. What time did you discover the body?"

"It was about 7:30 A.M. I needed to be at work by eight for a meeting, so it must have been around that time."

"So, you left your apartment around seven-thirty, walked to your car, and then what?"

Becca gave a wry laugh, "Then I opened the passenger door of my car and got the shock of my life! It isn't every day that one finds a dead body in one's car, Detective," she added with a note of disdain in her voice.

Warfel nodded in sympathy but continued his query. "Was your car locked?"

Becca thought for several moments before answering, "It wasn't, though I thought I had locked it yesterday when I arrived home. I rarely forget to lock my car, but yesterday I had my arms full of groceries and may have neglected to lock it."

13

The detective noted the response in his notebook. "Do you have any idea why someone would place a dead body in your car, ma'am?"

"I can't imagine! I don't believe I have any what you might call *real* enemies, although I'm sure some of the staff of Braxton Regional Hospital aren't overly fond of me. I'm the Chief Nursing Officer there, and my decisions are not always popular. It comes with the territory I'm afraid. There are always difficult choices to make in my line of work."

"What about your personal life? Have you had any disputes lately?"

"Nothing of any consequence. The dry cleaners ruined a silk blouse last week, and the neighbor upstairs complained about the noise when I had a carpenter repair a closet door that was sticking. Neither disagreement escalated to any degree of enmity, I assure you."

Warfel made an entry on his notepad. "What about family? Any problems there?"

"My father is deceased, my mother lives in Colorado with her third husband, and my only sibling, a sister, lives here in Braxton with her perfect husband and three perfect children. I get along with my family as well as anyone, I suppose."

The detective noted the cynicism in the narrative but refrained from exploring the cause for now. Instead, he asked, "Have you ever been married, Ms. Dorland?"

"A rather personal question, isn't it, Detective?" Warfel didn't answer, but simply waited for the answer. "Yes, many years ago. It lasted only three years before we decided to quit trying to salvage what wasn't working and divorced. I decided to return to my maiden name after the divorce. We have one son. He lives with

14

his father in Louisville. When he turned fifteen, we thought it best for him to have more male influence in his life. He was becoming a handful, and his father felt he could forestall any progression of the behavior he was exhibiting at the time."

"Such as?"

Becca wondered why the detective would need to explore her family so closely, "Why do you ask? Is it necessary for the investigation? I did not kill that poor woman, and I have no idea who she is, so why do you need to know anything about my family?"

Warfel sensed the rising emotion in Becca and decided to go in a different direction, "Have you lived here long?"

Becca had been prepared to defend her family's privacy and was caught off guard by the question. "I've been in this apartment for four years, if that's what you're asking. I've lived in Braxton all my life." Becca regained some control over her emotions and assumed a more assertive demeanor. "Detective, if you are finished with your coffee and your questions, I need to get to work now. Leave your card; I'll call you if I think of anything else that might be useful." Becca reached into her purse sitting next to her on the couch. "Here is my card with my direct office number. If I don't answer, just leave a message with Betsy, my assistant, and I'll call you back."

It was a firm dismissal and Tom could see the businesswoman persona take over the formerly frightened single lady who had just discovered a body in her parked car. He had the distinct impression that she was holding something back.

"Of course; I think we have enough for now. There is one thing, however. We need to take your car to our forensics lab. We need to check it over thoroughly to see if the murderer left any clue as to his or her identity and the identity of the victim. I hope you understand; we'll get it back to you as soon as possible."

Becca started to argue but realized it would be futile. Of course, the police would need to examine her car. A dead body had just been discovered in it! "I understand. I would appreciate its timely return, so please do your best to make that happen. Now excuse me, Detective, I must arrange for a taxi, so I can get to work."

"Yes ma'am. I appreciate your time; have a good day. I'll see myself out."

Tom Warfel needn't have made his last offer. Becca had already pulled out her phone and was searching online for taxi car companies. The detective and his investigation were already fading in her mind as she became occupied with her own immediate needs.

Warfel emerged from the red brick apartment building to find the medical examiner leaning over the body. Dr. Stephen Morley was a short man with the beginnings of a middle-age paunch. He was known for his ability to shut out everything around him when he was examining a crime scene. This talent to focus had produced spectacular results in the past, as he often discovered details lost to others. There was no one better in the field of forensic medicine, so Detective Warfel waited patiently with his partner for the medical examiner to complete his survey of the scene and the victim before he asked any questions.

Dr. Morley stood up and indicated to his assistant that the body could be zipped up in the polyethylene body bag for transport to the morgue. He would perform the autopsy later in the day. He removed his gloves and approached the waiting detectives.

"Good morning, Tom, Drew. The apparent cause of death was a single gunshot to the back of the head. The bullet is either still in her or it was lost when the killer placed her in the car. A quick search of the vehicle didn't find it, but the techs will do a more thorough search once the car is towed. I'll know more when I complete the autopsy; you're welcome to be there."

"Thanks, we'll see; it depends on the time."

"I should be able to get to this one by three o'clock. She's number four on the schedule today."

"We should be able to make it. Any indication of who she is, Doc?"

"No identification was found, but there's one clue. Her clothes are very expensive. The suit has a designer label and the name of the boutique where is was sold sewn into the jacket."

"That is helpful, thanks." Detective Warfel became thoughtful, "So how did a high-class chic like her end up in an Infinity sedan on a Tuesday morning in a quiet, tree-lined neighborhood?"

Dr. Morley chuckled, "I'm afraid that's for you to find out, Detective. Now, I need to get back to my office. The dead may not be in a hurry, but you police types are. See you around three o'clock, gentlemen."

Dr. Morley opened the passenger door of the coroner's van and assumed his seat. He gave a final head nod to the detectives as his assistant pulled the white van out into traffic.

# Two

Detective Warfel turned to his partner. "Drew, let's track down the boutique where our victim bought her clothes. I believe it's in Louisville. I recognize the name of the boutique found on the label. My wife attended a fashion show a few months ago at the new Omni Hotel as part of their grand opening. She went with a friend. I was terrified she would come home with an expensive outfit, but common sense prevailed."

Drew nodded. "On our salaries, it would take a long time to pay for some of those designer outfits. I'm glad my wife doesn't have expensive tastes. Okay, I'll find the boutique, but then what?"

"I don't know, but it's the only clue we've got. We need to look closer at Ms. Dorland. The body may have been placed in her car at random, but maybe not. There may be someone with a very personal grudge against her. That can wait, though. I'll call the forensics lab and see if they have found any clue to the victim's identity from the car. I'll check with missing persons also. Someone will report her missing sooner or later. I just hope it's sooner."

"I'll call you after I check out the boutique."

"Okay, Drew, take the car; I'll get a ride back to the station with one of the black and whites."

Three hours later, Drew called Tom to report on his visit to the boutique. It had been a dead end. "The owner said that even if she saw the suit, she would not have any idea who bought it. The clothing was sold during a show, and the buyer had paid cash. Since no credit card had been used, there was no record of the buyer's name. The owner checked her mailing list and the invited guests for the show but found no customer

18

from Braxton. She said the client who bought the clothing must have been a guest of one of the invitees, or the outfit was given to her. The owner emphasized, in a condescending tone, that her clothing was sold primarily to celebrities and local elite. Her demeanor suggested she found it distasteful to speak to a policeman, and she made it clear she wanted nothing to do with a murder investigation. She promised to check with her clerks who had worked the show where the suit was bought, but I sensed this was a way of extracting herself from the conversation. I doubt very much that I will hear from the shopkeeper. If needed, I'll press her for more information, but honestly, I hope I will not have to deal further with her," Tom confessed.

"She does sound rather dreadful. Well, we had to try; all we can do is push on, someone will report her missing eventually," Tom stated, with more confidence than he was feeling. He hung up and sat staring at the papers on his desk unable to concentrate when his phone rang again. *I hope this is good news,* he thought.

"Warfel here." The person on the other end identified himself. "Oh, hello, John. I hope you have something for me. Have your lab techs found anything?" the detective asked.

"Maybe. We found a dental appointment card under the front seat. It could belong to the victim, or owner of the vehicle, but it's worth checking out."

"It's more than I've gotten so far." Tom jotted down the name of the dentist's office, as well as the date and time of the appointment. "Thanks, John; this just might be the break we need."

"I hope so. We're not finished with the car yet, but I thought you'd want this information right away. I'll let you know if we find anything else."

19

Tom ended the call and immediately dialed the number for the dental office.

A pleasant female voice greeted him and asked how she could help him. Detective Warfel identified himself and told the receptionist what he needed.

"Could you please check with scheduling and give me the name of the patient who has an appointment at the date and time I just told you?"

The receptionist hesitated, "I'm sorry, sir; I cannot give out that information. We guard our patients' privacy."

"Of course, I understand. Could I speak with the dentist or your supervisor?"

"Uh, just a minute. I'll put you on hold—please wait."

It was a full five minutes before the call was picked up again. An impatient male voice came on the line.

"This is Dr. Butler; what's this about?" he demanded.

"Dr. Butler, my name is Tom Warfel, I'm a detective with the Braxton Police Department. I'm conducting a death investigation, and I need to know the name of a patient who has an appointment with you."

"A death investigation? What has that to do with me?"

"Maybe nothing, sir. In the course of our investigation, an appointment card from your office was found. I need the name of that patient. It may help our investigation."

"Detective, er what did you say your name was?"

"Warfel, W-A-R-F-E-L."

"Detective Warfel, you do understand I am constrained by HIPAA regulations, don't you?"

"Yes, I understand; however, our victim has not been identified, and this may be our only clue to her identity. We really need your help. I'm not asking for her medical information, just a name and address."

"I'll check with my attorney and call you back. That's the best I can do."

Warfel suppressed the comment he wanted to make and answered, "Thank you, sir. I look forward to your call."

The detective hung up the phone without further comment and wondered if the dentist would call him back. He would give the dentist an hour to return the call. If he hadn't heard back by then, he would get a warrant for the information. Next, Tom dialed the extension for missing persons, but received no help there either. No one matching the description of the body in the car had been reported missing. Tom had done all he could do for the moment, so he pushed back from his battered desk, grabbed his jacket from the hook on the back of the door, and headed to the deli on the corner for lunch.

Forty minutes later Tom was back at his desk looking through his phone messages when his extension rang.

"This is Detective Warfel."

"Yes, Detective, this is Dr. Butler. I spoke with my attorney, and he sees no reason why I can't give you this information—especially under the circumstances."

"Thank you, Dr. Butler." Tom waited for the dentist to provide the name of his Jane Doe.

"The patient with the appointment date and time is Cora Larkin. I have her address and phone number, too." The dentist proceeded to provide the additional information before adding, "If this lady is the victim, will you please let me know? She's a friend of my wife's as it turns out. I would prefer to tell my wife of Cora's death personally, and not have her find out from a news clip."

Detective Warfel wrote down the information before responding. "Of course, but I'm sure you realize we cannot release the information until next of kin is notified, and we are certain our victim is actually this lady. Please keep this information confidential for now, Dr. Butler."

"Yes, Detective, I will."

"Thank you for the information, Dr. Butler. When I can release the victim's identity, I'll give you a call."

"I appreciate that. Good-bye."

Warfel ended the call on his end and pulled up driver's license information on his computer. The photo for Cora Larkin certainly looked like the murdered woman, but it was somewhat difficult to tell for sure. At least it was a place to start.

By late afternoon, Detective Warfel had his positive I.D. of the victim. Although Mrs. Larkin had been divorced for over a year, her ex-husband agreed to view the body for a definitive identification. Dr. Mike Larkin was shocked to hear of his ex-wife's possible demise, but his emotions were tested further once he saw the body.

"Cora looks so violated, as if every shred of her dignity has been stripped away," Dr. Larkin stated while struggling to control his emotions. After some moments, he added, "Her children need to be notified. She had two by her first marriage. Will you please call them? We were never on the best of terms."

Tom carefully noted Dr. Larkin's response to

seeing the body and listened for any indication of duplicity as he spoke. The man seemed genuinely shaken by the experience, but that didn't mean he was not a suspect. In fact, as the most recent husband, he had been paying alimony to his ex-wife for more than a year. This gave him motive.

Detective Warfel responded to Dr. Larkin's request, "Of course, if you'll give me their names and contact information, I'll be glad to take care of notifying them."

Dr. Larkin provided the information. "I guess you had better call her son and let him call his sister. Cameron is the less emotional of the two."

"Noted, thank you. Now, I know this is a bad time to ask, Dr. Larkin, but it's my job. Can you provide an alibi for last night between midnight and three this morning?"

"Uh, sure. I guess the husband, or ex-husband in this case, is the most likely suspect. I was on call last night and had to go into the hospital around ten. I'm an orthopedist and I was called in to assist with three accident victims—multiple fractures, that sort of thing. I guess I left the hospital around 2:30 this morning. I arrived home about three. My home security system will show when I re-entered the house. I live alone since my divorce, so there was no one home to vouch for my arrival, but the security system should give you what you need. I logged in when I got to the hospital, so the desk clerk in the ER can tell you when I arrived and left the hospital. Is that all, Detective? I'm afraid I must go if you have no other questions. I have to operate on one of those accident victims from last night."

"Of course, Dr. Larkin. Thank you for coming in. I'm sure all of this has been quite a shock. I'll contact your stepson and notify him of his mother's death. I'll have some follow-up questions, however. Will you be available in the next few days?"

Dr. Larkin gave a wry smile, "Of course, I have no travel plans. As they say in the movies, I promise not to leave town. Good day, Detective."

Detective Warfel watched the physician as he walked away, not with the step of a confident and accomplished surgeon, but with stooped posture and slow gait. Cora's death had diminished him, as if the murderer had assaulted the doctor as well as his ex-wife. The seasoned detective's impression of the ex-husband was that he was a decent man, and not the killer he sought. The alibi would have to be checked out, though, as he could have paid someone to murder his ex-wife. Dr. Larkin couldn't be ruled out yet as a suspect.

Warfel's next call was to Dr. Butler. There was no wait to speak to the dentist this time.

"Detective Warfel, thank you for calling me. Is the victim Cora Larkin?"

"I'm afraid so. I know you want to tell your wife personally, but can you wait a little longer? I need to notify another family member before the news becomes public. I'm sure you understand."

"Absolutely! I want to break the news in person anyway, so it will be around five o'clock or so before I get home. I cleared my last two appointments so I could get home before she sees the news on television. From what you told me earlier, I felt sure it was Cora. She was a very nice lady, Detective. She will be mourned by a lot of people."

"Thank you for your help, Dr. Butler. I don't envy you the task of breaking the news to your wife. Good friends are hard to come by."

24

"That they are, Detective."

Warfel hung up and dialed the number for Cora Larkin's son. Notifying next-of-kin of a loved one's death was the least favorite part of his job. He took a deep breath as he heard Cameron Osborne's voice answer the call. *Lord, give me the right words,* he prayed.

# Three

Mac Osborne emerged from his barn leading a Palomino mare and her foal. The colt was two days old, and the birth had been traumatic for both him and his mother. Mac had kept the pair in a stall to allow them to recover and to ensure they were healthy enough to be put in the pasture with other mares and foals. They were both recovering nicely, so he opened the gate and allowed them to join the other mares and foals.

Mac was a retired police detective who had traded in his badge for a farm. He had been divorced from his first wife Cora for four years but had been remarried for two years. Before marrying Mac, Mary had been a highly paid publishing executive in Chicago. They had met through friends and had felt a mutual attraction immediately. The pair now enjoyed semi-retirement on the farm: Mac managed the farm, and Mary continued her career on a part-time basis as a freelance editor.

Mary, a stunning brunette with a trim figure, joined Mac at the paddock gate. "He's a beautiful colt; I'm so glad he and his mother are doing better."

"Yes, if his temperament is anything like his mother's, he'll make a fine riding horse. What brings you out here? I thought you were planning to work on Sarah's new manuscript all day."

"I was, but your son called. It seemed important, so I told him I would have you call him back as soon as possible."

"Cameron? It must be important for him to call during the day. His job keeps him so busy; he rarely has time for lunch, much less phone calls to his old man.

26

Did he say what it was about?"

"No, he just said to call him on his cell phone. His voice sounded strained; I could tell he was upset about something."

"Sounds like I'd better call him now. I'll wash up in the barn and be right in. Is lunch ready? I'm starved!"

Mary laughed, "You're always starved! Yes, Aggie has made a wonderful sandwich and potato salad as well. I'll ask her to set it on the table for you. I've already had my lunch, so I'll get back to work."

Mac checked on the mare and foal in the pasture to ensure they were okay before he returned to the barn to wash his hands in the utility room. He knew Mary would be occupied with Sarah's manuscript most of the day. Sarah and Sam Richards were the friends who had introduced Mac and Mary. Mac had assisted the young couple with investigations of murder in the past. Sarah, as a writer, was naturally inquisitive and had found herself involved in three murder investigations as a result. Mac had done his best to keep his friends out of harm's way, but both had narrowly escaped death as a result of their snooping. The arrival of their baby Anna had settled the pair considerably, and Sarah had become a successful author. With Sarah's quieter lifestyle, Mac had enjoyed two wonderful years with his new wife without being involved in any murder investigations. His bucolic existence on the farm in Central Kentucky suited him just fine.

Mary met Sarah in Chicago before her move to Kentucky. Mary had headed up Stinnett Publishing and had recruited Sarah to work full-time for her. The executive had traded her heels for farm boots, however, when she married Mac and had become a seasoned veteran of farm life.

Mac removed his shoes at the back door and slipped on a pair of Crocs before entering the kitchen. Aggie, the part time housekeeper and cook, greeted him as he entered. "I understand you're hungry, Mr. Osborne. Well, I think you'll get filled up with what I have ready for you."

Mac Smiled. "I'm sure I will, Aggie; you always make delicious meals for us. I need to make a quick phone call, but I'll be back to eat lunch in a jiffy."

Mac retrieved his cell phone from the kitchen counter where he had left it earlier and made his way to his study. He sat down in the worn leather chair behind the oak desk and punched in the numbers of Cameron's cell phone.

The call was answered right away. "Dad, thank goodness!"

Hearing the tension in Cameron's voice, Mac became alert instantly, "What's wrong, Cameron?"

"Dad, I got a call this morning from the Braxton police. It's Mom, she's…she's dead."

It required several moments for Mac to process what he had just heard. "What did you say?"

"Mom's dead! Murdered!"

Mac thought this must be some kind of a mistake. *How could Cora be dead?*

"Cameron, this can't be right. Who did you talk to?"

"I wrote his name down. I knew you'd want to talk with him." Cameron reached for the note he had written and recited Detective Warfel's name and phone number.

"I'll call him and get this straightened out. Have you called your sister?"

28

"No, I didn't want to alarm Amy until I spoke with you."

"Good, there's no sense in getting her upset. This has to be a mistake. I'll call this Detective Warfel and get back to you."

"Okay, Dad—thanks. I'll be at home. I left the office right after I got the call from the detective. I couldn't have gotten any work done—under the circumstances."

"I understand. Sit tight. I'll call you back as soon as I know more."

Mac hung up the phone and stared off into space. Cora—dead? It couldn't be. It had to be some sort of mistake. Mac stared at the phone number for Detective Warfel. He was in no hurry to check the veracity of the information. Although he had been divorced for nearly four years, he had pleasant memories of his life with Cora. The early years had been great. He had been a young patrolman on the local police force, and Cora worked for the phone company in the accounting department. Their jobs had kept them busy during the day, but the nights—oh the nights! With little money to take trips, the young couple had enjoyed the company of each other. Once the children came along, their time together was always family oriented. *Maybe too family oriented,* Mac thought. *We didn't take enough time for just the two of us. Maybe if I had tried a little harder to pay more attention to Cora...*

"Mr. Osborne? Are you coming to lunch?" Aggie asked from the doorway of Mac's office.

"What? Oh, sorry, Aggie. I'll be delayed a bit. I need to make some calls.

The housekeeper nodded but muttered under her breath as she went back toward the kitchen.

Mac dialed the number Cameron had given him for Detective Warfel. The call was answered quickly, catching Mac a bit off guard.

"Detective Warfel."

Mac attempted to respond, but his mouth had gone completely dry. He swallowed and identified himself as Cameron's father and Cora's former husband.

"Mr. Osborne, thank you for contacting me. Your son tells me you're a retired detective, is that right?"

"Yes, I served twenty-five years on the force before I settled down to farm life."

"Sounds like a dream; I hope to do the same someday." Warfel paused and drew in his breath, "Mr. Osborne, I'm sorry for your loss. Your son took the news rather badly, I'm afraid. It's never easy to lose a loved one, especially when it's murder."

"Detective, are you certain it's Cora?"

"I'm afraid so, Mr. Osborne. I will be attending her autopsy later this afternoon. We don't have an official cause of death yet, but the circumstances are very suspicious and lead us to believe she was murdered."

"What can you tell me?"

Tom Warfel hesitated as he decided how much to reveal to this possible suspect. Although Mac Osborne seemed to be an unlikely murderer, he could not afford to eliminate anyone this early in the investigation.

"All I can tell you right now is that she was found in a car this morning about seven-thirty. She had been shot and had been dead a few hours. I would like to sit down with you and discuss the case further. Could you come to Braxton, or would you prefer I come to you?"

"I can come there; what time would work for you?"

"Let's plan to meet in my office in the downtown police station around four-thirty. I should be back from the autopsy by then."

"I'll be there." The call ended and Mac let out a deep breath. *How could Cora have been murdered? Who would want her dead?"*

"Mac?" Mary's voice intruded on her husband's swirling thoughts. He looked up, and she knew immediately that something was wrong. "What is it, what's happened?"

Mac didn't speak for several seconds as if putting it into words would make it real. Mary stepped closer and put a hand on Mac's shoulder. "Darling, what is it? You look positively ashen."

Finally, Mac explained the situation. "It's Cora. She's dead—murdered it seems."

Mary stared at her husband, not able to comprehend what he had just said. "Cora?"

"Yes, I just spoke with a detective from Braxton. He said she was found dead in a car this morning. Apparently, she was killed during the night."

"I can't believe it! How did she die?"

"They either don't know or wouldn't tell me; her autopsy is this afternoon; they'll know more then."

Mary leaned over and wrapped her arms around Mac. "Oh, sweetheart, I'm so sorry. I've always admired how amicable the two of you have been toward each other."

"Yes, we actually became friends after the divorce. I know that sounds crazy, but once the divorce was final and we had a chance to recover, we reconnected on a different level. At first it was for the sake of the kids, but somehow, we both remembered how we had been such good friends before we married and were able to recapture that relationship. Without the strain of living together, we could appreciate each other again. We had drifted apart over the years, and gradually developed different interests. I blame myself. My job required long hours sometimes, and that put more strain on her. I should have made our time together a priority."

Mary let Mac talk as she held onto him. Once he finished, she reached for Mac's chin and raised his head so she could look directly at him. "Darling, I'm so very sorry Cora is dead, but please don't torture yourself with should-haves. All we can control is now. I've got the most wonderful man in the world as my husband, and I love you with all my heart."

Mac returned Mary's gaze and felt a lifting of some of the weight that had been sitting on his shoulders since Cameron's call. "I love you, too. You're my world."

Mary let the moment linger a bit before speaking, "I understand from what I heard of the phone conversation that you have to drive into town. Where do you have to go?"

"The detective I spoke to wants to see me. I'm sure he wants to know if I have an alibi for last night, as well as ask me general questions that might help the investigation."

"I'll go with you." Mac started to shake his head, but Mary quickly added, "After all, I'm your alibi for last night, and I'm not sure you should be driving at the moment. Now, Aggie has your lunch ready. You may not feel like eating but try to eat something."

Mac nodded, realizing how truly blessed he was to have Mary in his life. He had been happy living on the farm as a bachelor, but Mary had given him what he had not even realized was missing. Her love and support meant everything to him, and he was glad to have her by his side as he dealt with this tragedy. She stood beside him as he called Cameron.

"Cameron, this is Dad. Detective Warfel confirmed that your mother was the murdered victim. I'm on my way to meet with him. I'll call you again after I see him."

"Why do you have to meet with him; I don't understand."

Mac smiled. It would never occur to Cameron that Mac could have hurt Cora. "Most likely to hear my alibi for last night."

"Oh...but how could he think you could have killed Mom? You wouldn't hurt anyone."

"It's routine questioning, that's all. Husbands, even ex-husbands are prime suspects when a woman is murdered. Besides, I'll probably be able to get more information in person. I'd better go, I'll call you as soon as we finish."

"Okay, Dad—and Dad?"

"Yes?"

"I love you."

Mac's breath caught. "I love you, too." It took Mac a couple of minutes to regain his composure after the call, and Mary waited patiently without comment.

Aggie sensed something was wrong as her employers entered the kitchen, but wisely held her tongue. Mary poured a glass of iced tea for Mac and another for herself and sat across from him at the kitchen table. Aggie placed the sandwich and potato salad in front of Mac and returned to the prep for the evening meal.

Once Mary was satisfied that Mac was eating, she turned to her housekeeper, "Aggie, Mac and I have to drive to Braxton this afternoon. There has been a family emergency. I'm not sure how long we'll be gone, so let's save the stew for tomorrow. We'll get something on the way home."

Aggie sensed the tension in her employer's voice, and only responded with, "Yes ma'am," although she was very curious as to what the so-called tragedy had been. She would have to be patient, she concluded. It would all come out eventually.

Mac ate half his sandwich, none of the potato salad, and downed the tea. He pushed back from the table and said, "I need to take a shower and change clothes. The detective asked me to meet with him at four-thirty. That will give me time to arrange for some help here on the farm. It looks like the next several days will be rather busy."

Mary smiled and nodded as she cleared the table and gave final instructions for the day to Aggie.

\*\*\*

The drive to Braxton's police station took twenty-five minutes. The emerging colors of autumn went unnoticed as Mac and Mary drove in silence, each recalling memories of Cora Larkin. Mac had been pleased when Cora had married Dr. Larkin. He seemed to be a decent man, and he could give Cora the same companionship Mac had found with Mary. After a year, however, the marriage had ended in divorce. Cora refused to elaborate on the reason, and Mac had respected her privacy. Now, he wondered about his ex-wife's life after her divorce from Dr. Larkin. Had she

34

been lonely? Did she have friends? Regret mingled with shock as Mac grappled with the reality of Cora's death.

Mary sensed the turmoil in Mac and left him to his own thoughts as she followed country roads to Braxton.

Mary located the newly constructed police department and drove to a side parking lot designated for visitors. She walked with Mac to the front door. The building had a state-of-the-art security system and the pair had to identify themselves and whom they needed to see before the door unlocked electronically. Once inside, they had to pass through a metal detector. A petite older woman greeted them, asked Mary to wait in a small waiting room, and led Mac down a hallway to Detective Warfel's office. "He's expecting you; go right in."

Warfel was sitting at his desk when Mac appeared in his office doorway, but he stood and came around his desk to greet his visitor. He shook hands with Mac and indicated for him to sit down.

"Thank you for coming in. I know you must have a lot of questions and I'll try to answer them."

Mac took the offered chair and thought to himself how strange it felt to be on the other side other desk.

Warfel reclaimed his seat and got right to the point. "I just came from Mrs. Larkin's autopsy." Warfel paused.

"And?" Mac asked.

"Well, she died of a single gunshot wound to the back of her head. There were no other wounds."

Mac shook his head, "Poor Cora."

"Mr. Osborne, are you aware of anyone with a

grudge against your ex-wife?"

Mac thought for a few seconds before answering the question, "No, I can't think of anyone. When I was married to her she had lots of friends—everyone liked her. Since our divorce four years ago, I'm sure she developed new relationships, but I'm not aware of any ill feelings toward her. Have you spoken with Dr. Larkin about this?"

The detective sidestepped the question and asked, "How would you describe your relationship with Mrs. Larkin?"

Mac had expected this question; he would have asked it. "We've been good friends since the divorce. We get together for family celebrations, birthdays, Christmas, that sort of thing. She even invited me to her wedding to Dr. Larkin. I liked the guy. That seemed important to Cora. She told me my opinion mattered to her."

"I see. You know I have to ask this next question. Where were you last night between the hours of midnight and seven a.m. this morning?"

"I understand, Detective. I can assure you I was at home, sleeping until about six this morning. My wife can vouch for that, and our housekeeper can tell you I was home at seven o'clock this morning. That's when she usually arrives. I waved at her from the paddock when she got out of her car."

"I see. Tell me about your children; were they on good terms with their mother?"

Mac bristled at the intent of the questions, but hid his emotions as he answered, "They love their mother; they'll be devastated by this. Amy doesn't know yet. I didn't want to tell her until I was sure that the dead woman was really Cora."

36

"I can assure you that the victim is Cora Larkin. Dr. Larkin has already made a positive identification."

"I see."

"We'll be able to release the body by tomorrow morning at the latest. Given her divorced status, your son and daughter are the next of kin. Her body will be released to them.

"I'll let Cameron know. I'm sure he and Amy will want to use the funeral home our family has always used. This is devastating; our family is very close. Cameron is really shaken, and Amy will probably fall apart. She and her mother talked nearly every day."

Detective Warfel heard the catch in Mac's voice and was aware of the unshed tears glistening in his eyes. "Mr. Osborne, is there anything else you can think of that would help our investigation?"

"No, but if I think of anything else, I'll let you know. Right now, I can barely remember my name. This has been quite a shock."

"I'm sure it has. You have my deepest sympathy. Mr. Osborne, I do need to speak with your wife. How can I reach her?"

"She's in the waiting room. She actually drove me here. We felt it the safest thing to do."

"Very wise." Warfel made a quick call to have Mrs. Osborne brought to his office. A few minutes later, he was sitting across from her. Mac had been excused from the room. Warfel launched into his questions after acknowledging the tragic nature of the circumstances. "Mrs. Osborne, are you aware of your husband's whereabouts last night between midnight and seven this morning?"

"Certainly. We went to bed around ten-thirty. I read for a while, but Mac went right to sleep. He got up around six, I believe. I woke briefly but went back to sleep until seven. When I got up, Aggie, our housekeeper and cook, was fixing his breakfast. She said he had asked for eggs and bacon."

"Are you sure he was in bed all night, Mrs. Osborne?"

Mary suppressed a smile as she considered the question. Neither she nor Mac had slept well for the first part of the night and had made love around midnight. She decided to edit her response, however. "I'm a very light sleeper and usually wake up two or three times a night. Each time I awoke last night, Mac was beside me."

"Thank you, Mrs. Osborne. I appreciate your time. May I contact you if I have other questions?"

Mary sensed this was asked out of courtesy but knew the detective would not hesitate to question her further whether she agreed or not. "Of course, all of us want to see justice done for poor Cora. She was a good woman and a wonderful mother."

Detective Warfel heard the sincerity in Mary's voice, but withheld judgment as to Mac and Mary's guilt for now.

The couple left police headquarters with even more questions than before. It was beyond imagining why someone would want to murder Cora. Mary reached for Mac's hand and gave a squeeze. "I'm sorry, Mac; I really am. I know the next several days will be rough, but I'm here if you need a sounding board, or just a hug."

Mac stopped walking and looked at his wife. "How did I ever get lucky enough to find you?"

Mary smiled, "I think it was meant to be, darling."

Mac stood a little taller as he and Mary walked to their car. He dreaded his call to Amy but knew Mary would be there for all of them. That was enough for Mac.

# Four

Back at home, Mac sat down behind his desk and pulled out his cell phone. It was time to call Amy. As a detective, he had made this call many times to inform families of loved ones' passing, but this was personal and very difficult. This was his own daughter, and he was about to destroy her world. Mary sat beside Mac with a hand on his shoulder as he dialed the number and waited. Just as the voice message announced to leave a message, Amy picked up.

"Hello?"

"Amy, it's Dad."

"Oh, hi, Dad! How are you?"

"Uh, not so good; listen I have something to tell you that is really upsetting. I'd rather do this in person, but it can't wait."

"What is it, Dad? You're really scaring me."

"Amy, it's your mother; she's been...uh, she's dead."

There was no response from Amy. Mac wondered if the connection had been lost. "Amy? Are you there?"

"Y-yes, Dad, I'm here. Mom's dead? How? Are you sure?"

"Yes, I'm sure. I'm sorry, Amy; I know this is a shock. We don't have much information yet, but just come home, okay?"

"Of course, I'll get a flight out tonight; can you pick me up at the airport?"

"Sure, let me know when your plane is scheduled to get in. Will you be able to reschedule any work you miss?"

"That won't be a problem; my professors will let

40

me make up any work I miss," Amy assured her father. Mac could hear the tremor in Amy's voice and knew she must be crying.

"Amy, we'll get through this, okay?"

"Okay, Dad," Amy responded, her voice merely a whisper.

Mac sighed as he hung up the phone. He knew how close Amy had been to her mother. Now, he had to call his son. Mary gave her husband a hug and left. She needed to prepare two guest rooms and plan food.

Mac dialed the familiar number and Cameron picked up on the first ring. Mac could hear the tension in his voice. "Dad, what did you find out? What did the autopsy show?'

"She died from a gunshot wound, probably instantly. I didn't learn much more than that."

"This makes no sense; who would want to murder Mom?"

"I don't know, Cameron, but the police have already opened a murder investigation. I met with the Detective Warfel; he seems very capable."

"I don't know what to say, Dad. It seems like a bad dream. I just want to wake up and find Mom alive and well."

"I know; it seems so surreal. Cameron, I know this is very difficult, but you will have to arrange for the body to be released from the morgue. They require next of kin for that."

"Oh, okay. What do I do?"

"You have to give permission for her body to be moved to a funeral home. I'll text you with the number for the one we've always used."

"Yeah, I guess that's what we should do...uh, did Mom wanted to be cremated?"

41

Mac considered the option for a few moments. "I can't remember if she said what she wanted to do. It never came up. I guess we both thought we had lots of time before we had to worry about that."

"I know, Dad. I guess we can decide about all of that after the funeral home picks up her body." Cameron sighed, "I'm on the road already; I should be there in another thirty minutes. Have you spoken to Amy?"

"Yes, I just hung up. She's taking it about as well as possible. She's flying home late this evening."

"I can pick her up for you if that would help."

"Thanks, Cameron; I'll take you up on that."

No problem, glad to help out. Oh, and Dad?"

"Yes?"

"I'm really sorry; I know you and Mom still loved each other—in a non-romantic sort of way."

Mac was touched by the perceptiveness of his eldest child. "Yes, she was a terrific woman and a good friend, even after the divorce. I'll miss her."

"Yes, we all will." Cameron took a deep breath, "Okay, I'll see you soon."

Mac hung up and said a silent prayer of thanks for his kids. They had grown into wonderful adults.

\*\*\*

Amy's plane was on time, and Cameron was waiting for her. The young woman's eyes were red from crying, and she stifled a sob as her brother embraced her.

"It's okay, you can cry all you want. If there was ever a time for tears, this is it," Cameron assured his sibling.

"Oh, Cameron, is it really true? Mom's dead?"

Cameron only nodded and picked up Amy's carry-on suitcase and guided her toward the exit doors.

"We'll talk in the car."

Cameron drove away from the airport and to a nearby park. He pulled to the side of the road and turned off the ignition. Turning to his sister he said, "Amy, there's more. Mom's death was not natural."

Amy didn't understand what her brother was trying to tell her. The horrible shock had not sunk in yet, and she had not thought to ask how her mother had died. Now, she met her brother's gaze and asked, "What do you mean by not natural?"

"Amy, she was murdered."

"Murdered? What are you saying? Who would want to murder our mother?" Amy's voice was rising, and Cameron reached for his sister's hands in an attempt to calm her.

"We don't have many details yet, but we do know her death was not a natural one. There's been an autopsy. She was shot, Amy."

"Oh no! Cameron, could it have been suicide?"

"That's very doubtful. You see, she was discovered this morning in someone else's car, and the gunshot was to the back of her head."

"You're not making any sense, Cameron! I don't understand any of this."

"We don't have all the facts yet, but the car she was found in was parked along a street. It belongs to a nurse at the hospital. When she opened the car door, Mom, er, she fell out of the car. That's about all we know."

Amy sat staring at her brother, unable to make sense of what he had just said. "Poor Mother!" Amy's sobs tugged at her brother, but there was little he could say or do to comfort his sister.

After several minutes, Amy's crying subsided.

She pulled a package of wipes from her purse and bathed her face. "I must look a mess. I need to pull myself together before we get to Dad's. I'm sure he's experiencing his own grief and doesn't need to worry about me."

"Amy, it's okay. We're family, we'll grieve together."

Amy attempted a smile. Her brother always knew how to make her feel better. When they were children, it was Cameron who had gently washed away the blood and dirt on her skinned knees and elbows the summer she learned to skate. He had always watched out for her, and it was a comfort now to know he would be beside her as they faced the greatest challenge of their lives.

"Thanks, Cameron; you're the best big brother a girl could ever want."

Cameron smiled mischievously, "That's right, and don't you ever forget it, Ames!" Amy's smile widened as she heard the pet name her brother had coined for her when they were only toddlers.

Thirty minutes later, the siblings walked into the farmhouse and were greeted by Mary and their dad. Mac reached for his youngest child and gave her a long hug.

"Hey, sweetheart, I've missed you!"

"I've missed you, too, Dad!" Amy reached on tiptoes to give her dad a kiss on his check.

Mary stepped forward and wrapped her arms around her stepdaughter. "Amy, it's so good to see you. We have your room ready. Have you had anything to eat?"

Amy smiled, "It's good to see you too and, no, I didn't have anything to eat before I left. I'm not very hungry, though."

44

"We have some chicken. I could make you a sandwich," Mary offered.

"That would be great, thanks." Amy turned to her dad, "Cameron told me about Mom, about how she died. This doesn't seem real. Who would want to murder her?"

Mac's face took on a pained expression, both for the circumstances of his ex-wife's death, and for the misery it was causing his children. "I don't know, sweetheart. I met with the detective in charge of the case, but he didn't, or couldn't, tell me much. We'll know more soon, I'm sure. Now, why don't you go upstairs, get settled, then join us in the kitchen."

Amy nodded, and followed her brother who was carrying her suitcase up the stairs. The answers to her questions would have to wait.

# Five

The next morning, the phone at Serendipity Farm rang. Sam and Sarah Richards were having breakfast with their two-year-old daughter, Anna. Sam excused himself and picked up the phone in the hallway.

"Mac, good morning! How are you this beautiful fall day?"

Sam listened as Mac related the events of the day before. The smile on Sam's face was replaced by sadness. At the end of the narrative, Sam attempted to reassure his friend, "Mac, we're here for you. Anything that Sarah and I can do, just ask. What about Cameron and Amy? Do they know?"

"Yes, and they're both here. I just wanted you to hear about this from me before you see it on the news. I've already gotten several calls from media this morning. It's awful. The circumstances of Cora's death will create a news sensation, for sure."

"I'm so sorry, Mac. Are there funeral arrangements yet?"

"No, not yet. Cameron will call the funeral home today so they can pick up Cora's body."

"Mac, I don't know what to say. This is a terrible tragedy for your entire family."

Mac let out a long breath, "Yeah, but we'll get through it somehow. I appreciate your concern. I'll let you know about the funeral arrangements."

"Mac, I'm sure Sarah will want to bring food to the house. She and Mrs. Hoskins can provide whatever you need."

"I appreciate that. I'll have Mary call Sarah to work it out. Well, I'd better go. Today will be busy."

"Okay, take care, Mac. We'll check in with you

later today."

Sam hung up and turned to find Sarah standing close by. "Sam, what is it? What happened?"

"It's Mac's ex-wife, Cora. She's been murdered."

Sarah gasped, and tears immediately filled her eyes. Mac was like a father to her, and his pain affected her deeply. "Murdered? How?"

"She was shot. She was found in a parked car on a quiet neighborhood street yesterday morning. Apparently, someone placed her body there after she died.

"How horrible for Mac and his family! What can we do to help them?"

"I told Mac that you and Mrs. Hoskins would help provide food. Cameron and Amy are home, and there will be a meal at the house after the funeral."

"Of course, we'll be glad to help with that. Mrs. Hoskins and Aggie can coordinate together."

"Mac said he would have Mary call you today."

"Okay. Did he say when the funeral would be?"

"No, the arrangements haven't been made. Her body is to be released to the funeral home today."

"I see. I wish there was more we could do for them. Their hearts must be breaking!"

Sam reached for his wife and held her as she cried. He knew once the tears dried, his wife would be a force of nature in her efforts to comfort and provide for Mac and his family. For now, he would comfort her as she grieved for their friends.

\*\*\*

As the news of the murder spread across the news outlets, Detective Warfel met with his partner, Drew Samuels. "Drew, we need to get ahead of this and

47

fast. The media has already dubbed this case, 'The Corpse in the Car.' The unusual circumstances have piqued the imagination of the press, and we'll have a regular circus on our hands before long. We need to check on her ex-husbands' alibis first thing. Get anything you can on both of them. Where they go, who their friends are, how they got along with the deceased. I'll explore the life of Mrs. Larkin. If the murderer is not one of her ex-husbands, and I don't think it is, then she made someone very angry, or very nervous. We need to determine who that was."

Detective Samuels nodded, "I think you have the hardest job. I agree. I don't believe either ex-husband committed this crime. Mac Osborne had no apparent motive, and Dr. Larkin has enough money to cover his ex-wife's alimony with plenty to spare. That could hardly have been a reason to murder her. I'll check out the husbands, then help you with investigating Mrs. Larkin's past. I'm sure if we kick up enough sand, something will turn up."

"It always does. Before you get started on the husbands, check with the medical examiner to see if he has anything new to tell us."

"Will do. I'll check in with you this afternoon."

\*\*\*

Detective Warfel parked his car in front of the office of The Palisades Apartments. He flashed his badge and identified himself to the elderly receptionist and asked for the manager. Adam Baxter emerged from his office as soon as he was notified of the visitor. The receptionist made no attempt to conceal her interest in Warfel's visit.

"What can I do for you, Detective?" Baxter asked.

"I need your assistance. I'm sure you've heard of the death of one of your tenants, Mrs. Cora Larkin."

"Yeah, it's all over the news, a real shame."

"Yes, well, I need to get into her apartment."

"No problem, let me just get my master key."

The two men walked a short distance to the apartment where Cora Larkin spent her last days. Mr. Baxter inserted his key in the lock and pushed the door open. "Do you need anything else, Detective?"

"I don't think so. Once I'm finished, our crime scene crew will arrive."

"Crime scene crew? She didn't die here. I heard on the news she was found dead in a car across town."

Detective Warfel pushed back a feeling of impatience, "We need to know everything we can about Mrs. Larkin to help us determine why she died and who wanted her dead. Now, if you'll excuse me, I need to get on with my investigation. I'll probably have some questions for you after I finish here."

The manager took the hint. "Of course, Detective. I'll be in my office."

Warfel pulled a pair of latex gloves from his pocket as he entered the silent space. He scanned the living room, looking for any sign of a struggle. He saw none; everything was in its place. Mrs. Larkin had kept a clean and orderly home.

Entering a victim's home always made him feel as if he was violating the deceased a second time. He often wondered how people would prepare their home if they knew it would be the last time they would see it and that it would be invaded by the police after their death. They would surely discard anything personal that would reflect badly on them, possibly discarding evidence that could lead to the arrest of their killer. It was fortunate for him that victims couldn't know they were about to die. It made his job easier.

He continued his tour, taking a quick look in the kitchen before walking down a short hall to the two bedrooms and baths. The guest bath was very neat, with matching towels and shower curtain. The room was clean and the waste can was empty. The guest bedroom held a twin bed, a small desk and chest. The room apparently doubled as a home office of sorts.

The master bath was also decorated tastefully, but was not as neat as the guest bath. Various items of makeup were spread across the counter and a towel was on the floor next to the shower. Two pairs of earrings lay next to the hairbrush, as if the deceased had tried on several pairs of earrings before deciding on the pair she would wear to her death. The detective opened drawers and looked under the sink. There was the usual collection of toiletries, cleaning supplies, and miscellaneous items.

The master bedroom displayed a definite feminine touch, with light pink accents. The bed was neatly made and the wastebasket was nearly empty. Warfel reached down into the basket to retrieve the one crumpled piece of paper at the bottom. The paper was cream colored and of good quality. He smoothed out the note and walked to the window to see the handwriting better: "Find a safe place to keep this for me; I'll explain later". The note was signed, B.D. The crime scene crew would get their crack at the apartment, but Detective Warfel had wanted to get a look at it first. He pulled out his phone and requested the technicians. He spent the interim completing his cursory search of the apartment. Once the crew arrived, he turned over the space to them. If he were lucky, a fingerprint or other identifying feature of Cora's attacker would be found. He placed the note in an evidence bag. After letting the apartment complex office receptionist know he was finished, he returned to the station.

As he entered the lab, his phone rang. It was Drew. "Hey Drew, have you come up with anything?"

"Maybe, I'm still tracking down leads on the husbands. Both had busy lives with various interests. So far, everyone speaks glowingly of both men. Both work hard and have achieved professional recognition. Dr. Larkin works long hours, probably hard on a marriage, I would think. He didn't seem to socialize much. Mr. Osborne is a retired police detective, as you know, and he now has a farm with horses. He's married to his second wife, an editor. I don't think there's anything there. The son and daughter are with him now and planning the funeral. I wasn't able to get much from them. I'll circle back after the funeral."

"So, what about the medical examiner?"

"Well, that's what's interesting. The toxicology reports will take at least four weeks, but Doc did find something when he combed out the victim's hair. He found a broken fingernail and sent it to the lab. It might have broken off as the murderer struggled to get her body into that car."

"That's great news! I guess it's too much to hope that we can match the DNA to someone in the system. I understand that DNA nail clippings are not as detailed as DNA obtained from blood or bone, but it could possibly catch us a killer."

"Doc sent the broken nail to the lab already. We should get the results back in a couple of days. Did you have any luck at Mrs. Larkin's apartment?" Detective Samuels asked his partner.

"I believe I did. I found a note in a wastebasket asking Mrs. Larkin to keep something safe. It was signed with the initials B.D. I'm taking it to the lab now."

"B.D. I wonder if that could be Ms. Dorland. I heard one of the neighbors who passed by on the sidewalk refer to Ms. Dorland as Becca."

"That's interesting; perhaps our Ms. Dorland knew the victim after all. She became pretty evasive once she recovered a bit from the shock of finding the body."

"This case is already throwing a few curveballs. I'd like to wrap this one up quickly. It's getting a lot of notoriety already."

"I agree, Drew, but we still have a lot to explore—Ms. Dorland, for one thing. Why was the body placed in her car? There are a lot of easier places to dump a body," Warfel mused.

"Do you want me to check her out, or do you want to take care of that?" Drew asked.

"I'll probably have to handle it; I got a sense she was holding something back when I first interviewed her. I want to push a little harder and see if her story holds up. Get back to the husbands; make sure they have all their fingernails. Ask them if they would give a voluntary DNA sample so we can rule them out as suspects."

"Got it. Good luck with Ms. Dorland."

"Thanks, Drew. I'll touch base with you later."

# Six

Becca Dorland was sitting at her desk with next year's budget worksheets in front of her. She had a meeting the next day with her nursing managers to discuss budget needs for the following year, and she needed to prepare for it. Her mind, however, was not on the figures she had scribbled on the worksheet. She gazed out her first-floor window in the executive suite. It was a beautiful autumn day, and the foliage in the green space had turned to bright gold and orange. What her mind's eye saw, however, was a corpse falling out of her car with its eyes open staring into darkness. Reporters had discovered that the murdered woman had been placed in Becca's car. It hadn't taken long for the calls to start, both at her apartment and at work. Becca had instructed her administrative assistant to refuse those calls, but the gruesome news had created quite a disturbance in the office for two days.

Becca shook her head to clear the macabre image and stood up. She wouldn't be able to get any work done until she banished that picture from her mind. Not patient by nature, she found it difficult to keep her voice steady as she approached her administrative assistant's desk. "Stephanie, am I still getting calls from the media?"

The trim blonde nodded and looked up from her desk. "Yes, ma'am, quite a few. I told them you are not taking calls and asked each one to please not call back."

"Then let's hope they comply with that request. We'll never get any work done until this whole thing dies down. Do I have any other messages?"

"Just one; Mr. Banks called and wants a word with you as soon as possible."

*Uh-oh,* thought Becca, *he must want to speak with me about the murder. I guess I'll get this over with.* To Stephanie she said as nonchalantly as possible, "Okay, anything else?"

"No, it's been quiet except for the calls from reporters. I guess everyone's busy working on budgets. It's that time of year."

"I guess so." Becca proceeded down the hall to the office of the CEO, Hal Banks. Mrs. White, his administrative assistant, looked up as Becca entered. A twenty-year veteran of the position, little rattled the white-haired grandmother.

"Good morning, Mrs. White; is Hal in?"

"Yes, go right in; he's expecting you." The smile on Mrs. White's face was perfunctory and was quickly replaced by her usual scowl as she returned to her work. What she lacked in personality was more than made up by her efficiency and four CEO's had benefitted from the fact that she was very good at what she did.

Becca felt a wave of nerves as she reached for the handle to Hal's office. *Get a grip, you've met with Hal dozens of time,* Becca coached herself. She took a deep breath in an attempt to become calm and walked through the door. She fixed her face in as pleasant a way as possible as she greeted her boss.

"Good morning, Hal."

"Good morning, Becca. Have a seat." Becca complied and took a seat in front of Hal's massive walnut desk. She positioned herself on the front of the upholstered chair, too wired to sit more comfortably farther back. She folded her hands on her lap in an attempt to mask a slight tremor. She sat quietly, waiting for Hal to begin.

"Becca, I understand you had a very nasty shock

yesterday morning." Becca nodded, but refrained from comment. "A very unfortunate situation, and I'm sure it has shaken you to your very core."

Hal paused, and Becca saw that he expected a response. "Y-yes sir, it has been very unpleasant, to say the least."

The CEO detected the tremor in his CNO's voice. "Do you feel you need some time off to deal with this?"

Becca was surprised at the question. She had a reputation as very hard working, putting in long hours to get the job done. "I don't think so. Work is probably the best thing for me at the moment. If you'll give me just a bit of leeway as I deal with the situation, I'm sure I'll be back to my old self in a few days."

Hal regarded her over his reading glasses. "Hmm, are you sure? I would certainly understand if you took a few days off."

"Thank you for your kind consideration, but it's budget time, and being away from work right now would only cause me more stress."

"Okay, but if you need some time, please don't hesitate to ask. We'll manage, even with the budget issues. Is there anything I can do to make your job a bit easier at the moment?"

*Goodness! Does he think I'm an invalid?* "I appreciate the offer, but I'm doing fine." Becca tried to sound as if she meant it, although it sounded hollow in her own ears.

"All right; thank you for coming in. I'll check in with you tomorrow."

"Thanks, Hal." Becca rose and returned to her office. As she attempted to study budget sheets, her assistant rang. "Yes, Stephanie?"

"Ms. Dorland, there is a Detective Warfel here to see you."

Becca sighed and sat back heavily against her chair. *Oh brother! That's just what I need right now!* To her assistant, however, she merely said, "Send him in." Becca smoothed her hair and rose to greet her visitor.

"Detective Warfel, it's a pleasure to see you again," she lied as she extended her hand.

The detective accepted the offered hand and nodded, "Ms. Dorland, I hope I'm not disturbing you."

The CNO suppressed a wry smile. He would never know how much it truly did disturb her. "Of course not, please sit down. What can I do for you?"

Warfel sat in the offered chair as his host turned away to place a folder on the credenza behind her desk. As she did so, Warfel glanced at a notepad on her desk. The paper was identical to the note he found in the wastebasket at the victim's home and, although it was difficult to tell for sure, he thought the handwriting was similar.

As Becca sat down in the matching chair next to Warfel, he adjusted his chair so he could look directly at her. "I'm just following up on our conversation from yesterday. I don't like loose ends, and the reason the perpetrator placed a body in your car is a very loose end. Why your car specifically?"

Becca considered the question before answering. "As I told you yesterday, Detective, I have no idea. I have never met the dead woman. It had to be a random act. My car was unlocked and available. I wish I had off-street parking, but I make do with what I can find." *Will he believe me? Did I sound nonchalant? His gaze seems to look right through me.* Becca's thoughts were racing through her mind faster than she could process them.

56

"Yes, so you said. So, there's no one with whom you are at odds with presently? No one you've argued with?"

"No, Detective; no one."

Warfel spent another twenty minutes exploring Becca's movements over the past several weeks: places she had visited and people she had met. He was looking for any common element with the victim, any acquaintances in common, for instance. He took careful notes as the questions were answered. He detected a definite unease in the woman, and again got the impression she was hiding something. She was already nervous; he was sure she would eventually tell him what he already suspected. He would lay odds that she knew the deceased, and possibly knew why she was killed. He would give her some time to come around. Her defenses were still up today, but they would gradually weaken as she worried if she would be the next victim. He hoped for her sake that she confided in him before that happened. He finally stood and thanked Becca for her time and made his exit. He would have liked to hear her next phone call. He felt certain she would make a call, he just didn't know to whom.

Becca closed her eyes and tried to control her breathing. She had held her breath at times during the interview. She stood up, closed the door to her office and reached for her cell phone. With trembling fingers, she punched in a number from memory and waited for the call to be answered on the other end.

Detective Warfel exited the building and made his way around to the outside of the executive wing. He located the window to Becca's office and stood unmoving as he watched her bring her cell phone to her ear. He could barely make out the movement through the slightly tinted glass, but she definitely made a call as soon as he left. Nodding, he smiled and said out loud, "I thought so. Now, we just need to connect the dots."

# Seven

Sam made the familiar turn into the graveled driveway of Mac's farm. Mary walked out onto the porch as she heard the crunch of tires. She waited until Sam and Sarah exited their truck before she called out to them. "Hi, you two! It's so good to see you!"

Sarah reached the top step and hugged her friend. "Oh, Mary, how are you? This is such a nightmare for all of you!"

"I know; it's very upsetting. Poor Amy is taking it the hardest, I think. She was very close to her mother."

Sarah stepped aside, and Sam leaned down to hug Mary and to kiss her cheek. "I'm so sorry, Mary. How's Mac holding up?"

"Oh, you know Mac; he wants everyone to think he's so tough, but we all know how tender hearted he is. He and Cora may have been divorced, but they have maintained a wonderful relationship. I've never seen a more amicable divorced couple. Mac told me that once he and Cora were divorced, it was easier for them to communicate. They no longer had reasons to argue, so they rediscovered what they really liked about each other. He's taking Cora's death very hard, too."

Mary continued, "Thank you for coming this evening. We could all use a break from making funeral arrangements. The police let us into Cora's apartment earlier today to choose an outfit for her funeral. After that, I helped Amy select flowers while Cameron and Mac chose the casket. We were all pretty wiped out after that. Aggie is doing her best to take care of all of us, but your offer to bring a casserole for dinner allowed her to take a much-needed break."

"It's our pleasure to find some way to help you.

59

Our hearts are breaking for you guys. I only wish there was more we could do for you," Sarah said with a concerned look.

"You're doing more than you know by just being here with us. We need a new set of faces to look at after non-stop togetherness for two days," Mary laughed. "Now, come inside and let's eat that delicious-smelling casserole."

Sam and Sarah followed Mary inside. "Welcome! What is that heavenly smell?" Mac embraced Sarah and Sam in turn. Sam offered his condolences to Mac, and received a quick, "Thank you," in return. Sam put his arm around his friend's shoulders as they walked to the kitchen. The two women followed behind, and, before long, the four were digging into the casserole and a pie provided by a neighbor.

"Mm, this is delicious!" Sam exclaimed. "Who baked this?"

"Mrs. Patterson; she lives nearby and is well known for her baked goods. She can always be counted on to provide a pie or cake for any occasion," Mac explained.

"If we weren't already spoiled by Mrs. Hoskins, I'd offer Mrs. Patterson a job!" Sam offered.

Everyone laughed. Sarah looked around and asked, "Where are Cameron and Amy?"

Mary explained, "They're at a mutual friend's house. They needed a night out. This is very tough for them. It will do them good to be with other young adults."

Sam asked, "Mac, how is Cameron doing in his new job?"

"It's going great! He has always had an affinity for numbers. Now that he's a CPA and working in a good firm, he seems really happy. He has a steady girlfriend, and Mary and I expect an engagement announcement soon. We heard him on the phone with a jewelry store discussing a ring. We haven't let on; we want him to tell us when he's ready."

"And, what about Amy? How are her studies going?" Sarah asked.

"Straight A's," bragged Mac. She only has this semester and next, then she'll be off to medical school."

"Has she heard from her med school applications?"

"Not yet," explained Mary, "but we're very convinced she'll be accepted. Her interviews went well, and she was all but told she would be accepted. Both the University of Louisville and the University of Kentucky have great med schools, so either one is a good choice."

"She'll make a fine doctor," Sarah said.

Mac smiled. "We think so, too."

Companionable silence settled over the group. Finally, Sarah asked, "Will Cora's funeral be on Thursday?"

Mac answered, "Yes, at two o'clock. She'll be cremated the next day. It's what the kids wanted – a full funeral, but no burial. They want to scatter her ashes near the mountain cabin where we vacationed when they were younger. I spoke with the owner of the cabin, and he has no objection."

"Sounds very respectful and thoughtful," Sam said. Silence settled again on the group, eventually broken again by Sam, "Mac, how's your new colt doing?

Mac's face brightened, "He's coming along nicely. He'll make a fine addition to your equine therapy program someday. Would you like to see him? He's in the barn with his mother. It's getting chilly at night, and I don't want him to suffer a setback."

"I'd love to! Sarah, are you coming?"

"Thanks, but I'll stay here and help Mary with the dishes."

Mac and Sam left for the barn, and the women began clearing the table. "How's little Anna?" Mary asked.

"She's so busy! I have a hard time keeping up with her. I never knew a two-year-old could find so many ways to get into mischief! When she takes a nap, I sit down and use that time to write. Mrs. Hoskins takes her for a while after that so I can finish writing for the day."

"How is the new novel coming?"

"A bit slowly, but I think I have it all figured out. I love the characters and may use them again in my next book."

"I can't wait to read it. Maybe it will become a movie like your first book."

"Oh, once was enough! All that attention was exhausting! I do love to write, but I don't like to be away from Sam and the farm for more than a couple of days. Anna is getting harder to travel with, too. Mrs. Hoskins came along on the book tours, but Anna was just a baby then. It would be harder now. I think I'll take a break from touring until Anna is a bit older."

Mary smiled. "I understand completely. I put my career on hold when Susan was born. I just knew no one could take care of her as well as I could. When she started school, I eased back into work, but didn't work full time until she was in high school."

"You climbed the corporate ladder quickly after that."

"Yes, I guess I did. I loved every minute I spent with Susan, and I loved my fast-paced career, too. Now, though, Mac and the farm are my focus. I do some editing, but I certainly do not work the long hours that I did in Chicago. I love my life here with Mac. Thank you for bringing us together."

"All we did was invite both of you to our wedding. You were on your own after that."

The two worked in companionable silence for the next several minutes, but the quiet was interrupted by Mac's voice as he burst through the back door. "Mary, call 911!"

Both women stood in the center of the kitchen with surprised looks on their faces. Sarah finally looked around and asked, "Mac, where's Sam?"

Mac answered, "He's hurt, call 911."

Mary picked up her cell phone and made the call as Sarah threw her kitchen towel down and ran outside. Mac ran after her, "Sarah, wait!"

"Sam...Sam!"

"Over here, Sarah." Sarah followed the voice and discovered Sam lying on the ground. He was rubbing his head.

"What happened Sam?" Sarah cried, as she fell to the ground and reached for Sam's hand.

"I, I don't know. I was walking along with Mac when I suddenly felt a sharp pain in the back of my head. I don't know what happened after that. I blacked out."

Mac and Mary caught up with Sarah and assured the couple that an ambulance was on its way. Sam raised up on one elbow, "I'm all right, I..." Before Sam could finish his sentence, he fell back again. "I'm a little dizzy."

Sarah looked at Mac with wide eyes, "Mac, what can we do?"

"Sarah, the ambulance is coming. Let's just keep him comfortable until then."

Sarah noticed, for the first time, that Mac was holding a revolver. "Mac, why do you have your gun? What's wrong?"

"I'm afraid the person who attacked Sam could still be around. We caught him poking around in the shed next to the barn. Sam came up on him first; that's why he was attacked. I was a couple of steps behind. The guy pushed me and ran away."

Sam opened his eyes again and Sarah prevented him from trying to sit up this time. "Careful, darling. Lie down, okay?"

Sirens broke the night silence, and Mary directed the EMT's toward the barn. Sam's vital signs were assessed, and his bleeding head wound was cleansed and bandaged. "We need to take you to the hospital; you probably have a concussion."

"I doubt I need a hospital; I'll be fine."

"Sam, do as they say; I want to make sure you're okay," Sarah instructed, her voice indicating there would be no further discussion.

Sam acquiesced as he realized it would be futile to argue. When the EMT's moved Sam to the stretcher, he cried out in pain. Something was wrong with his left arm. One of the EMT's skillfully felt along the shaft of the humerus. There was no bone displacement, but a nondisplaced fracture was likely. The EMT's supported Sam's arm with a folded blanket placed under the elbow. The arm was then secured to the stretcher with a strap.

Sarah followed the ambulance to the hospital.

Mac and Mary drove behind her in Mac's truck. At the hospital, there was little Sarah could do but wait anxiously with her friends while Sam was being assessed and treated. She called Mrs. Hoskins to explain why she and Sam would be late coming home. She tried to convey more confidence than she was feeling about Sam's condition.

Sarah waited anxiously in the ED waiting room as Sam was evaluated. Sarah called home periodically to check on Anna. Mrs. Hoskins assured her employer that the toddler was sleeping soundly. She expressed concern for Sam, and assured Sarah that Anna would be fine until her parents were able to come home. After completing the call, Sarah turned to speak to Mac and Mary, but was interrupted. "Mrs. Richardson?"

Sarah turned around, "Yes?"

"Mrs. Richardson, I'm Dr. Poole. I examined your husband, performed a brain scan, and x-rayed his ribs and left arm. He has a mild concussion, bruised ribs, and a nondisplaced fracture of his left humerus; that's the upper bone in the arm. He needs to wear a sling for a few weeks. I doubt your husband will need anything more, but it's probably best to have it checked out further by an orthopedist. He's a lucky man; this could have been much worse."

"Thank you, Dr. Poole. Will he need to remain in the hospital?"

"No, he can go home. There's no swelling in his brain. He may have a headache for a couple of weeks, especially with bending over, but that will resolve in time. The ribs will heal by themselves but will be painful for a few days. He's been given pain meds in his IV, and I wrote a prescription for oral pain medication that can be filled at our in-house pharmacy

65

before you leave."

"When can I take him home?" Sarah asked.

"He'll be ready to go as soon as the nurse instructs you in his care and what to watch for that could signal a complication. He should be fine, but it pays to heed the precautions and report any changes right away. If you'll follow me, I'll take you to him."

Sarah turned to Mac and Mary, "If you guys need to get home, I should be fine now. I can get Sam home."

Mary objected. "No way, Sarah, we'll follow you home. We want to make sure Sam is settled before we leave you."

"Thanks, you guys are the best." She smiled at her friends, and then hurried to catch up to Dr. Poole.

Mac followed Sarah's SUV as she drove Sam home. Once both vehicles were parked, Mac hurried to help Sam out of the passenger seat. His gait was unsteady because of the pain meds, so care was taken with the porch steps. Once inside the house, Sam was guided down the hall to the family room. His favorite chair, a recliner, was waiting for him.

"I think I'll stay right here tonight. I don't want to move until morning," Sam whispered.

Sarah reassured her husband, "Honey, you can sleep wherever you want. We have pain medication to help you rest. I filled it at the hospital pharmacy before we left." Sarah retrieved a pillow to support Sam's injured arm and another one to put behind his head. She helped Sam take his medication and covered him with an afghan. He was asleep in seconds.

"Is there anything you need before I go to bed?" Mrs. Hoskins asked.

"No, I'm sure we're fine for the night. I would

appreciate it you could tend to Anna in the morning as I'm sure I'll be up some tonight helping Sam."

"Of course. Good night, everyone."

"Good night, Mrs. Hoskins, and thank you for all you do for us."

The housekeeper smiled and nodded in response.

Everyone tiptoed from the family room, and Sarah checked on Anna before joining her friends in the kitchen. It was nearly midnight as the friends sat down together at the kitchen table.

Mac spoke first, "Sarah, I'm really sorry about tonight. I have no idea who that could have been or why he was searching our shed. Stuff was scattered on the floor, and two file cabinets were pried open. We keep farm records in there. I'll have to look tomorrow to see if anything was taken and file a police report."

"Mac, I have a question. How did Sam bruise his ribs and break his arm? I thought he was hit from behind on the head."

"He was, but when he fell, he hit the water pump in the paddock. It all happened so fast, I wasn't able to break his fall."

"Poor Sam," Mary commiserated. "I'm glad his injuries weren't even worse."

"Me, too," Sarah agreed. "Can I get anyone something to drink?"

Mac declined. "Thanks, but we'd better get going. I called Cameron from the hospital, so he and Amy are aware of what happened and where we are. He called the police to report the incident and said a deputy came out but couldn't see anything in the dark. He told them I would file a report in the morning. He turned on the floodlights and checked on the horses. I think our attacker is gone—at least for tonight. If Sam has any problems, be sure to call us. We can be here in five minutes."

"Will do. I'll sleep on the couch near Sam tonight, and let Mrs. Hoskins care for Anna in the morning. I'll call you by noon to let you know how Sam is doing."

"Okay, Sarah, get some rest," Mac said as he parted.

The next morning, Sarah awoke to Anna's voice. Sarah pushed her blanket aside to get up, but Mrs. Hoskins spoke quietly from the doorway. "It's okay, Mrs. Richards, I have her. You go back to sleep."

An hour later she was awakened as Sam called out to her. "Sarah?" Sam's voice sounded very far away as she struggled to come up from the dream she was having. She opened her eyes and tried to remember why she was sleeping on the couch before it all came rushing back to her. She realized Sam had called out, and she hurried to him with a look of concern on her face.

"Whoa! I'm fine, sweetheart," Sam assured his wife, with more conviction than he felt.

"Oh, Sam, I just had the worst dream. You were at the hospital, and I couldn't find you. I searched down dark hallways, but all the rooms were empty! I'm so glad you're safe and sound at home."

"Well, mostly sound," Sam joked, with a wry smile.

"Are you in a lot of pain, sweetheart?"

"Not too bad, but I'll take another of those pain pills when I have my breakfast."

"You got it! Mrs. Hoskins got up with Anna. I'll go check on them, then I'll get you something to eat."

"Okay, but first, I need to get up and go to the bathroom. Can you help me up?"

"Sure, honey."

Sam headed to the bathroom while Sarah quickly changed into jeans and a sweater. She then went in search of Mrs. Hoskins and Anna. She found them playing in the backyard and watched as her daughter twirled and scurried through the fallen carpet of leaves before she threw handfuls up in the air. The toddler laughed as she played. It was pure joy, and it lifted Sarah's mood as she watched. Mrs. Hoskins waved to Sarah before turning her attention back to her young charge. Sarah turned from the doorway and started putting a simple breakfast together. She put everything on a tray and returned to the family room as Sam eased himself back into his recliner. Sarah set her portion of the breakfast on a side table and placed the tray on Sam's lap.

"It's not much, I'll make it up at lunch."

"Looks good to me. Bagels, fruit, and coffee make the perfect breakfast after such an eventful night."

Sam spread cream cheese on his bagel and took a bite. He munched for a while before expressing a theory about the attack of the night before. "Sarah, I was thinking about why someone would be rummaging through Mac's shed. I don't believe the man who hit me intended to confront us. We surprised him, and he simply reacted. The real question is why he was there to begin with." Sam was thoughtful, then added, "Do you think it could possibly have anything to do with Cora's murder?"

Sarah stopped chewing and swallowed hard, "Are you saying that man could be the same person who killed Cora?"

"I don't know. It just seems an odd coincidence, if that's what it is. Mac once said he doesn't believe in coincidence. I wonder what he thinks about last night."

"Well, you can ask me," Mac said from the doorway.

"Mac! Where did you come from?"

"I saw Mrs. Hoskins in the yard. She let me in. How are you doing, Sam?"

"I think I'll live."

"So, what did you want to ask me?" Mac asked, as he chose a chair near Sam.

Sam cleared his throat, "Well, do you think the man who attacked me last night was somehow tied to Cora's murder?"

Mac was thoughtful for several seconds before responding. "I suppose it's possible. Of course, it could be totally unrelated."

"Mac, aren't you the one who said you don't believe in coincidences?" Sam reminded.

Mac laughed. "You're right, I did. Okay, so let's assume the two events are related. What could Cora's murderer want from my shed?"

"I guess that's the question we need to answer. Mac, you need to get through Cora's funeral, and I need a couple of days to heal, but this weekend we'll both be in a better position to pursue this."

At the mention of Cora's funeral, Mac became quiet.

"Mac, what's wrong?" Sarah asked her friend.

Mac sighed, "The kids want me to speak at the funeral, but I don't know if I can. After all, I wasn't her only husband. Dr. Larkin might have something to say about what's included in the funeral. Her sister Beth will be there, too. Things got a little strained with Beth after Cora and I divorced. She blamed me for the break-up. I let her believe it was my fault because it was easier than

70

spoiling her image of her sister. I just couldn't tell her about Cora's affair; it served no purpose. I have no idea if Cora ever set the record straight. If not, Beth would take umbrage, I believe, if I participated in the service. I loved Cora, but her sister might feel that I was being a hypocrite. To tell the truth, I'll be glad when the service is over."

Sarah attempted to comfort her friend. "Mac, we'll be there to support you and your family. You're not alone."

"I know, and I appreciate it. Are you sure you'll feel up to it, Sam?"

"Sure, I just need to move a bit slowly. The ribs are the worst part. It hurts even to breathe. The pain meds help, though."

"That's good; pain is no fun, but if you wake up tomorrow and feel you're not up to it, don't try to come to the service."

"You won't be able to keep me away. You can't get rid of me that easily," Sam quipped.

"Mac, would you care for something to eat?" Sarah offered.

"I've had breakfast, thank you, but I think I'll go ask Mrs. Hoskins for a cup of coffee. I just heard the backdoor squeak. I think she and Anna are back inside."

Mac stood up and headed to the kitchen. As he passed the front door, the doorbell rang. "I'll get it, Mrs. Hoskins." He opened the door and exclaimed, "Detective Warfel, good morning! What brings you out here?"

"Mr. Osborne, your wife told me you were here. May I come in?"

"Of course! Do you want to speak with Sam and Sarah, too?"

"Yes, I would."

"I was just on my way to the kitchen for coffee; would you like a cup?"

"I would love a cup, thank you."

"Okay, I'll show you into the family room, then I'll get our coffee."

Mac led the detective to the family room and announced the detective's arrival.

"Come in, Detective. Have a seat," Sarah invited. "Pardon our appearance; we had a very late night."

"So, I heard; that's why I'm here. I'm glad to catch all of you together. I'd like to hear what happened last night at Mr. Osborne's farm."

"Sure," Sam replied as Mac returned with two coffees, cream, and sugar.

"I wasn't sure how you take your coffee, Detective."

"Black is fine, Mr. Osborne; thank you."

"Please call me Mac; everyone does."

"Okay, Mac. I was just telling Mr. and Mrs. Richards that I would like to hear about last night."

Sam interjected, "We're Sam and Sarah, Detective. Feel free to call us by our first names if you are comfortable doing so."

"Thank you, I'm Tom."

Mac smiled, "Well, now that we have that settled, what do you want to know about last night, and why are you, a homicide detective, interested in a simple break-in and knock on the head?'

The detective took a sip of his coffee before answering, "Mac, have you considered the possibility that the death of your ex-wife and the incident last night are related?"

Mac and Sam exchanged a glance. "As a matter

of fact, Sam and I were just discussing that very possibility. Do *you* believe they are related?" Mac asked.

"I'm entertaining the idea," Warfel replied. "Why do you think the man broke into your shed last night? What do you keep in there?"

Mac was surprised that Detective Warfel knew of the break-in. "I keep some file cabinets in there to store farm records and some miscellaneous stuff. There's nothing important, I assure you."

"What is and what isn't important is a matter of perspective, Mac. There may be something there that ties into Mrs. Larkin's murder. How many people know you store records in that shed?"

Mac thought for a minute before he said, "Well, it's no secret. There have been several hired men on my farm since I bought it four years ago. I'm sure all of them saw me in the shed filing paperwork at one time or another."

"I see; would you be able to provide a list of those hired men? Contact information would be helpful, too."

"Names are no problem. Tax records had to be kept for each man except short-term hires who received less than the required amount for withholding. These are men I hired for a day or two to help with a big project such as building a fence. Contact information is another story altogether. Most of these guys move around a lot. The addresses I have could be completely inaccurate now."

"I understand. It would give us a place to start, though." Warfel dropped his eyes and hesitated before continuing. "I believe Mrs. Larkin's funeral is tomorrow; is that correct?"

"Yes, at two o'clock."

"I'd like to attend, if that's all right with you. As a rule, I attend murder victims' funerals. I try to be unobtrusive, and I stand in the back. This gives me a chance to look over the mourners. I look for anyone who seems uneasy or out of place. Killers often attend the funeral services of their victims, especially if they had known the victim and their presence would seem natural. After the funeral, do I have your permission to search the shed with you?"

"Absolutely! Sam and I had already planned to do just that, except we were going to do it Friday. I don't know how long we'll have friends visiting after the funeral."

"It could wait until Friday, I suppose," Warfel conceded.

"That's settled then. We'll get started early Friday morning. Come around eight o'clock and Aggie will have breakfast ready."

"Now that sounds like an offer I can't turn down," Detective Warfel answered. A broad smile lit up his face; transforming it from the crusty no-nonsense detective to a man Mac felt he could call his friend. Tom finished his coffee and wished Sam a speedy recovery. He left Serendipity Farm more determined than ever to bring closure to the case.

# Eight

The day of the funeral brought cold autumn winds and intermittent rain. The leaves that still clung to their branches were being buffeted and brought down in a cascade of color. Streets and sidewalks were strewn with the wet leaves, making surfaces slick and hazardous. Mac stood at his back door watching the falling rain. Mary walked up from behind and wrapped her arms around him. She rested her head against his back. The gesture caused Mac to smile, and it eased a bit of the sadness he felt. "Thinking about Cora?" Mary asked.

Still looking out the door with his back to Mary, he said, "Yes, she can't even get a pretty day for her funeral." Mary remained silent, waiting for Mac. "She always did have the worst luck. I was hoping for a sunny day for her. The dismal weather seems to make it all worse, if that's possible." Mac finally turned around and held Mary close, with his chin resting on her head. "Thank you for being so understanding about all of this. You've been amazing. A lot of women would be jealous of her husband's friendship with his ex-wife. I don't have the same feelings I had for her when we were married, but I did care for her. It's hard to explain, but we had a lot of good years together, and a couple of terrific kids."

Mary stepped back a half step and looked up at Mac. "Sweetheart, I know you love me. That's enough for me. Your feelings toward Cora are a compilation of years of shared memories. She was a good woman. I understand that. Your feelings toward her in no way diminish our love. If there is anything I've discovered about you, Mac Osborne, is that you have a very large

75

capacity to love. That's why people are drawn to you, and why you take in horses no one else wants. I would never want to change that about you. As long as you continue to look at me with love in your eyes, I'll be a contented woman."

Tears stung Mac's eyes as he pulled Mary close to him. "How did I get so lucky as to have the love of such a wonderful woman?"

Amy walked into the kitchen but stopped when she saw her dad and Mary embracing. "Oh, sorry, I hope I'm not interrupting something important."

Mac and Mary laughed at the comment and separated from each other. "Amy, you're looking at two people who love each other very much. I guess you could say that is very important, but so are you. What can I get you for breakfast?" Mary asked.

"I'm not very hungry; I was just going to get some coffee."

"I just made it; help yourself, but I'm making blueberry pancakes and I made enough batter for everyone."

"That's sounds delicious. I guess I am a little bit hungry. Where's Aggie?"

"We gave her the morning off. She was here late last night getting food ready for this afternoon, so we felt she needed to sleep in this morning. Is Cameron up yet?"

"Yeah, he should be down soon. He was getting ready in the bathroom when I came down."

"Good, I'll start the pancakes. Mac, will you take care of the bacon? You always get it crispy without burning it."

"Sure. Feed me blueberry pancakes, and I'll do anything you want," Mac teased.

76

Cameron bounded into the kitchen, "Yum! What smells so good?"

"Your breakfast, silly!" Amy quipped.

Cameron laughed at his sister's teasing and tugged at the back of her hair.

"Hey!" Amy pretended to be angry but started laughing at her brother's antics. He sat down next to her and reached for the pitcher of orange juice Mary had placed on the table. He poured four glasses and asked everyone to take one. When all had their juice, he proposed a toast.

"To Mom and the many years of love she gave us, and to our family. As long as we hold onto each other, we can weather anything." The glasses clinked together in a show of unity before everyone sipped the golden liquid.

A few hours later, the family rode together to the church where Mac and his family had worshipped when the children were young, and where Cora had continued as a member. The drive took forty minutes and gave everyone time to reminisce. No one felt the need to break the silence in the car. It was a collective time of grief and reflection, and it prepared them for the service to come.

Mac felt a growing sense of unease as he anticipated coming face-to-face with Cora's sister. He hoped there would not be a scene, but he remembered all too well Beth's parting words to him. She made it clear she considered Mac's divorce from Cora to be his fault. How would she react to Cora's murder? Would she blame Mac in some way? Mac's stomach churned, and he doubted he would be able to deliver the speech he had prepared.

He pulled the car into the parking lot of the

church and helped Mary out of the car. Cameron and Amy emerged from the back, and the four of them walked along the flagstone path to the front of the stone church. They climbed the steps and were met at the entrance by the minister.

"Good afternoon, Mac. It's good to see you again." The two men embraced and Mac introduced Mary. "I've heard so much about you from Mac. I feel I know you already."

"It's been several years, Reverend, but do you remember my children, Amy and Cameron?"

"I do remember both of you! I was very sad to hear of your mother's death. I'm so sorry; she was a good woman."

"Thank you, Reverend. That's very kind of you," Cameron replied.

Reverend Jennings led the family into the church and explained the order of the service and seating arrangements. "Of course, all of you will enter last. I'll show you where you can wait."

The family entered a room with comfortable upholstered chairs. "We hold Bible studies in here for small groups, but we also use it as a waiting room for funerals, weddings, and such. There's coffee, water, and soft drinks on the counter. Help yourself. The restrooms are across the hall. Is there anything else you need?" the minister asked.

"I don't think so. Thank you for your hospitality. Oh, there is one thing," Mac said, "when will we know when to come into the sanctuary?"

"Someone will come for you. Until then, please make yourself at home."

"Thank you," Mac replied.

The family sat down and tried to settle their

nerves. Saying good-bye to a loved one was never easy. A knock on the door startled the family, but before anyone could answer, the door slowly opened and a petite gray-haired lady entered.

"Beth!" Mac exclaimed.

"Hello, Mac. Could I speak with you privately for a few minutes?"

"Uh, of course." Mac turned to Mary and his children, "I'll be back in a few minutes."

Beth led Mac to a nearby Sunday school room. She sat down and motioned for Mac to do the same.

Mac complied and waited for Beth to speak.

"I'm sure you're wondering why I want to talk with you. You can relax; I'm not going to rehash old accusations. In fact, I want to apologize. I've been unfair to you. Cora told me about her affair. While I don't condone it, I think I understand it. She said your marriage had stalled, and there was little in common. She said the affair made her feel attractive and young again, but it only lasted a few weeks. She finally came to her senses, but the damage was already done. When you found out about the affair, there wasn't enough left between the two of you to salvage the marriage. It happens. I understand that now. Can you forgive me for what I said to you?"

"Beth, thank you for having the courage to come to me. It means more to me than you know. I loved Cora, even after the divorce, and I'll miss her very much. As for forgiving you, there is nothing to forgive."

"Thank you, Mac. I'm glad we can put the past to rest. Do you think I could talk to my niece and nephew now?"

"I'm sure they would love to see you, Beth. I would also like to introduce my wife Mary to you. She and Cora got along beautifully, and I hope you like her, too."

"I'm sure I will."

The rest of the day was a blur, with the funeral, the reception at the farm afterwards, and cleaning up after the last of the guests had left. Sam and Sarah helped with the cleanup, and finally sat down with Mac and Mary in the kitchen for a cup of coffee before heading home.

"It was a very nice service, Mac," Sarah remarked.

"Yes, Reverend Jennings gave a great eulogy," Mac agreed.

"I thought Dr. Larkin's tribute to Cora was touching. He certainly seemed to be fond of her still. I could hear the emotion in his voice. Your comments were beautiful, too, Mac. Cora would be pleased."

"Thanks, I meant all of it. She was a wonderful mother to our children and a good wife to me. I still wonder where it all went wrong for our marriage. It's hard to pinpoint a time or event that knocked the train off its tracks. We just grew apart gradually."

Mary reached out for Mac's hand across the table. "It's too easy to second guess ourselves, sweetheart. You're only human like everyone else in the world. We all make mistakes."

"I suppose you're right; I'll try to let it go." He gave Mary's hand a squeeze, and started to say something else, but was interrupted by the doorbell.

Mac stood up, "I wonder who that could be. Everyone we know already visited."

Aggie arrived at the door ahead of Mac. Detective Warfel was introducing himself to Aggie when Mac walked up behind her.

"Tom, come in! You're just in time to partake of the feast before we put it all away."

The detective smiled, "Thanks, I could use a sandwich and something to drink, but I don't want to intrude."

"Not at all, everyone's gone except Sam and Sarah. Come on into the kitchen and have a seat."

"Thank you." The men entered the kitchen and Tom took a seat. "Hello, everyone."

The greeting was returned. Mac prepared a roast beef sandwich for the detective. "Are you officially on duty, or can you have a beer?"

Tom smiled a bit sheepishly, "No, I'm not on duty, and a beer would be great, thank you." Tom took a bite of his sandwich and a sip of his beer before revealing why he was there. "I attended the service, very nice by the way." Mac nodded. I stood in the back and watched people's expressions and body language during the service. Almost everyone was attentive, several cried, but one man with red hair sat stone still. He didn't speak to anyone, and no one spoke to him. He didn't sing or follow the liturgy. He just sat there. He sat on the back row, all the way to the end of the pew, next to the windows."

"Who was he?" Mac asked.

"I don't know, but one of my men followed him. We had hoped he had driven a car so we could get a license plate number, but he walked a few blocks toward town and went into a diner. He must have gone immediately out the back door. My man walked around to the alley and back through the restaurant, even checked the men's room, but couldn't find him. He may have nothing to do with Mrs. Larkin's murder, but his actions were very suspicious."

Mac looked directly at the detective, "I want to get whoever did this to Cora. They can't get away with what they did to her."

Tom noticed the emotion behind the words. *He still cared for her.* Out loud he said, "We're making this case a priority. No one deserved what happened to Mrs. Larkin."

"It's dark now, but we could get flashlights and start tonight," Mac offered.

"No, thanks, it can wait until morning; we'll have better light then. I don't want to overlook something in the dark."

"Okay, whatever you want."

"I can help, too" Sam offered.

"If you're up to it, we could use the help. I have most of my team following up on several leads. If you help, that would free up one of them."

"My arm and ribs are feeling a bit better today. I saw an orthopedist this morning, and he said I could get by with just the sling. The break doesn't need surgery. By tomorrow, the initial pain from inflammation should be gone."

Sarah spoke up, "Listen to you; you sound like a doctor."

"Nah, I'm just repeating what the nurse told me at the hospital. Anyway, I want to help."

"Thanks, Sam," Mac replied.

The next morning dawned sunny and crisp. The rain of the day before left cooler temperatures in its wake, and bright sunshine replaced the gray clouds of the day before. Amy and Cameron said tearful good-byes after breakfast, and promised to come home for Thanksgiving. Mac watched them drive away, and then he went into his study. He searched through a file drawer in the desk until he found what he was searching for.

"What's that?" Mary asked from the doorway.

"It's a master list of the files in the shed. I'm glad I kept this list. It will show if anything is missing. I have to keep records for tax purposes. I've always been organized, I guess it's the cop in me."

Mary laughed, "You could give lessons on organization to Martha Stewart! While you're looking through the shed, I'll be working. I'm a bit behind on my editing. Let Aggie or me know if you need anything."

"Will do. I think I hear either Tom or Sam coming up the driveway now. We'll get started after breakfast."

Tom's unmarked department issue sedan was followed closely by the crunch of tires on gravel as Sam joined the other men. Mac made two copies of the list of files and handed one to each man. "Let's eat the eggs, biscuits, and gravy Aggie fixed, then we can go through the files." Mac suggested.

Sam readily agreed. "You don't have to ask me twice; I love Aggie's cooking!"

The men entered the kitchen to the inviting aroma of a large country breakfast. Aggie beamed with pleasure as each man ate everything on his plate. As Aggie cleared the table, the men pushed back from the table, thanked the housekeeper for the wonderful breakfast, and made their way to the shed by the barn.

"The list you gave us helps a lot, Mac. Where do you want to start?" Tom asked.

"Well, I guess we each take a file cabinet. That should take a while."

"Okay, sounds good. Let's go," replied the

detective.

The men worked all morning looking through files. They carefully scrutinized each page to prevent overlooking anything important. As the last file was replaced in its cabinet and the drawer was shut, Sam dropped his list, and it floated behind one of the cabinets. "Just leave it," Mac directed, but Sam had already begun to move the cabinet with his one good hand. Tom bent to the task and finished moving the cabinet to the side. He leaned over to pick up the list when he noticed a torn piece of paper under it. He pulled a pair of latex gloves from his pocket and picked up both pages.

"Mac, what do you think this is?"

Mac looked over Tom's shoulder at the torn remnant. "I don't know. I don't have anything like this. It's a document of some sort. The decorative edging is not familiar to me, though."

"This may be nothing, or it may be connected to the case. May I take it?" Warfel asked.

"Sure, I've already had my fingernails inspected and my cheek swabbed for my DNA, why would I object to handing over a torn piece of paper?" Mac joked.

Tom smiled, "Thank you for being so cooperative. You and Dr. Larkin have been great to work with. It made it easier to eliminate you as suspects.

"As a former police detective, I know how hard investigation is. I'm happy to do anything that will help find Cora's killer."

Tom retrieved an evidence bag from his coat pocket and placed the paper in it. "I'll take this to the lab and let them get a crack at it. I'll let you know if we find anything."

"I'll either be here or at Sam's. With his arm in a sling, he needs a little help today," Mac stated.

The detective nodded, removed his gloves, and walked back to his car. Mac and Sam traded looks, each leaving unsaid what they wanted most—Cora's killer.

\*\*\*

Sam and Mac arrived at Serendipity Farm two hours later, and were greeted by Mrs. Hoskins before they made it to the front porch.

"Now, Mr. Richards, you come in here and get settled. Can I get you anything? Have you had your lunch?"

"I'm fine, Mrs. Hoskins and thank you for offering, but we had lunch on the way. I plan to rest a bit while Mac checks on a couple of the horses."

The gray-haired housekeeper started to say something further, but Anna woke from her nap and began calling for Mrs. Hoskins. With a final look of concern for Sam, she nodded and turned to tend to the toddler.

Mac helped Sam get comfortable in his recliner. "You're looking a bit on the pale side, my friend. Are you okay?"

"Just tired, but I could use half of one of my pain pills. They're on the table by the couch."

"Just half?"

"Yeah, I'm tapering off. I don't like to have a fuzzy head. Half of one will take the edge off the pain."

"Okay, here you go. Now, you get some rest, just tell me what needs to be done, and I'll get started," Mac offered.

"Thanks, Mac. I'm sure Howard can take care of most of the chores, but I would appreciate it if you'd help Howard get ready for this afternoon's therapy session. The kids from foster care really look forward to coming, so we decided to go ahead with it."

"Sure, no problem. Are there any special instructions on the kids?"

"No, not with this group. They're between the ages of ten and twelve and have been coming for six weeks, so they know the drill. We've already seen several coming out of their shells as they work with the horses. Starting an equine therapy program for at-risk foster kids was the best possible use of the money Sara inherited from her father."

"Yes, it was. Okay, I'll check with Howard first and let him know I'm here. Your farm manager is very protective of his four-legged charges, so I don't want him to think I'm butting into his business."

Sam attempted a laugh, but his ribs protested. "Yes, Howard takes his job here very seriously, and we're really glad he does. He and Mrs. Hoskins let Sarah and me believe we're in charge, but the truth is, we couldn't run this place without either of them."

Mac chuckled. "Aw, you two are doing pretty well for a couple of city slickers, but I'm glad you appreciate what you have. Now, you just rest awhile and I'll take care of the class."

"Thanks, Mac."

Mac left the farmhouse and headed to the paddock. As he came to the bottom of the back door steps, his peripheral vision caught movement at the left corner of the house.

"Howard?" No answer. *He must not have heard me.* With a shrug, Mac turned to his right, toward the paddock. He could see Prissy just beyond the gate. The young filly caught the scent of her former owner and met Mac at the gate to the paddock.

"Hi, girl, how do you like it here?"

As Mac gently stroked the mare's neck, Howard emerged from the barn.

"Hey, Mac, it's good to see you," Howard said as he led one of the horses from the barn.

"Howard? But, you were...weren't you just behind the house? I thought I saw you when I came down the steps."

"I've been in the barn cleaning stalls. It wasn't me you saw." The two men looked at each other with rising concern.

Mac asked, "Could it have been one of the hired men?"

"No, Lonnie is in town picking up feed for the horses, and Jake is in the barn. I left him to finish cleaning up. What did you see, or think you saw, Mac?"

With a look of concern, Mac told Howard of the man he had seen walking around the side of the house. It took only a moment for them to realize the significance of what Mac had seen before both men took off at a run. They searched outbuildings and around bushes but found no one.

Finally, Howard asked, "Did you get a look at him?"

"Not really," Mac responded, "his back was to me, but he had red hair and was wearing a blue denim shirt and jeans."

"Hmm, there's no one around here except me with red hair. I don't like this. Do you think it could be the same person who struck Sam?"

"Maybe, but we can't take any chances; we need to post someone to watch the farm until this all gets cleared up. Sam's resting now, but when he wakes up; we'll let him know what happened. I'm sure he'll agree to hiring guards."

"What's this about guards?" Sam asked.

Both men turned around at the sound of Sam's voice. "Sam, I thought you were resting," Mac stated.

"I'm too restless, what's going on?"

Howard explained the situation to his boss with added details from Mac.

Sam gave a low whistle. "I don't understand any of this, but I agree with getting 'round the clock guards. Howard, can you arrange that?"

"Sure, no problem."

"Good, I don't want the ladies of the house to be frightened. Mac, do you have any idea what's happening? First, Cora is found dead, then someone searches your shed and cold cocks me, and, now some stranger appears at my house."

"I don't, Sam—at least not yet, but I don't think these are unrelated incidents. I'll call Detective Warfel and tell him about this. I'm sure he'd want to know."

"Okay, sounds like the best plan," Sam agreed. "Now, can we get ready for the kids?"

# Nine

It was late Friday afternoon, and Becca looked forward to the weekend. Most of the budget was finished, with only the capital items to be completed. Donations had dwindled in recent months, so several of the capital requests would be denied. Finesse would be required to prioritize the competing proposals without incurring the displeasure of key members of the medical staff. Becca sighed as she thought of the battle ahead. She glanced at the clock, was surprised that it had gotten so late, and decided she was at a good stopping point for the day.

What a week! It had started off with finding a dead body in her car and made worse by that nosy detective. He didn't seem satisfied with his last visit. Would he come back? The thought chilled her, but he wasn't her only concern. Was Cora's murder a warning? Would Becca be next? Fear had replaced her usual self-assurance, and it was consuming her every thought. *I have to find a way out of this mess,* she decided. With a small shake of her head, she pushed aside her concerns as she prepared to leave for the day.

Becca reached into the bottom right hand drawer of her desk and retrieved her purse. Maybe she would shop on the way home. It always made her feel better to buy something new, and the anticipation made her step lighter as she walked toward the parking garage. The sun was low in the sky, and without warmth from the sun, the air had become cool. Becca pulled her coat closer around her and became uneasy as she entered the dark parking garage. Long shadows extended into the corners of the structure. *I can't believe it's nearly dark already. I miss the longer daylight hours of summer,* she thought as she spied her new car.

Becca approached the black Mercedes Benz SLC Roadster. It had been an extravagance, but she loved the feel of it as she drove. She justified the purchase by realizing she would see Cora's dead body tumbling out of her car each time she opened the door, Cora's eyes staring back at her.

The dealership, not knowing of the dead body that had occupied it only days before, made a great offer for her low mileage trade-in. Besides, with the extra money she had earned recently, she could afford it. Her personal trainer at the gym where she worked out had told her she could receive a generous bonus for attracting women to the gym. A fleeting feeling of guilt crossed her conscience, but was quickly replaced by justifications for her actions—albeit false ones. She couldn't change anything now, even if she could give the money back. She wondered again what had really happened to the women and girls she had lured to the gym with offers of free membership fees and other perks. Her imagination conjured up visions of forced prostitution and physical abuse. *How did I get myself involved in human trafficking? I should have seen through the deception. It's too late now, though. If I could only find the bonds I could disappear. Four million dollars would go a long way toward a new life. But, what if I don't find them?* The thought made her shudder. She opened the door of the luxury car and slid behind the wheel. She turned to her right and placed her Louis Vuitton purse on the passenger seat. A movement caught her eye and she looked up as the passenger door was flung open. A man shoved a gun in her face as he got into the car, pushing the expensive handbag to the floor.

90

"Drive!"

Too shocked to respond, Becca merely sat there staring at the intruder.

"I said, drive!"

With trembling hands, she started the car and put it in reverse. "Wh-where are we going?"

"Take a right out of the garage, then go straight. I'll give you directions as we go along."

The frightened woman drove, making turns as directed. She considered jumping from the car, but the gun's barrel remained pressed against her ribs. If she even reached for the door handle, she would be killed. She had no viable course of action except to follow the man's instructions. Becca drove past familiar neighborhoods, finding it remarkable that the homes' occupants were going about their daily routine, unaware of the menace just beyond the safety of their front door.

The assailant barked new orders, and the sporty car sped out of town as the last vestiges of sunlight dropped below the horizon.

Becca's heart was beating nearly as fast as her car was driving. She was negotiating countryside curves faster than was wise, but her fear controlled the car. With each passing mile, her terror increased. *What does this man want with me? Will he kill me and dump me like Cora?* Darkness descended silently, a fitting shroud for the occupants in the sleek roadster.

Finally, the man broke his silence. "Turn right here—at the stop sign."

Becca's hands trembled and her palms were sweaty. The instruction had been given too late to slow the car for a smooth turn, and she nearly lost control as she negotiated the maneuver. The man beside her paid no attention to the car's swerve as he strained to see

91

ahead of him.

The narrow road transitioned to a rough gravel path, but Becca was instructed to continue on. A mile further, and Becca could just make out a dim light ahead. Now, her heart skipped a beat as this appeared to be the place where she would die.

"Pull over the to the left and stop," growled the nameless menace beside her.

Becca struggled to find her voice. "Wh…what are you going to do?"

A strange laugh escaped from her captor. "You got that wrong, lady; it's what *you* are going to do. Now, get out!"

Becca did as he instructed but wasn't sure her legs would hold her. A trickle of urine made its way down her leg and into her Christian Louboutin leather and suede boots.

A rough hand grabbed her right arm and pulled her in the direction of the dim light. As her eyes adjusted, Becca could see the outline of a small cabin. A final push sent her sprawling onto the steps leading to the rough, wooden porch. Blood oozed from the corner of her mouth as a tooth pierced her lip.

The strange laugh again. "Get up! You're the honored guest tonight."

Becca struggled to her feet and continued up the steps and onto the porch. The front door swung open, and a man's outline could be seen against the light of the room. Without a word, he stepped aside and motioned for Becca to enter.

Bile rose in Becca's throat as a strong stench assailed her nostrils. The cabin's interior was filthy with an ancient brown couch taking up a large part of the space in the front room. Beyond, was a primitive kitchen. The adjoining room held two sets of bunk beds, their thin and sagging mattresses stripped bare. Becca averted her eyes so her mind wouldn't dwell on the dark stains sullying the ticking. The hospital executive knew she was in real trouble. Her mind raced, searching for a way out of the dire situation.

"Sit down!" a voice behind her commanded. Becca hesitated, but another hard push landed her in the middle of the soiled couch. She sat up straight, unwilling to touch more of the fabric than necessary.

The sound of a wooden chair scraping across the floor caused Becca to jump. A few seconds later, she was face-to-face with her worst nightmare. The one person she had hoped never to see again leaned in close to her and his fetid breath covered her face.

"Ah, Becca, we meet again. I trust you got my messages." The voice was menacing, innuendo intertwined with threats. "The question is, Ms. Dorland, why didn't you respond?"

The question hung in the air, seemingly unable to find a place to land. Becca had no answer, at least none that would satisfy the man sitting inches from her. How could she tell him she didn't have the bonds, and had no idea where they were? *I was a fool to trust Cora with them.*

"Come, now. You can tell me your little secret. I'll get it out of you—one way or the other, no doubt about that."

There it was again, the threat. Becca had received the letters and phone messages from her nemesis. She had known for some time this day might come, but she had convinced herself that Cora must have revealed where she had hidden the bonds before she died. Why, then, was she here? She had nothing to offer them, nothing to use to bargain in exchange for her life.

"Michael, I…I don't know what to tell you. I don't have the bonds; I thought you had them back."

"Me? I don't have them. If you think you can play some kind of game with me, you're very, very wrong. You ought to know enough about me by now to know that I always get what I want, and I don't care to…uh…shall we say break some eggs in the process. Save yourself a lot of misery and tell me where you hid them, or I'll let Murray have a go at you. It won't be pretty, I assure you. I'll let you have a little time to think it over. You'll stay here tonight in our deluxe suite. Several of the girls you gave us spent time there. I'm sure you'll be more cooperative once you get a taste of our hospitality."

The chair legs pushed back and Michael rose from his seat. With a single nod of his head, he directed Murray's next actions.

A bag was placed over Becca's head and her arms were pulled behind her. Zip ties secured them tightly. A new wave of panic swept over her as she was hauled up from the sofa and dragged back outside. She half walked, half stumbled for several yards before Murray jerked her back and told her to wait. A metallic scraping sound in front of her caused Becca to recoil, but Murray kept a strong, restraining hand on her.

When the scraping sound stopped, she was pushed forward onto her knees. Bare ground greeted her as she heard the metallic scrape again as the door was closed behind her. She sensed she was in some sort of enclosure. She could hear muffled voices outside. Murray. Apparently, this was the prelude to their plan. Becca knew the treatment would get worse, but just short of killing her, as long as they thought she might give them what they wanted. But she couldn't. No matter how much she was tortured, she couldn't give them the bonds—because she had no idea where they were.

She had trusted Cora, a dupe, to hold the bonds for her. Cora had no idea what was in the locked case Becca had given her. Something had gone wrong. All Cora had to do was take the case home and keep it until Becca asked for it. Somehow, someone had found out that Cora had the bonds. Nothing made sense. If Michael had found the bonds, why was she here?

Becca's tired mind struggled to find a way out of her predicament. Her kidnappers had made it very difficult for her to escape, but she had to find a way to get out of the shed. If she failed, she would be tortured, raped, maybe killed. *I wish I had never gotten involved in any of this. Everything has gone from bad to worse.*

Becca reflected on how she had gotten into this predicament. First, that stupid physical trainer at the gym sold her some energy drink that turned out to be loaded with illegal drugs. She was hooked before she realized what was happening. As she needed more and more of the mixture just to function, it all became too expensive to buy. That's when Michael was introduced to her. He told her she could have all the drugs she wanted if she would help him procure some teenage girls and young women. Becca rationalized her complicity by telling herself these girls had no one to care about them anyway and, after all, Michael had assured her that the girls would be well treated.

Through charity work sponsored by her hospital, Becca had direct access to a significant number of underprivileged women and girls. Each had been

95

desperate for money and a better life. Michael promised them both. Once the girls were lured with promises and a little cash, Becca never heard from them again. Becca bought Michael's story that most of the girls were relocated to cities where they could find jobs. Jobs indeed! The only work they would know would take place in a bedroom. When Becca stopped kidding herself about why Michael wanted help finding girls, she tried to get out of the dirty business. Michael had only smiled and told her that was impossible; he would tell her when she was done.

In desperation, Becca turned to Gus Averill, her trainer at the gym. After all, he had gotten her into this mess in the first place. Gus told her he knew how they could get their hands on several million dollars in bearer bonds. The bonds could be their ticket to get away from Michael. It would take them both to make his scheme work, he had told her. By this point, Becca was desperate to escape Michael's reach. The money would mean a new life for her. She had already amassed a tidy sum from the payments she had been given to procure the girls for Michael, but it wasn't enough to escape his clutches. So, she decided to go along with the plan to steal the bearer bonds from the gym's office safe. She and Gus had planned the theft down to the second and the operation went smoothly, or so she had thought. She had come under suspicion almost immediately. After the theft, Gus told Becca to hold onto the bonds until they could plan their escape. Once Becca was suspected of stealing the bonds, she handed them off to Cora for safekeeping. No one would suspect the demure, middle-aged woman. Becca fully expected to retrieve the bonds within a few days, but Cora became spooked and hid them. Now, Michael believed that Becca knew where the bonds were—but she didn't! Becca had felt sure that Cora had revealed where the bonds were hidden before she was killed. If Michael didn't have them, who did?

Becca was pulled back to her present predicament as the voices outside her prison faded away. Now was the time to make her move. Removal of the hood was the first task. She pulled her legs up as far as she could and snagged the hood's fabric between her knees, but it had been fastened with a cord and knotted around her neck. She would have to find another way. She scooted on the dirt floor until she came into contact with garden tools stacked in a corner. Being careful to make as little noise as possible, she sorted through them. The process was slow and difficult as the zip ties offered little mobility.

Finally, she felt a sharp jab. Further examination revealed the object to be garden shears. She used her teeth to unfasten the clasp and eventually opened the blades. She then leaned the blades against a box and backed up until she could position her wrists between the sharp edges. The process was slow and more than once she felt the blade slice through her skin, causing blood to trickle down onto her hands. *It would be ironic if I managed to slit my wrists and die,* she thought.

Suddenly, the zip ties gave way and her hands came free. The knotted cord securing the hood took a few more minutes as she fumbled with blood-soaked hands. Once free of the covering, Becca looked around at her surroundings. The shed was about ten feet square and had a dirt floor. She had given little thought until now as to what had happened to the young girls she had lured into Michael's snare. Each of them must have been as frightened as Becca was now. A flicker of guilt pricked her conscience but was quickly discarded. She had no time or energy to waste on regrets; her priority had to be escape.

Becca had heard the click of a padlock after Murray shut the door, so it would be impossible to escape through the door. She needed to find another way out. She turned again to the collection of tools and found a shovel. She started digging the dirt floor next to a wall.

The process was slow, and Becca expected Murray and his sidekick to return any moment, but fear pumped adrenaline into her muscles, aiding her efforts. She dug into the packed dirt until she had created a space of sufficient size to squeeze her body under the sidewall. Becca removed her coat so she could fit into the opening easier and pushed it out ahead of her. Next, she lay on her stomach and wiggled headfirst until she was outside the shed. Nearly exhausted, she retrieved her coat and stood on wobbly legs. With her heart pounding, she looked for any sign of Murray or the others. From the dim light that escaped the cabin, she could see her Mercedes about thirty yards away. She considered the possibility of reaching it and driving away before being discovered, but then she remembered that Murray had pocketed the keys when they arrived. No, she would have to walk. She looked down at her very expensive, but now ruined boots and regretted her choice of such high heels, but they would have to do. With only the light from a half moon, she found the road she had driven earlier and retraced her path.

## Ten

Becca walked along the rutted dirt road until she reached the highway. She looked over her shoulder every few feet expecting Michael or one of his minions to find her. She wouldn't last long in the open and considered trying to hitch a ride. Her appearance, however, would not be in her favor in seeking a ride back into town. Blood, urine, and dirt covered her torn clothing. She knew she must look like a crazed woman, so she continued on foot.

The rattle of an old Chevy pickup announced its arrival from behind, and the squeak of its brakes told Becca it was coming to a stop. She heard the door of the truck open, and then slam shut. Afraid to turn around, she kept walking, now with a marked limp with each step.

"Hey, lady!" came a voice behind her. "Do you need a ride?"

Becca stopped. Was this a Good Samaritan, or another potential killer? Near exhaustion, Becca made the decision to turn around. The man standing next to the truck was elderly, with wisps of white hair covering his ears. His faded overalls covered a once white tee shirt. He looked harmless enough. She decided if her appearance didn't scare the man away, maybe she would be rescued. She didn't return his greeting, but merely stood in place to let the man decide his next move once he saw her better.

He got out of his truck and stood a few feet away. "Now, aren't you a sight? It looks like you need some help. Get in and I'll drive you where you need to go."

Becca hesitated briefly, but decided this was her

best, and maybe only chance to get home. She nodded, and made her way to the truck, hoping the old man wouldn't change his mind once he got a good whiff of her. The man walked to the passenger side as Becca approached. He extended a weathered and wrinkled hand. "My name's Ben Haddock. Let me help you up into the truck."

"I'm Becca, uh, thanks for the ride; I was about to fall down with exhaustion."

"No problem." Ben walked back to the driver's side of the old truck and hoisted himself up into his seat with a practiced motion. If the man's nose smelled anything out of the ordinary, he kept that to himself as he turned over the motor and put the truck in gear. "So, where do you need to go?"

Becca gave Ben directions to her apartment. She was gambling that her escape had not been discovered yet. She wanted to pack a bag and get the cash she had on hand. It would buy her a little time—and a shower— she definitely needed a shower!

"It's none of my business, ma'am, but you look like you're in trouble."

"You're right, it's none of your business. I appreciate the ride, but let's skip the small talk."

Ben credited the rudeness to the woman's dire circumstances and directed his attention to the road, and she was right; it was none of his business. He made no further attempt to engage Becca in conversation and pulled up in front of her apartment thirty minutes later. He exited from his side of the truck so he could help her, but before he could reach her she already had opened her door and was getting out. As her feet made contact with the ground, Becca nearly fell. Her legs felt like rubber after walking so far in four-inch heels. As she stepped onto the curb, she waved a quick thank-you to Ben, and hurried through the front door of the four-plex.

Ben shook his head as he pulled away from the curb. "Now, that lady is headed for more trouble, that's for darn sure," he said aloud to himself.

Becca retrieved the extra key to her apartment from her next-door neighbor. To avoid questions, she made up a story about falling down an embankment while out for a stroll. The neighbor didn't buy it but sensed that any probing would be unwelcome.

After a quick shower, Becca threw enough clothes into a suitcase to get her through a few days. She didn't know when she would return. A hidden stash of six thousand dollars was removed from the backside of a dresser drawer. It would take several days to replace her ID, debit, and credit cards, so she would need to make the money last several days. Her personal cell phone was in her purse at the cabin, but fortunately, she had forgotten her hospital issued cell phone at home that morning. She threw it and the money in a purse and headed out the door.

Five blocks away, she entered an all-night diner. It was ten-thirty, but seemed much later. A great deal had happened in the past five hours and now Becca was hungry. She ordered coffee and a sandwich. When she reached into her purse to get money to pay for her food, she noticed Tom Warfel's business card.

"How did this get here?" she asked under her breath. Then she remembered that he had given it to her during their first meeting. She had stuffed it into her purse and forgotten about it. She fingered it for several minutes, attempting to decide whether to call him or not. How much could she tell him without implicating herself in the theft of the bonds and the luring of women and teenage girls into prostitution? No, it was too risky.

Becca had almost finished her meal when movement at the entrance to the diner caught Becca's attention. It was Murray and his goon sidekick! They had their backs to her as they spoke with the counter waitress. Becca left money for the food, grabbed her things and made a hasty retreat to the back of the diner. She only hoped there was another door there. Her luck held and she darted outside into an alley. She paused as she decided whether to run away as fast as possible or hide and wait until the men left. She decided on the latter.

Within seconds of Becca's positioning herself behind a dumpster, the men walked past! Becca thought they must surely hear her heart beating. She waited in her hiding place for a full twenty minutes after the men passed by. Slowly, she crept out from her hiding place and kept close to the shadows of buildings as she surreptitiously made her way in the opposite direction to another restaurant several blocks away. She again chose a table near the back of the restaurant, was seated, and pulled out her cell phone.

# Eleven

Tom Warfel was at home watching television with his wife when his cell phone rang. He had barely answered before the person on the other end rushed to speak. Tom listened carefully. He recognized the voice as that of Becca Dorland, though she was obviously very upset. "Slow down, where was this? Did you recognize any of the men?"

Becca hesitated. How much should she tell the detective? "I...uh, I'm not sure. I just left my apartment; I don't feel safe."

"Where are you? I'll meet you." Tom reached for pen and paper and wrote down an address. "Okay, I'll be there in fifteen minutes. Stay put."

The detective's wife was accustomed to emergency calls at all hours and already had Tom's shoes and coat ready for him. "Thanks, Honey, sorry about tonight." He leaned down to give his wife a quick kiss and rushed out the door. He pulled out his cell phone and chose Drew's number from his list of 'favorites'.

"Drew, can you meet me at Coleman's Restaurant? Becca Dorland just called, and she's gotten into some trouble."

"Sure, no problem. I'll be there in ten minutes."

The two detectives met up outside the popular downtown restaurant, informed the hostess whom they were meeting, and were directed to a back-corner table. Becca was sitting with a menu hiding her face. Detective Warfel spoke, startling the woman.

"Oh, Detective, it's you. I've been watching the door, afraid that those awful men will find me."

The two men sat down across from her without

103

being invited, gave the server their drink order of coffee, and refused any food. Once the waitress brought the coffee and moved on to another table, Tom broached the kidnapping. He could tell how upset the woman sitting across from him was, so he kept his voice calm and low.

"Ms. Dorland, you told me on the phone that a man forced his way into your car, had you drive out of town at gunpoint, tied you up and left you in a locked shed, is that correct?"

"Essentially, yes. I was so scared; I just knew he was going to kill me—like Cora." Immediately, Becca caught her mistake. I mean, er..."

Tom's eyes widened at the unintended gaffe. "I thought you said you didn't know the deceased lady who fell out of your car."

"Well, I, you see...we went to the same gym. I really didn't know her at all. I just saw her there sometimes when we attended the same class. I didn't recognize her that morning because it was such a shock. I looked away from her body; I was too upset to think straight." Becca hoped Detective Warfel believed her hasty fabrication, because she wasn't ready to reveal more.

Warfel sensed the evasion, but let Becca believe she had gotten away with it. Instead, he asked her to sit down with a police artist in the morning. "You've had enough excitement for one night. Where are you staying?"

"Staying? I hadn't given it much thought. I guess a hotel."

"You told me when we met that you have a sister; could you stay with her? It would be safer not to use your credit cards."

"Oh, I'll use cash. I don't really have anyone I

can ask for such a big favor. In my line of work, I can't afford to make friends. It makes it too hard to administer discipline."

"I see, well where would you like to stay? We'll drop you off."

Drew realized that even though he and Tom had driven separately, it would not be a good idea for either of them to be alone with Ms. Dorland—even to drive her to a hotel. She was an unreliable witness and a possible suspect.

Becca chose a very expensive hotel. Warfel raised his eyebrows and shot a look at Samuels as he turned away from Becca. He wondered how she could afford to pay in cash for such an expense. Tom considered the expensive new car, a big wad of cash, designer clothes and shoes. *Where did all this money come from, and what is she not telling us?* Tom mused.

Becca was dropped off at her chosen hotel after she gave directions to the location where she had been held. It was doubtful anyone was still there, but there might be some information to be gained from the cabin They called for a patrol car with two officers for backup, drove out of town, and slowly made their way along the rutted country lane to the cabin where Becca had been taken. They found little that could help to advance their investigation. No men, no drugs, no cash—nothing except Becca's car. Ms. Dorland's account of her evening seemed to check out. The door or the shed where Becca had been taken was standing open, with the padlock hanging from the handle. Drew aimed a flashlight into the opening, but neither man entered to prevent additional footprints in the soft ground. The shed still held the usual rusty tools one might expect to find. The shovel used to enable the escape was still lying next to the cleared space under the wall of the shed. Tom chuckled when he imagined how shocked the men were when they found their prey missing. They had underestimated Ms. Dorland. Tom knew he needed to be careful not to make the same mistake.

Arrangements were made to get a crime scene unit out to the remote cabin in the morning. It would be useless to search the area in the dark. The Mercedes was still parked by the cabin's steps, and Tom wondered why the men had not taken it. He would arrange for it to be towed, and once the car was processed for prints and other evidence, it would be returned to its owner. For the second time in a week, a car belonging to Rebecca Dorland would be examined for evidence of a crime.

"Okay, Drew, let's call it a night. It's already two a.m. I'm bushed."

The younger detective nodded and followed Tom to the car. On the drive back to town, the men discussed the case.

"It would seem that our victim could also be a suspect in this case," Drew mused.

"I believe you're right, Drew. She's involved in this whole mess up to her eyeballs. We'll discover her secrets; it's only a matter of time."

"She's not a pleasant woman."

Tom chuckled at the understatement. "Yeah, she's a piece of work. I know she's hiding something; I've sensed that from the beginning. It's obvious that she knew Cora Larkin. The question is what is the connection? What did they get mixed up in to cause the death of one and the kidnapping of the other? One thing's for sure, Ms. Dorland isn't safe, no matter how much she spends on a hotel. I'll arrange for police protection for her. She should be safe enough during the day at the hospital."

"I can speak to the head of security there Monday morning. He's a former police officer; we went through the academy together. He left the force after he lost his right leg from a gunshot wound. He went through rehab and eventually landed the hospital job. He has a great attitude toward life and seems to be doing well at his new job."

"That sounds good; that will free up our guys during the day to chase down information instead of playing babysitter to Ms. Dorland. There's something about this case I really don't like, and I'm afraid it will only get worse before we solve this one."

"One thing's for sure: if the ladies went to the same gym, we had better check out that location." So far, it's the only common denominator between the women," Tom concluded.

"Funny, I didn't take our Ms. Dorland for a gym rat," Drew offered.

Tom gave a short laugh and continued to drive even as his body screamed for sleep. He needed rest in order to stay a step ahead of the bad guys—and Rebecca Dorland.

# Twelve

Saturday night was clear and chilly, with bright stars shining down on Mac's farm. He and Mary were standing by the fenced paddock and gazing up at the stars.

"How amazing! I could never see stars like this in Chicago. There, I was lucky to see any at all, even on a clear night. It's beautiful here! Mac wrapped his arms around his wife from behind and gazed upward. The celestial array was indeed impressive. The pair remained unmoving for several minutes as they picked out various landmarks in the sky: Orion's belt, the Big Dipper, and Taurus. They stood transfixed by the display, unaware of a stealthy figure approaching from behind. Mac received the first blow and fell to the ground with a heavy thud. He had been holding onto Mary, and his weight caused her to fall to her knees. She raised her hands to ward off the blow she saw coming, but the heavy object caught her on the side of her head. She fell backward onto the cold earth.

The assailant ran to the house and searched every room. He cursed under his breath as he searched the last drawer in the kitchen. His search had yielded nothing. *Where were they?*
***
Aggie arrived at Mac and Mary's farm the next morning and drove around to the back of the house. She pulled the backdoor key from her purse. She didn't usually come in on Sunday morning, but it had been an unusual week, and she wanted to give her employers a good breakfast before she headed to church. She reached for the door to insert her key, but found the door unlocked. She was surprised. Mac always locked the

108

door back when he got up early to tend to the horses. Mary usually slept in a bit, and he was very careful when it came to his wife's safety. As Aggie pushed the door, she felt resistance but managed to open it enough to squeeze through. Once inside, she saw the source of the problem. The door was partially blocked by an overturned chair. Dishes and pans were everywhere. All the cabinets were open and the contents strewn over the kitchen. She called out to her employers but got no answer. She stepped to the next room and found similar disarray. Panic began to rise in her as she screamed for Mac and Mary. Receiving no answer, she rushed out the back door and headed to the barn. Maybe Mac was there. As she rounded the corner of the house and approached the paddock, she saw them lying on the ground. As she drew nearer, she saw the blood. Aggie screamed as she rushed to the couple.

She checked Mary first. She had a pulse. Letting out the breath she had been holding, she next checked Mac. He also had a pulse, though very weak. Their faces were cool to the touch, but both had been protected somewhat by heavy winter coats and gloves. Aggie pulled her cell phone from her purse and dialed 911. Her hands trembled so badly it took three tries to hit the right numbers. She ran to the house and pulled the comforter from the bed and ran back out to the paddock. As she spread the comforter over the couple and tucked it around their sides, she could hear sirens in the distance. She knelt beside her employers and prayed. *Dear God, these are good people. Help them! Please!* The EMT's arrived and gently helped Aggie to her feet before kneeling next to the injured couple It was decided to get them in the ambulance quickly, start IV's, and apply warming blankets. There was little more they could do until the couple could be seen in the hospital.

Aggie followed in her car after she called Sarah. She knew Sarah and Sam would want to know what had happened, and would provide moral support. Sarah assured Aggie that she and Sam would come to the hospital right away. The reassurance took away some of Aggie's anxiety; she would not have to face this crisis alone.

When Sam and Sarah arrived, they found Aggie in a private consultation room in the emergency department. She was relating what had happened to a policeman and a nurse, and appeared overwhelmed. Sarah sat beside the housekeeper and laid her hand on Aggie's. The couple listened with growing horror at the narrative.

Sam brought Aggie a cup of water and sat down across from her. "What have the doctors said?" he asked, with obvious concern etched on his face.

"They're doing tests, but Mac seems to be in better shape than Mary. The EMT's said he woke up in the ambulance and talked to them before going out again."

Sarah's heart lurched as she heard that her dear friend was badly hurt. This couldn't be real; it must be only dream and she would wake up soon. Sarah began to tremble, and tears fell. *First Sam, now Mac and Mary. Who was doing this? Why?* Sarah wondered.

As Sam was doing his best to comfort both Aggie and Sarah, the door opened and a doctor walked in. He was wearing scrubs and a white lab coat. The embroidered name on his coat identified him as Brian Coulter, MD. In confirmation of his identity, he introduced himself and extended his hand to Sam who had risen from his chair. "Are you family of Mr. and

Mrs. Osborne?"

"Technically, no, but as good as. We've called their children. Mac has a son and daughter, and Mary has a daughter. It will be a while before they can get here as they don't live close by."

"I see. Well, I am bound by HIPAA regulations, so I cannot discuss their situation with anyone except next-of-kin."

Sarah stood, "Dr. Coulter, we *are* family. We've been there for each other during some really rough times. It's also very possible that they were attacked by the same person who attacked my husband, giving him this broken arm," Sarah explained as she pointed to Sam. "We're as close to those two as their own family."

"Well, I don't know…uh"

A voice came from behind the doctor. "Maybe I can help, Dr. Coulter."

"Detective Warfel, are you involved in this case?"

Tom stepped forward. "Yes, it's the most recent chapter in a very ugly story, I'm afraid. I can vouch for what Sarah told you. Mr. and Mrs. Richards and the Osbornes are very close and involved in this investigation."

"Okay, on your say-so, here's what we know so far. Both were hit on the head with a blunt, but unknown object and both suffered concussions. Mr. Osborne bled out quite a bit, but the cold temperatures actually worked in his favor, and stopped the bleeding by constricting his blood vessels. We expect him to make a full recovery."

"What about Mary?" Sarah asked in a quiet voice.

"Mrs. Osborne was not as lucky, I'm afraid. She

111

has been taken to surgery to remove a subdural hematoma. Her injury was to the right temporal lobe, the side of her head. Blunt force trauma to this area is more serious than some other areas of the brain. Her injury has been classified as moderate, as she scored eleven out of fifteen on the GCS."

Everyone displayed confused looks. Sarah asked, "GCS?"

"The Glasgow Coma Scale. It's how we assess head trauma. Mr. Osborne scored thirteen. The difference between a score of eleven and thirteen is significant, and Mrs. Osborne has the hematoma, which must be removed immediately. She also presented with hypotension, low blood pressure. We stabilized her, of course, before sending her to surgery. Her prognosis is uncertain at this time, so she will go to ICU once her operation is completed. Mr. Osborne will be taken soon to our transitional care unit, where he will be closely watched for a few days. A neurosurgeon was called in to assess Mrs. Osborne and he is doing her surgery."

The physician gave his audience a few moments to absorb the technical information before asking, "Do you have any questions?"

Sam spoke for the group, "This has all been such a shock. You see, Mr. Osborne's ex-wife was murdered last week; she was buried on Thursday."

The veteran physician showed only mild surprise; he had seen it all in his twenty years of emergency medicine. "That *is* a great deal for one family to experience; I'm very sorry." He looked at his watch. "Well, I need to get back; it's a busy night for us. Be assured that Mr. and Mrs. Osborne are getting the very best care. You are welcome to visit Mr. Osborne here in the ED before his transfer to the TCU. Then, you might want to check in with the hospitality desk in the surgical waiting room on the second floor. They will give you updates on Mrs. Osborne. Take the elevators down the left hallway, just beyond the ED. Signs will direct you from there." The doctor started to turn away and return to his other patients, but he turned instead and added, "I'm very sorry that your friends have been injured. We're very hopeful that Mrs. Osborne will make a full recovery, prayers help, too. There is a chapel on the second floor, near the surgical waiting area."

Once the doctor was out of earshot, Aggie was the first to speak, "I only understood about half of what that doctor said, but I did hear the part about the chapel. I'm going there now."

Sarah smiled, "Add our prayers to yours, Aggie. We want to visit with Mac; he must be beside himself with worry."

"Give him my best and tell him I'm praying for him and Mrs. Osborne."

"Will do. Thank you for calling us, Aggie. Mac and Mary are like family to us."

"I know; they talk about you two all the time, so I know how fond they are of you. Well, I had better start praying; it sounds as if Mrs. Osborne needs all the prayers she can get."

Sarah forced a smile and nodded as she fought to push down the lump in her throat. She watched as Aggie headed down the hallway that would lead to the second-floor surgical area and the chapel.

Detective Warfel addressed the young couple. "I'm even more convinced now that all of these incidents are related. If you'll excuse, me I need to bring my team up to date and start this investigation. Please tell Mac I'm already working on who did this and that I'll check in with him as soon as possible." He then excused himself and set his team in motion with a phone call.

After Tom left, Sam turned to Sarah, "Let's go see Mac."

The clerk at the ED waiting room desk directed the couple to bay nine. Each bay had solid walls on the sides and a glass front, with a wide sliding door. A privacy curtain was drawn halfway across the glass wall. Sam and Sarah entered cautiously, not wanting to interrupt any care being given. They found Mac alone, however, with the bedrails up and the head of his bed elevated about halfway. His eyes were closed, but they opened as soon as he heard footsteps.

"Oh, thank goodness you're here!"

The couple rushed to Mac's bedside. "Mac, we came as soon as Aggie called."

"I'm glad you did. Has anyone told you anything about Mary?"

Sam related what the doctor had just explained about her condition. "She's faring a bit worse than you, it seems. She's in surgery right now to remove a blood clot from her brain. She'll be taken to ICU from there."

Mac let out a breath, "Yeah, that's what he told me. I just wanted to hear someone else say it. I was afraid she might be dead. I came to after it happened, but Mary was still out. I couldn't seem to stay conscious long enough to call for help, so I crawled closer and tried to cover her with my body to keep her warm. When Aggie found us, I could hear her, but I must have passed out again because the next thing I remember was waking up in the ambulance."

Sam reached for his friend's hand. "Mac, what happened?"

114

"I don't know. We were standing at the paddock gate looking up at the stars. It was such a clear night and we could see individual constellations. I remember a pain on the back of my head. I fell, and Mary fell on top of me. That's all I remember. Poor Mary; she must've been so frightened." Mac began to sob, prompting a nurse to enter the room.

"I'm sorry, but you'll have to leave now."

Sam gave Mac a final squeeze of his hand and assured him they would let him know as soon as Mary was out of surgery. The nurse injected medicine into Mac's IV, and he calmed down a few seconds later.

As they waited for the elevator, Sam turned to Sarah, "That must have been a sedative."

"Yes, I'm sure it was. Poor Mac; he must be worried sick about Mary."

The surgical waiting area was found easily. The couple checked in with the attendant at the optimistically titled 'Hospitality Desk', and found Aggie already waiting. They chose seats on either side of her.

She turned to Sarah with a concerned look and asked, "How's Mr. Osborne?"

"He's doing fairly well. We spoke with him for a few minutes. He's worried about Mary, though," Sarah explained.

"Of course, we all are," Aggie agreed.

The friends sat in silence for several minutes before Sam spoke, "I forgot to call Mrs. Hoskins. She asked me to call her as soon as we knew something." Sam excused himself and stepped into the hallway to make his call.

When he returned, Sarah asked, "Is everything okay at home?"

Sam gave a short laugh, "Well, I heard Anna

squealing in the background as she played with the dog, the timer on the dryer sounded, and Howard must have come into the kitchen because I heard him ask if he could get a thermos of coffee. It all sounds under control, though. It takes a lot to ruffle Mrs. Hoskins' feathers. She's able to handle almost anything, I believe."

Sarah smiled, "I agree; she's a trooper."

Sam resumed his seat and the trio waited two hours longer before they heard, "Will the family of Mary Osborne please go to consultation room six."

The attendant directed them to the correct location where they found a comfortably furnished room with upholstered chairs and a Georgia O'Keefe print on the wall.

In a few minutes, the surgeon appeared. He remained standing, dressed in green scrubs, his surgical mask dangling from two straps around his neck. He introduced himself and immediately began relating the specifics of the surgery. Sarah winced as he described the Burr hole he drilled into Mary's skull to remove the hematoma.

"Mrs. Osborne is in recovery now, but will be taken to her room shortly. She woke up in recovery, so that's a very good sign. The next couple of days are critical, but I'm optimistic for her recovery."

"May we see her?" Sarah asked.

"Once she's in ICU, you'll be permitted to visit for fifteen minutes, but only one of you at a time. It will be at least an hour before you can see her, so get some lunch while you wait. Our cafeteria food is really quite good."

Sarah thanked the doctor, and he rushed from the room. "Wow, these doctors are certainly in a hurry

116

around here," she quipped.

Sam agreed, "I guess they're really busy. If you gals would like to head to the cafeteria, I'll find the TCU and let Mac know how the surgery went."

Sarah agreed. "Sounds like a plan." Turning to Aggie, she said, "Come on, Aggie, let's sample the hospital's food." The two women said good-bye to Sam, and he agreed to meet them in the cafeteria after he visited Mac. Aggie pulled out her cell phone to update Mrs. Hoskins. The two housekeepers had become fast friends, their friendship bridged by their employers.

Sam found Mac's room with the help of a friendly nursing assistant. Sam entered to find two nurses in attendance. He offered to come back later but was assured by one of the nurses that their work was nearly done.

"We're just finishing; come on in," one of the nurses said as she excused herself and left.

Sam smiled and teased, "Mac, how did you manage to get so much attention?"

Mac returned the smile, but quickly asked, "What about Mary?"

"The operation went well; the hematoma was removed from her brain. She's in recovery and is awake. The doctor seems very optimistic for her recovery—his exact words."

Mac visibly relaxed. "I've been so worried; I've never felt so helpless in my life. If I had just heard the attacker coming up behind us, I could have done something." As he spoke, he slammed a fist onto the bed. A beep on Mac's monitor got the attention of the remaining nurse in the room.

"Mr. Osborne, you need to remain calm or I will have to ask your visitor to leave." Her voice was soft but carried a definite tone of authority.

"Okay, I'll try, but you see, my wife was attacked too. She's in worse shape than I am. It's hard to be calm when I'm so worried about her."

The nurse nodded but repeated her caution. "I understand, but *you* are *my* concern." She turned to Sam to get her point across, "He's had a serious injury; he needs time to heal."

Sam assumed a serious look, "Yes, ma'am. I'll do my best to keep him calm. Thank you for your concern."

The nurse smiled, and then addressed Mac in a gentle tone. "I just want you to get well so you can take care of your wife when she comes home. Now, please try to remain calm." She gave one last look of caution to Sam and left the room.

Sam turned to his friend, "You'd better mind the boss. With all those wires attached to you, she'll know if you hiccup."

Mac sighed, "I'll try. She's just doing her job, but I'm not worried about me; I'm worried sick about Mary."

"I know, but let me take a portion of that worry off your shoulders. I'll visit Mary as often as permitted so I can report her condition to you."

"Sam, you're a good friend. Thanks."

"You'd do the same for me. Now, is there anything I can get for you from your house?"

"Yeah, there are a few things. Mac started to list his requests when there was a knock on the door. Mac and Sam looked up to see Tom Warfel standing in the doorway.

"Tom! We need to stop meeting like this!" Mac exclaimed.

Tom's rueful smile indicated his agreement. "May I come in?"

"Of course," Mac replied.

Sam started to leave, but the detective stopped him. "Sam, I'd like you to stay if you can."

"Sure, no problem." Sam offered Tom his seat next to the bed and chose another by the window.

"Well, we certainly didn't expect this. Apparently, our guy thought you might have what he was looking for. He ransacked your entire house. It's quite a mess; I have a team there now processing the scene."

"What could he possibly be looking for?"

"I believe I might have the answer to that question," interjected the detective. "Do you remember the name Rebecca Dorland?"

Mac nodded, "Sure, Cora was found in her car."

"Yes, well, she had her own adventures this weekend. She was kidnapped Friday night, but managed to escape. Her apartment was also ransacked, but the guy didn't find what he was looking for there either."

"Oh?"

"Yes, we think he was after stolen bearer bonds," Warfel revealed.

"Bearer bonds?"

"Do you remember the scrap of paper with the decorative edges that we found in your shed?"

Mac nodded.

"Well, we've discovered that it was a corner of a bearer bond."

Sam spoke up. "I'm confused; what is a bearer bond and why was there part of one in Mac's shed?"

"A bearer bond," Tom explained, "is a type of

119

bond that is not registered. Whoever is holding it, owns it. There is no proof of ownership other than having it in one's possession. This makes them very portable and valuable in the drug trade." Sam's frown and Mac's confused look indicated to the detective that the pair didn't see the connection.

"It's one way to launder drug money. Money that comes in from the sale of drugs has to be accounted for somehow. A lot of money can flow through the purchase of these instruments. Our sources on the street tell us that bearer bonds worth several million dollars have disappeared, and the men who were robbed are plenty angry."

Sam nodded understanding. "But why was one in Mac's shed? It doesn't make any sense."

"That's what we don't know. The only connection is Cora Larkin. Who else would use Mac's shed to hide the bonds? It's possible that Mrs. Larkin obtained the bonds somehow and was killed when the owner of the bonds found out. The guy who attacked Sam at your farm, Mac, may have taken the bonds—or, Mrs. Larkin moved them before he searched the shed.

Still under the influence of pain meds, Mac was struggling to keep up with the conversation. "Are you saying Cora had these stolen bearer bonds? That's preposterous!"

The monitor behind Mac's bed beeped and a nurse appeared. "I'm afraid your visitors will have to leave now, Mr. Osborne. You're getting too excited."

Detective Warfel apologized to the nurse. "I'm sorry, ma'am. We'll leave now."

The nurse was satisfied that her patient's visitors were leaving, so she gave a curt nod and left the room.

"Tom?" Mac said in a weak voice. "Cora wasn't

a criminal; there has to be another explanation. If she was mixed up in this, she must have been tricked or forced. She was a good woman. Please find out the truth. Amy and Cameron have already lost their mother; they shouldn't lose the image they have of her, too."

"We're working on it, Mac. Don't worry, just focus on getting well. Give Mary my best when you visit her." With a final nod to Sam, the detective left the room.

"Mac, I'll leave now too. Get some rest. I'll check on Mary and come back later. I don't want to wear out my welcome with your nurse."

Mac, too weak to argue, merely nodded his head and allowed his mind to slow down and drift into sleep.

Sam caught up with the detective down the hall from Mac's room. They walked together down the hallway toward the elevators. Neither spoke until they reached the end of the hall, out of earshot of Mac.

Warfel turned to look at Sam and asked, "How's Mary?"

"Before I came to see Mac, we spoke with the doctor, the surgeon actually. Mary had a hematoma on her brain. It was removed surgically. We'll know more in a couple of days, but the doctors are optimistic."

"I'm sorry, Sam, about all of this. This guy is determined to find those bonds, it seems."

Sam spoke up, "What does all of this have to do with Cora? She seems a most unlikely villain."

"We don't know the answer to that yet, I'm afraid."

"Do you really think she was killed because she had the bonds?" Sam asked.

"That's what we're trying to figure out."

"None of this makes any sense. I didn't think

Cora knew Ms. Dorland."

"Apparently, she did; they went to the same gym."

"I see; yes, that would explain their connection. This all seems so out of character from what Mac and Mary have told me about her, though. There is a lot we don't know, Tom."

"That's for sure. One thing to keep in mind, if Mrs. Larkin told someone where to find the bonds, then that person probably killed her. He would also likely be the man who cold-cocked you, Sam, although I think there's more than one person looking for them. These guys play for keeps, so please be on alert. Well, I have to go, but I'll keep you guys informed. Let me know if there's any change in Mac or Mary."

"Thank you for keeping us in the loop. I hope you catch this guy soon. None of us will rest easy until you do."

"We'll do our best, I assure you."

"I know you will." With a final nod, he turned down a side hallway and followed signs to the cafeteria. Sam decided he would wait to relay the new information to Sarah. He didn't want to worry Aggie needlessly. She didn't live in as Mrs. Hoskins did, and there was no reason for anyone to believe the housekeeper would know where the bonds were hidden. *What a mess! I pray this all gets straightened out soon.*

# Thirteen

Later that day, Sam returned with Sarah to the hospital after packing a bag for Mac. They had not been allowed in Mac's house because the crime scene unit was still processing it, so they shopped for the few items on Mac's list. The couple sat down in a small waiting room at the end of the TCU hallway. Aggie had already left for home to get some much-needed rest.

Sarah looked at Sam and asked about his visit with Mac. Sam replied that Tom Warfel had joined them and updated them on the case. Sarah sat transfixed as the details of the investigation were shared with her.

"Bearer bonds? Does Tom think the murderer is the same person who's been to Mac's farm twice?"

"Probably. Rebecca Dorland's apartment was ransacked, too. He was presumably looking for the bonds."

"You said he; are we sure the murderer is a man?" Sarah asked.

Detective Warfel is fairly sure. DNA was found at Ms. Dorland's apartment on a broken figurine. The person who searched the apartment cut himself on the edge of the figurine. The DNA indicated the blood came from a male." Sam explained.

Sarah's eyebrows rose at the mention of the DNA, but Sam added, "The DNA was not a match to anyone in the system. However, if a suspect is identified, his DNA can be compared to that on the figurine."

"What about the fingernail found in Cora's hair? Did they police get DNA from that?"

"Only the sex, a male. They couldn't determine more than that," Sam explained.

"So where do the police go from here?" Sarah asked.

Sam was thoughtful. "I suppose they need to delve into the lives of Cora and Ms. Dorland— who they knew and where they might have gotten the bonds."

Sarah became very quiet. Sam had seen that look before, and it had brought disastrous results.

"Sweetheart?" Sam asked.

Sarah looked up.

"I hope you aren't planning to help the police."

Sarah's expression turned sheepish. "You know me too well, Sam Richards. No, I won't get actively involved. I was just thinking about the bonds and how greed can cause so much heartache. This case stirred the memory of the extreme measures my biological father took to hoard money, that's all."

"I'm sure you'll never forget that experience for the rest of your life. In fact, it nearly took your life. The possibility of you being in danger again is too painful to consider."

"Don't worry, darling. You and little Anna are my world. The only sleuthing I plan to do these days is for my books."

"I'm glad to hear it."

Sarah stood up. "I need to go home now and help Mrs. Hoskins. She has cared for Anna a lot these past few days and I'm sure she needs some rest. How long do you plan to stay?"

"At least until visiting hours are over. I promised Mac I would check on Mary periodically. The nurses in ICU told me it would be okay to come into the unit between posted visiting times, as long as I was very quiet and didn't stay too long. They are very sympathetic to Mac and Mary's situation, and are

124

willing to bend the rules a bit until Mary is more stable."

"Does Mac have everything he needs?"

"I believe so, except Mac did ask if he could have his cell phone and charger when you come back. Maybe the police will let you into their house soon."

"I'll check. Give Mac my love; I don't want to disturb him if he's asleep."

Kiss Anna goodnight for me."

"I will. I'll wait up for you if you are later than you anticipate."

Sam reached out to embrace Sarah. "Make sure everything is locked up tight. Check with Howard to see if he has obtained a night watchman. I don't want the murderer to come calling at our house."

"We'll be fine, and I'll remind Howard. Now, quit worrying about us."

Sarah left the hospital and found her car in the visitor's lot. The day had seemed like a week and she felt the tension of the day's events in her neck and shoulders. A nice hot bath would be a welcome treat after such a trying day.

Sarah arrived home to the happy sounds of two-year-old Anna at play. She could hear the squeals coming from Anna's bedroom. Mrs. Hoskins met Sarah in the hall, so Sarah wondered whom her daughter was talking to. Mrs. Hoskins laughed, shook her head, and returned to the kitchen. This left the young mother more confused than before. Not knowing exactly what to expect, Sarah quietly opened the door to the nursery. The scene before her took a few moments to take in fully. Anna was sitting with her back to the door, having a tea party with Teddy, Rabbit, and the dog! Benny was sitting in one of Anna's little chairs, with a bib, and a scarf on his head! The little dog was watching Anna closely as she doled out animal crackers to the group. He licked back saliva as he waited patiently for his portion. Sarah watched in amazement as the tableau unfolded before her.

"No, Benny, that belongs to Teddy, here's yours."

The dog waited until animal crackers were placed on his plate and Anna withdrew her hand. Looking first at his young mistress for her approval, the dog then quickly grabbed the cookies and finished them off in one bite. He sat back and watched again as the rations were distributed.

Sarah stifled a laugh as she watched, trying not to interrupt the party. Eventually, though, she could no longer hold back her laughter. Anna turned around at the sound and ran to Sarah.

Sarah bent over to hug the toddler.

"Mommy, I havin' a tea party!" Benny came running up behind Anna, his tail wagging, and the bib dragging the ground.

"Why, Benny! You're all dressed up!"

"Yeth, Mommy, he came to the tea party."

"Well, he looks very nice in his party clothes. Can we take them off now so he can go play outside?"

"Okay. He was eating all the cookies anyway!"

Sarah leaned over, freed the dog of his party finery, and picked up her daughter. "Anna, I love your tea party! Did you have a good time?"

"Uh-huh, but Mrs. Hoskins said she had to pour the juice. Benny didn't drink his, so I drank it. Bunny said I could have his, too."

"My, you must have juice sloshing all around your tummy!"

Anna giggled as Sarah tickled her. The

youngster put her arms around her mommy's neck and squeezed. "I love you Mommy!"

"I love you, too, Darling! Let's go see what Mrs. Hoskins has planned for our dinner."

The pair entered the kitchen and found the housekeeper stirring a pot of soup.

"Mmm, that smells delicious!"

"It's broccoli cheddar, and there are turkey sandwiches with avocado."

"I can't remember what we ate before you came along." Sarah leaned over and kissed the cheek of the older woman. "I hope you know how much we appreciate all you do for us, and how much we love you."

"Thank you. I'm so happy here with you, Sam, and little Anna. My own children live so far away, so I see my grandchildren very seldom. Being with Anna is like having one of my own grandchildren close to me. She's such a sweet little girl, so full of life—and imagination! She can think up more to do than five children!"

Sarah laughed. "Yes, she can. I'm afraid she gets that directly from me. That little tea party I just saw took me back to my own childhood. I was an only child, so my stuffed animals and my dog were my friends. Benny seems to take it all well though. He adores her, so I guess he'll do anything she wants, especially when cookies can be had!" Both women laughed as Anna wiggled to be let down. Sarah deposited her onto the floor, and Anna ran back to her room.

"I forgot; it's time for Bunny and Teddy to take a nap. They'll get so gwumpy if they don't take a nap."

Sarah and Mrs. Hoskins laughed again as they watched the plump little legs scamper down the hall.

Mrs. Hoskins lowered the heat on the soup and asked about Mary and Mac. Sarah caught her up on their progress. "It looks good for Mac to come home soon, but it will take Mary a bit longer; she will have a long recovery, but it could have been so much worse. As bad as it was, they both should make a full recovery."

"That is such a blessing," Mrs. Hoskins said as she returned to the preparations for dinner. "Do the police know who attacked them?"

"No, so all of us need to be on our guard. Detective Warfel believes whoever is responsible is looking for some valuable bonds. I feel better knowing we have an armed guard protecting us and the farm."

"Me, too, Mrs. Richards. The guard was in here about an hour ago—I already gave him dinner. He said he was heading back out to make rounds again."

"Good." Sarah listened for sounds of her daughter playing but couldn't hear her. "Mrs. Hoskins, I'll check on Anna, then I need to write for a while."

"Okay, I'll keep an eye on our girl while you work."

Sarah smiled at the expression. Indeed, Mrs. Hoskins was a big part of Anna's life, and the little girl was thriving as a result. With a satisfied sigh, she left the kitchen and caught up with her daughter in the nursery.

"Hey, little one, what do you...oh!" Sarah screamed and reached for her daughter. Sweeping her up into her arms, she ran back toward the kitchen. She ran headlong into Mrs. Hoskins.

"Mrs. Richards, what's the matter?"

"Lock all the doors! Hurry!"

Mrs. Hoskins stared only a moment at her

employer before complying with the urgent plea. As a rule, Mrs. Hoskins kept all the doors locked except the door leading into the kitchen from the paddock area. She rushed to secure that door as Sarah followed her.

Sarah, still holding Anna, reached for her cell phone on the kitchen counter. She dialed Sam's cell phone and the call was quickly answered. "Sam, someone is outside the house. He was looking in Anna's bedroom window!"

"Sarah, where are you now? Are all the doors locked?"

"Yes, Mrs. Hoskins has locked them. I don't know where the guard is; Mrs. Hoskins saw him an hour ago, just before he was to start his rounds."

"Sarah, listen to me. Stay on the line but have Mrs. Hoskins call Howard on her phone. Do it now."

The instructions were relayed and the housekeeper quickly dialed Howard's cell. The phone rang five, six times without an answer. The call went to voice mail.

"Sam, he doesn't answer!"

"Okay, stay put. Leave Anna with Mrs. H. and go to our bedroom closet. Get the gun out of the lockbox. Have Mrs. H. take Anna to the guest room upstairs. I don't want her to see the gun."

"Got it. Sam, we'll be fine, but can you hurry home?"

"I'm already out the door. When we hang up, call the sheriff."

Sarah did as instructed, and it wasn't long before there was a knock on the front door.

"Mrs. Richards? It's Douglas Hamilton. Remember me? I'm a sheriff's deputy."

Relief flooded Sarah as she descended the stairs

and pulled the front door curtains aside to see the young deputy. She put the gun back on safety and opened the door.

"Thank goodness! I'm glad you were so close by."

"I understand there was an intruder?"

"Yes, I saw him looking in my daughter's bedroom window."

"Okay, I'll take a look around. Stay here with your doors locked."

The deputy turned and descended the porch steps just as Sam drove up. "Mr. Richards, I was just about to look around. Don't y'all have a farm manager?"

"Yes, we do, but he's not answering his phone. We have two other men and a twenty-four-hour armed guard, but I don't see anyone here."

The young deputy made no comment as he pulled out his phone and called for backup. He hung up and turned to Sam. "Where would Howard usually be at this time of day?"

"Uh, he would be either in the barn or in the paddock. He's training a couple of young foals."

"I'll start there, then."

"I'll come with you. Just give me a second to get my gun. It's in the house."

Sarah didn't question Sam's request for the gun, but it took all her willpower to refrain from falling into his safe arms. She handed the pistol over to him with a plea for him to be careful. Sam flashed one of his wide, signature grins in an effort to allay his young wife's fears. Sarah returned the smile but said a prayer as she closed and locked the door.

Sam joined the deputy and they approached the barn. The only sound was a gentle neighing from one of

130

the horses. Where was Howard? Jake? Lonnie? The hired guard?

The pair slowly entered the large structure and stood just inside the door. The deputy looked at Sam and raised a finger to his lips. The men waited, listening. At first, there was no sound, but then a soft moan reached their ears. Each man looked at the other to be certain of what he had heard. Each nodded. They had both heard the moan. The sound seemed to come from one of the stalls at the far end of the barn. Walking slowly, they checked each stall as they passed. Prissy whinnied in greeting as Sam passed, but he had no carrot for her today. As they approached the last stall, the moaning sound came again. This time, both men were positive the sound came from a human. Sam was the first one to peer into the stall.

"Howard!" Sam exclaimed as he rushed forward to aid his farm manager and friend. Howard was lying at the back of the stall, half raised up on his right elbow, with blood oozing down the left side of his face.

"Sam, help me."

"I'm right here, Howard. I'll get the first aid kit."

Sam ran to get the well-equipped first aid kit that was kept in the barn. He was back beside his friend in mere seconds. He opened the kit and retrieved the items he needed. As he cleaned and bandaged Howard's wounds, the deputy asked about the two hired hands.

Howard answered. "Lonnie was planning to meet me here after he checked on all the horses. Jake went into town for supplies."

"What about the guard?"

"He was here. I saw him about forty-five minutes ago when he was making rounds."

Douglas had a terrible feeling in his stomach. The last time he had experienced the same feeling, he had been searching for a missing family. They had been camping but didn't return home when family expected them, so they called the Sheriff. Everyone's worst fears were realized when, first a teddy bear, then a child's shoe, were found. Eventually all five family members were discovered, but it took three months to find all their remains. The area was deeply forested, and the family must have become disoriented and lost. Douglas had been the one to find the little girl's shoe. Now, he had another family depending on him. He mustn't blow it this time. The young deputy straightened his spine, called for an ambulance, and established that the women and little Anna were still safe in the house.

"Further searching will have to wait until backup gets here. Howard, can you walk?"

"I think so."

"Then, let's get Howard into the house. Mr. Richards, you stay with him."

Sam started to protest but was interrupted by the deputy. "You're a civilian, and with only one good arm. I can't allow you to put yourself in harm's way. It's my job to protect you, and that's what I'm going to do."

Sam gave no argument, and helped the deputy get Howard to the house. Sarah saw them coming and had the door open when they reached the top of the porch steps.

"Bring him into the den. We can put him in your recliner, Sam."

Once Howard and Sam were secured in the house, the deputy invested his efforts in finding Lonnie. He returned to the barn to start his search. As he passed the stalls of the young foals, he noticed how skittish they were. Their animal senses knew something was off, that danger lurked nearby. Douglas searched the barn quickly. He decided to leave the loft area until backup arrived. He would be too exposed and vulnerable if he climbed the ladder to reach the space. Each bale of hay was a potential hiding place for the assailant.

Douglas left the barn, and stood just outside the back doorway, surveying the area behind the barn. A movement just to the left of a small rise caught his attention. He held his gun ready in his right hand as he left the paddock and walked toward the spot where he had seen the white object. He had only walked about twelve feet when a shot rang out. The bullet caught him in the right arm, near his elbow, causing his gun to fall to the ground. A fleeting moment of panic surged through his body as he realized he had been shot. His gun, where was his gun? Douglas searched around him frantically for his service revolver. He was a sitting duck, a wounded one at that. He located the revolver, and picked it up with his left hand. He assumed a crouched position as he sought cover in the barn. He found refuge in the first stall and sat down on a bale of hay.

He listened for several moments but heard no sound except the horses' pawing and whinnying in response to the fired shot. It took him some minutes to remember to check his wound. To his horror, blood was seeping from the wound and making its way through the fabric of his shirt. His entire right sleeve was drenched in his own blood. *The bullet must have nicked a blood vessel,* he thought almost dispassionately. He felt as if the entire situation was a movie he was watching, not a drama in which he was the star player. Finally, a sense of self-preservation kicked in and he tore the left sleeve from his shirt and tied it around his right biceps. He used his teeth to pull the knot tight and hoped it was enough to stop the bleeding even as his vision blurred. He fought to stay conscious as he heard sirens speeding toward the farm.

Sam heard the shot from the farmhouse. He was with Howard in the downstairs family room. Sarah and Mrs. Hoskins were busy upstairs attempting to keep Anna amused with some toys. Thankfully, Anna's chatter and squeals of delight had masked the sound of the gunfire.

Sam was torn between staying with Howard and rushing out to check on the deputy. The decision was made for him however, as three patrol cars and an ambulance appeared in his driveway. Not wanting the officers to encounter gunfire, he walked out onto his porch to warn them of what had just occurred.

The officer in the first car waved his acknowledgment of the warning and motioned for Sam to return to the house. Sam turned to comply when another shot rang out. Sam crumpled onto the wooden porch. He lay there wondering why he was no longer standing, when a deputy and two EMT's appeared and moved him inside to safety. As he was half-carried into the house, he was aware of a burning sensation in his leg.

Sarah came running down the stairs and saw Sam lying in the entry with blood covering his left lower leg. She stifled a scream and ran to his side.

The EMT's moved with efficiency to examine Sam's wound. They cut away the pant leg and searched for the bullet wound. It was a clean entry and exit wound in the calf muscle, so they applied pressure to stop the bleeding and bandaged the wound. Transport to the hospital had to wait, however, until the shooter was found and neutralized.

Additional backup was requested from the Kentucky State Police, but only one officer was nearby. He joined the scene at Serendipity Farm to add what support he could. The officers on the scene quickly developed a plan of action. They would start with the barn and spread out from there in pairs.

As they neared the barn, however, another shot rang out. The six men on the scene sought cover where they could find it. Seconds passed. A minute. The men inched toward the barn and entered the dark space. They gave their eyes time to adjust to the relative darkness of the barn. Once they could see clearly, they saw a motionless form lying at the far end of the barn. Douglas, holding a gun in his left hand, was kneeling over the body of the assailant.

"He's dead. I shot him as he walked past the stall where I was sitting." Douglas announced. He attempted to get on his feet.

The officers rushed forward to assist Douglas as he started to fall.

"I think there's someone lying in the pasture," Douglas informed the group. " I was just about to check on it when I got hit."

Two officers cautiously approached the area indicated by Douglas. The lifeless form on the ground was Lonnie. He had been shot in the head and must have died instantly. Just beyond the body of the farmhand, the body of the hired guard was also found. He had his pistol drawn, and it was still in his hand as he lay in the verdant field.

The injured were loaded into ambulances and whisked away to receive treatment at the hospital. The

Coroner arrived to collect the dead. Sarah hurried out the front door to follow the ambulances to the hospital but was delayed by a deputy.

"Officer, I understand you need a statement from me, but my husband and our farm manager are on their way to the emergency room. I need to be with them. If you need anything further, you'll have to talk with me there."

Without waiting for a reply, Sarah turned to Mrs. Hoskins, who was holding Anna, and explained what she wanted her to do. Then, she grabbed her purse, jacket, and keys and ran to her car and sped away. The trip was made in record time as Sarah followed the ambulances. She found a parking spot at the hospital and pulled out her phone to call Detective Warfel. He would need to know what had happened.

Tom Warfel was sitting at his desk looking over phone records for Rebecca Dorland and Cora Larkin. He entered the phone logs of both women into a spreadsheet and did a search for any numbers in common, and possible calls to each other. It didn't take long to find the connection he was looking for. Each woman had called the other numerous times, and both women had calls to the same gym, as Ms. Dorland had said. It was the type that offered a variety of services—something for everyone it seemed. It was clear that the two women knew each other far better than Rebecca Dorland had claimed. It reinforced Warfel's suspicion that she was concealing information key to the case.

The calls to each other began three weeks before Cora Larkin's murder. The last phone call Becca Dorland made was to a number she called frequently. Warfel would need to match the number with a name. He then opened two other folders and scanned the

136

financial records of both women's accounts. Mrs. Larkin's accounts reflected her monthly alimony payments and her retirement income. There was nothing to indicate any influx or outgo of large amounts of money.

Becca Dorland's financial records told a different story. For the past six months, she had deposited large amounts of cash each month. Her spending increased at the same time, and her shopping had shifted to higher end labels. *But where were the bearer bonds?* Tom still had no idea how the bearer bonds figured into the relationship between Ms. Dorland and Cora Larkin, but at least he now had a place to begin. He would start with the gym where the two women had met.

He had to wait, however, as the call from Sarah interrupted his plan. He listened with heightened concern and assured Sarah he would join her at the hospital. He grabbed his jacket and rushed out the door. The case was escalating out of control with a rising body count.

Warfel remained at the hospital to be sure the deputy, Howard, and Sam were going to recover. While he waited, he stayed in touch with the crime scene unit at the farm. Several spent cartridges had been recovered, and the lab would have the task of matching them to the guns used. There wasn't an identity yet on the shooter, but his description matched that of the man Mac had seen at Sam and Sarah's farm a few days earlier.

All three men were released from the hospital later that evening. Sarah took Howard and Sam home before driving to Mac's farm to pick up Mrs. Hoskins and Anna. Sarah had instructed the housekeeper to take

Anna to Mac's to avoid all the crime scene activity. Aggie and Mrs. Hoskins had kept little Anna busy by baking cookies.

# Fourteen

The next day, Warfel walked into the gym shortly after it opened. He flashed his badge and asked the receptionist if he could speak with the manager. He was told to wait, and the receptionist left her desk and knocked on the door of an inner office. *I wonder why she didn't just use the intercom?* Tom wondered. The petite blonde returned in a few minutes and assured the detective that the manager would be with him in a few minutes. Time ticked by, and it was a full thirty minutes before the manager emerged.

Tom had expected a person with a trim physique, but was surprised when a middle-aged man with an overlapping belly and a receding hairline walked toward him with hand outstretched.

Tom shook hands and noted the sweaty palm. "Robert Snow, Detective; I'm so sorry to keep you waiting; I was in an interview and couldn't break off. Please come into my office."

Warfel followed the man into a well-appointed office with masculine touches. Prints of Kentucky Derby winners provided decoration for the dark tan walls. The detective was offered a chair in front of the manager's desk. Mr. Snow took the seat beside Warfel but turned it to face his guest. Tom adjusted his chair as well.

"Now, what can I do for you, Detective?"

"Mr. Snow, I'm here to get information on two of your members. It's in regard an active investigation."

Mr. Snow started to object but was interrupted by Warfel. "Before you object, you need to know that one of these women is dead."

The detective let that sink in before adding,

139

"Murdered, actually."

Snow's eyes widened and he was speechless. Finally, he sputtered, "How? I mean who?"

"The *how* I am not at liberty to say. By the *who,* I assume you mean the woman and not the murderer. Cora Larkin was the victim."

Snow took a minute to regain his composure. He took a sip of tepid coffee from a mug on his desk. "Detective, Cora Larkin's name is not familiar to me. Let me look in our files." The manager turned to his computer and pulled up the membership. "Ah, here she is. She joined only two months ago."

"Can you tell from your records if she attended the same exercise class, or had an athletic trainer in common with Rebecca Dorland?"

"Ms. Dorland? Has she been murdered, too?"

"No, I just need to know if Mrs. Larkin and Ms. Dorland attended a class at the same time."

"That's a relief; Ms. Dorland has been a client of ours for over two years." The manager paused and looked blankly at Warfel, seemingly oblivious to Warfel's request.

"Mr. Snow? You were going to check class schedules."

"Oh, oh, yes. Just a moment."

Warfel noted that Mr. Snow's hands had begun to tremble. The news of Mrs. Larkin's murder had obviously upset the man—or, he had not expected the police to make the connection to the gym.

The manager typed in several keystrokes on his computer and squinted at the screen. His reading glasses were lying untouched nearby. "Our members register for their classes in advance, and we assign a trainer to them when they join. Let me see…yes, here's the class both attended. It met three times a week: Tuesdays and Thursdays at six p.m. and Saturdays at ten a.m. Their trainers' names were…no, they both had the same trainer, Gus Averill. They also attended Kathy Meyers's yoga sessions from time to time."

"Could I speak with Ms. Myers and Mr. Averill?"

"Of course; Kathy is here now and doesn't have another class for twenty minutes, but Gus won't be here until three this afternoon, I'm afraid."

Warfel hid his disappointment. He had hoped to interview both employees immediately. This would give Gus Averill time to learn of the investigation. If he had something to hide, he would be able to prepare his answers in advance.

To Mr. Snow he said, "That's fine; I'll speak with Ms. Myers now and return this afternoon to speak with Mr. Averill."

"Fine, fine, now let me find Kathy for you. You can use my office for the interview."

"Uh, I'd rather speak with her outside, if you don't mind. There's a picnic table on the side of the building under an awning. Is that the employee break area?"

"Yes, we have an indoor one also, of course, but on pretty days our staff prefer to take their breaks outside." Mr. Snow appeared disappointed. Tom suspected the manager had intended to listen in on the intercom during the interview.

Kathy Myers was located and, after donning a light jacket, accompanied Tom to the outdoor break area. If she was nervous or suspicious, she hid it well because Warfel couldn't detect it. They sat down on opposite sides of a picnic table and Warfel began. "Ms.

Myers, I would like to ask you some questions about two women who were in your yoga class."

Kathy chewed on a piece of gum, shrugged, and merely said, "Okay."

Tom identified the two women, but withheld the fact that Cora Larkin was dead. Kathy scrunched up her face in an attempt to remember the pair. "Ms. Dorland, I know her really well; she's a regular and has been coming for some time. Cora Larkin...let's see...oh, I remember, she's the one who just joined a few weeks ago. She's a timid little mouse. I introduced them to each other. Cora needed someone to encourage her with her exercises. Becca, that's Ms. Dorland, took Cora under her wing and helped her with the exercises and some of the machines. The two of them have been chummy since then."

"What do you mean by *chummy?*" Warfel asked.

"Well, you know...they work out a lot together, and I heard them talking one day about meeting later for dinner."

"I see; what else can you tell me about them?"

"Why're you askin' so many questions? Did they do something wrong?"

"No, not at all. Now, is there anything else you can tell me about them?"

"Not really, I mean, I didn't see them that much, just here at the gym."

"Okay, here's my card. If there's anything else you can tell me, please give me a call."

Kathy studied the card and squinted up at the detective. "It says here you're from the homicide division. Are they dead?"

"Cora Larkin is." Detective Warfel was surprised the young lady knew nothing of the death. He surmised that she didn't watch the news much. He thanked the young woman, who now simply stared at him wide-eyed, and returned to the gym's office.

Tom found the manager in the outer reception area. He was leaning over the receptionist in such a way as to have a good view down her blouse. Upon seeing Tom's approach, he stood up quickly, clearly embarrassed to be caught leering at the ample breasts of his employee. Tom outwardly ignored what he had seen, but thought, *I knew I didn't like this guy.*

"Mr. Snow, I've finished speaking with Miss Myers. Could I have a phone number and an address for Mr. Averill?"

The request was met with a blank stare. "Well, uh...you see, we don't have a phone number for him. We do have an address, though. I'll get it for you."

Tom wondered why the simple request caused Mr. Snow such discomfort. He was definitely nonplussed. The manager returned in a few minutes with the address. Tom noticed the man was sweating and flushed. The change in demeanor was significant, and Mr. Snow's hand trembled as he passed a piece of paper to Warfel with an address scrawled on it.

"Thank you, Mr. Snow; I appreciate your help."

"Sure, anytime."

Tom left the gym and tapped the address into his phone. Gus lived about ten minutes away. Warfel started his car and pulled away from his parking spot. As he backed up, he could see Mr. Snow watching him from his office window. *I believe I've poked the hornet's nest*, Tom concluded.

Tom drove the short distance to Gus Averill's apartment, found a parking spot marked for guests, and turned off the engine. The area was strewn with

143

discarded items: food wrappings, soda cans, and other trash. The shrubs lining the property were half dead and overgrown. It was clear that management didn't spend any of its budget on grounds maintenance. Tom pulled into a parking spot and reached to open his door. Before he could exit his vehicle, an orange Dodge Charger sped past him, its tires squealing as it made the turn out of the complex. Tom noted the license number and suspected he already knew the name of the driver. As the car sped out of view, Tom climbed a flight of stairs to the second-floor apartment level. He knocked on Averill's door but received no answer. He knocked again and waited.

Tom met up with his partner at police headquarters and updated him on the morning's events. "The manager became very nervous when I asked for Gus Averill's phone number and address. He claimed the trainer didn't have a phone, but I'm fairly sure he called Averill before I could get to his apartment. Snow's hands were literally shaking when he handed me the address. It was obvious he didn't want me to call the man. If I had to guess, Averill's phone number will match the calls made recently by Rebecca Dorland. I was just about to check on the license plate number when you walked in."

"It seems we need to take a closer look at this gym," Drew offered.

Tom nodded in agreement and sat down behind his desk. He pulled up license plate information. "Yep, here it is. The Dodge Charger that sped out of the parking lot belongs to Augustus Ray Averill. His picture is a bit grainy, but I believe he's the same man I saw at Cora Larkin's funeral. I had a feeling he would show up again in our investigation. I wonder why he didn't want to speak with me."

"Maybe it's his apartment he doesn't want you to see. Could be drugs."

"I'm sure that's a good guess, and I would bet that Mr. Snow is aware and perhaps complicit. I think he knew about Ms. Larkin also, but was very surprised that we had made the connection to him and the gym so quickly. We don't have enough for a search warrant, but I'll go back to the gym at three o'clock. That's when he's to report to work today."

"Do you think he'll show up?"

"He might if he thinks I'm not there. I'll drive my own car this time and wait in the parking lot of the fast food place next door. I'll be able to see his orange car easily from there."

"Did you say orange?" Samuels asked, his face registering surprise.

"Yeah, orange—bright orange, with a black stripe on the hood. Not a good color for someone trying to keep a low profile."

"For sure. Okay, you said you interviewed the yoga instructor, too?"

"I did. She gave me some good information, but I doubt she knew the significance of it. Apparently, the two women met at the gym. Kathy Myers, that's the exercise instructor, introduced them. She depicted Cora Larkin as a timid little mouse," the detective said as he consulted his notes from the meeting.

"So, what brought these two women together?"

"The exercise instructor said Ms. Dorland took Mrs. Larkin under her wing at the gym and showed her how to use some of the equipment. They took the same exercise class. It could be that Ms. Dorland was looking for someone like Mrs. Larkin to be her dupe. We now have the connection between the two women and I believe we can start putting some pieces together."

Drew was thoughtful for several minutes, and then asked, "So you think Ms. Dorland and Mrs. Larkin were partners in some financial scheme?"

"Maybe; the bearer bonds seem to be missing, and someone is going to great lengths to find them. Mrs. Larkin's murder was likely an attempt to get her to reveal their location. The incidents at Mac and Sam's farms would indicate that the bonds haven't been found. It isn't a stretch to think all the recent events are related," Warfel asserted.

"What we can surmise so far is that the women met at the gym, Ms. Dorland reached out to Mrs. Larkin, untraceable bearer bonds were stolen, possibly by Ms. Dorland, somehow the bonds fell into Mrs. Larkin's hands, she was killed, and now the bonds are missing," Tom summarized.

"It's like a bowl of spaghetti noodles; everything is intertwined," Drew commented. "What's the next step?"

"I think we had better get back to the gym before Gus Averill arrives for work. We'll go together; if Averill gets any ideas about running, or if he starts a fight, two of us can handle him better than one of us alone. I think Averill and probably Snow, are involved in all of this; I just don't know how yet."

The detectives drove in Tom's car to the fast food restaurant next door to the gym. From this position, they could watch the parking spaces designated for the gym's employees. The orange Dodge Charger would be easy to spot. The two detectives spent the time regaling each other with exaggerated stories of past heroic acts.

"Yeah, I had to climb out a second story window

146

and make my way onto the roof just as the kid's hands slipped. I grabbed him before he could fall from the roof onto the concrete drive below," Drew explained.

"What was he doing up there?" Tom asked.

"His mom had been washing windows in the upstairs bedrooms. The phone rang and interrupted her. She left the room to answer it, and the temptation was just too much for a four-year-old. He scampered out the window and onto the roof while his mom was on the phone. When she returned, she looked for her son, couldn't find him, and suspected he had gone out the window. She had warned him specifically to stay away from there. There's nothing more attractive than forbidden fruit."

Tom laughed, "That's for sure. My girls take great delight in finding ways around the rules of the house instead of doing what I say. It's a universal truth that children will do the one thing you don't want them to do. They seem to go out of their way to get into trouble at that age."

Drew resumed his narrative, "When the mom returned, she found the window open and little Jerry missing. It didn't take her long to discover where he was. She tried to go after him but was overcome with a severe case of vertigo due to an extreme fear of heights. She called 911. I was close by when the call came in, so I covered it. I'm just glad I got there when I did. Jerry would have been badly hurt—or worse. By the time a patrol car could have gotten there, Jerry might have already tumbled off the roof."

"That was a close call, how did...hey, there he is!"

A bright orange Dodge Charger made a sharp turn into a parking spot. Gus Averill stepped out of the

147

flashy car, locked it, and proceeded toward the gym. He kept his head down but looked furtively around the parking lot before entering by a side door.

The detectives waited a couple of minutes before following their target.

Drew said, "I'll cover the side door. He's likely to leave by that door if he realizes you're here for him."

Tom nodded and proceeded to the front entrance. There was no need to identify himself to the receptionist; she remembered him from before. Her eyes widened with recognition, and her fingers paused above her keyboard as if she had been frozen by an arctic blast.

Tom scanned the room but did not see Gus Averill. He decided to check the men's locker room located just behind the main exercise area. Tom pushed open the door and came face-to-face with the subject of his visit.

Gus looked up as Tom pulled his badge out of his pocket. Realizing he was trapped, he decided to use bravado.

"A cop? Well, there's no reason to talk to me about anything; I can't help you," Gus stated with more confidence than he felt, and tried to push past the detective.

"Not so fast, Mr. Averill; I'd like to talk with you. I need you to come with me. I came by your apartment earlier, but it seemed you weren't home."

Tom gave the younger man a look that made it clear it was useless to argue. Nevertheless, Gus ignored the look and again attempted to push past Tom.

"I can't talk to you right now; I have clients waiting for me."

"I'm afraid you'll have to re-schedule, Mr. Averill; you're coming with me."

148

Gus Averill's eyes narrowed, and he pulled his shoulders back. He knew he could take the older man, but also knew the consequences would outweigh the temporary advantage.

"Okay, let me tell the office. I'll be right back."

"I'll come with you if you don't mind. I wouldn't want you to change your mind. And don't get any ideas about running out the side door; my partner is waiting there."

Anger and frustration marked the face of the personal trainer. His complexion took on a reddened hue and his breathing was fast, but he offered no resistance as he was escorted outside to the waiting car.

\*\*\*

Gus offered no conversation during the ride to the police station. He sat in the front passenger seat with Drew directly behind him. The detectives placed Gus in an interview room, provided a bottle of water, and made him wait for twenty minutes before joining him. He sipped the water as he waited impatiently, and glared at the detectives when they entered the room. They sat across the gray metal table from the angry young man. The table and chairs were bolted securely to the floor. A metal rail to lock handcuffs ran along the underneath edge of the table on the side where Gus was sitting. It was a not so subtle reminder that this room was also used to interrogate prisoners. The implication was not lost on Gus, but he held his tongue in spite of his pent-up rage.

Tom opened a notebook and silently reviewed some notes before addressing Gus.

"Mr. Averill, are you aware of the recent death of one of your clients, Cora Larkin?" Without waiting for a response, he charged ahead. "We know from your work schedule that you provided one-on-one personal training for the deceased in the past few weeks." *And, you attended her funeral,* he thought, but didn't say. This time, Tom waited for Gus to fill the silence.

"Yeah, I know about it. She was in my aerobics class—so what?"

Tom continued in a firm, yet almost quiet voice. "What can you tell us about Mrs. Larkin? You must have had conversations with her during her exercise sessions."

Gus stared back at the detectives and answered in a defiant tone. "We worked on her core strength, that's all. I don't stand around and listen to small talk."

"Is that so? Some of the other trainers said you paid particular interest to Mrs. Larkin; that you actually flirted with her."

"I wouldn't call it flirting. I encourage all my clients to do their best and compliment them when they succeed, nothing more."

"Are you telling us that you didn't specifically ask for Mrs. Larkin to be put on your schedule? You didn't have her moved from another personal trainer's schedule to yours?"

Gus, not knowing how much the detectives knew, struggled for a way to explain his actions. "Well, uh…I needed the money, and my schedule wasn't full. I was hoping she would sign-up for individual training. I get paid extra for that."

Tom made a notation in his notebook before looking up. His expression showed he didn't believe the explanation. Instead of addressing the obvious lie, he changed direction.

"Mr. Averill, Ms. Rebecca Dorland has been a client of yours for over a year." It was a statement, not a question. "Did you ever see her outside of work?"

Gus attempted to take the measure of his interrogator. He wondered how much the police had discovered and how much they were only guessing.

"I saw her around—at a couple of clubs, that sort of thing, but we weren't dating if that's what you mean."

"I'm not implying anything; I'm just trying to establish how well you know Rebecca Dorland. Have you ever arranged to meet her outside of work?"

Gus felt his temper rising and struggled to control it. He mustn't let himself be goaded into giving too much away. They were just fishing, he told himself.

"Now why would I do that? She's at least ten years older than me. I don't have any trouble getting chicks my own age, and a lot prettier, too."

"Just answer the question, Mr. Averill; I'm not concerned with your dating history."

"No! Is that plain enough for you?"

"Quite plain." Detective Warfel suppressed a grin as he continued the interview. An hour later, Gus Averill was permitted to leave, but refused the offer of a ride back to the gym. He called Uber instead. A uniformed officer escorted Gus from the building.

Drew turned to his partner, "Tom, he definitely knew Rebecca Dorland better than he admitted. Each time you mentioned her name, his face reddened and his breathing became more rapid. Those two are mixed up in something, that' s for damn sure."

"I believe you're right, Drew, and we need to find out what that is."

"How is Mrs. Osborne?" Drew asked, as the pair returned to Warfel's office.

Tom took a deep breath. "Not good. She had to have a blood clot removed from her brain and she's in

ICU."

"What about her husband?"

"He has a concussion and will have quite a headache for a while, but he'll make it. He's a tough one. I looked into his career; he was quite the investigator in his day. I'm trying to keep him in the loop so he won't go out on his own looking for answers—he's the type who would. He's been involved in some recent local cases since he retired."

"Once a detective, always a detective?"

"In this instance, yes," Tom answered. "Time to go home, but I have a couple of patrolmen keeping an eye on Gus Averill. With the pressure we put on him today, he just might be spooked enough to do something foolish."

Drew answered. "It always makes our job easier when suspects get nervous and make mistakes, but this case doesn't seem that simple. Mr. Averill doesn't seem to be the leader type."

"I agree. We've only scratched the surface on this one, and Gus Averill is likely only a minor player in it. He could lead us to the person making all the decisions, though. There is more going on at the gym where he works than exercising; I would bet a paycheck on that,"

"I believe you're right, Tom. This case is more than one homicide; it has the feel of much more. We've stirred things up a bit so we should know more soon."

"Yeah, that's what I'm afraid of. I only hope we can get to the bottom of this one before someone else gets hurt or killed."

# Fifteen

The next days at Serendipity Farm were sad ones, as the family prepared for Lonnie's funeral. The security guard's funeral was the same day as the farmhand's, but Sam and Sarah sent flowers for the guard's service and Sarah visited the grieving widow before attending services for Lonnie.

After Lonnie Tipton's service, Sam approached Lonnie's wife. "I know you have two children to raise and educate. Sarah and I want to help out," Sam offered as he pulled an envelope out of the breast pocket of his jacket.

Sue reached for the envelope with a trembling hand, too overcome to speak. Her father stepped forward and put an arm around her. "That's a decent thing to do, and totally unexpected. We're very grateful for your generosity, Mr. Richards."

"Just Sam. Mr. Richards is my Dad," Sam corrected with a smile. "We were very fond of Lonnie and he did good work for us. It's the least we can do."

Sue swallowed hard as she struggled with the roller coaster emotions inside her. "Thank you, Sam. You and Sarah have always been good to Lonnie. He always came home in a good mood with stories from his day. He especially enjoyed working with the foster kids. He told me how the horses sensed how fragile some of the kids were, and how they provided the children unconditional love."

Sam nodded. "Yes, the horses allow the children to trust again and ask nothing in return. We've seen some pretty amazing changes in the children. Sue, please call on us if there's anything you need, and bring the kids by to ride the horses."

154

Sue smiled. "Thank you, I'll do that." Other guests were waiting to speak with Sue and she turned her attention to them, but she held onto the envelope throughout the afternoon. Its contents represented stability, and for the first time since the shooting, she had hope that she and the children would be okay.

That evening, Sarah sat with Anna on her lap, rocking and singing to her two-year-old. Anna fell asleep in her arms. Sarah held her for another thirty minutes before she relinquished the sweet-smelling toddler to her bed. She wanted to hold her daughter close forever, keeping her safe from all the bad things in the world.

Sarah made sure the baby monitor was working properly, turned on the night light in the nursery, and joined Sam in their bedroom. She felt as if a month had passed in the past few days and wondered if she would ever feel safe again.

\*\*\*

The next morning, Sarah parked her car in the visitor's lot at the hospital. Upon entering Mac's room, she found him sound asleep. Mac had been moved to a general medical floor the evening before and he expected to be discharged soon. Sarah quietly set her purse down and found the nurses station.

The unit secretary looked up at her approach. "May I help you?"

"Yes, thank you. My friend, Mac Osborne, is in Room 328. I'm told he will be discharged possibly as soon as today. Can you check on that for me? I need to get some things ready for him at home."

The young woman assured Sarah she would get someone to help her. A few minutes later, a nurse approached the counter. "I understand you were inquiring about Mr. Osborne?"

"Yes, I need to know if he's going home today. I need to prepare for his homecoming."

"Are you family?"

"No, but Mr. Osborne has listed my husband and me as being able to share his medical information. I believe he signed something to that effect."

The nurse checked the computer and returned to Sarah. "What is your name?"

"Sarah Richards."

"Yes, we have that. The hospitalist came in this morning and signed off on the discharge, but the neurologist hasn't yet. I heard him paged a few minutes ago, so I expect him to do rounds here soon."

"Okay, thank you."

Sarah then made her way to the ICU to check on Mary. She was surprised to see her friend sitting up in bed.

"Mary, you look so much better! How are you feeling?"

"Hi, Sarah. I'm feeling more human, that's for sure. I'm waiting for transfer to another room. It'll be nice to get out of this fish bowl. I can't yawn without someone rushing in to check on me."

Sarah laughed. It was good to hear her friend make light of her situation.

"Sarah, have you seen Mac this morning?"

"Yes, he's taking a nap at the moment. I spoke with his nurse. He can go home today if the neurologist feels he's ready."

"That's a relief. I guess we're lucky, considering, but I can't help but be somewhat angry. I don't understand how Mac and I got mixed up in all of this. What was Cora doing?"

156

"That's still being determined, but it mustn't have been very good. Apparently, Cora had something that belonged to someone else, and they want it back."

"It must be pretty valuable to cost Cora her life and nearly mine and Mac's."

Sarah had decided against telling her friend about the recent tragic events at Serendipity Farm, but did share one bit of information. "The police think it was bearer bonds—a very large sum."

"Bearer bonds? Where on earth would Cora have gotten bearer bonds?"

"That's a good question, and I can't answer it for you, at least not yet."

"Sarah, I see a familiar gleam in your eye. What do you plan to do?"

Sarah laughed. "I believe you know me almost as well as Sam. You both needn't worry; I only intend to do a little research and work on putting the puzzle together."

"Oh, Sarah, you must be careful!"

"Please don't worry about me, Mary. You just concentrate on getting well so you can come home."

"Sarah Richards, you have a talent for getting yourself in trouble with that super sleuth nose of yours. Need I remind you of past close calls?"

"No, I remember very well the harrowing events related to searching for my biological father and the murder investigation of the bourbon distilleries the year after. I assure you I don't plan to do anything to put myself or anyone else in jeopardy. But, I am good at research, and there might be something I can do to shed light on this situation. When my good friends are attacked in such a vicious manner, I take that rather personally." Sarah's mind recalled the horror of recent days but hid the shock and sadness from her friend.

Mary considered the young woman standing before her. Sarah was indeed headstrong, but she also had a head for ferreting out details others did not see. It was true that Sarah had not deliberately risked her or Sam's life, but both had faced danger as a result of her prying. She hoped this wasn't another such situation but had to trust her dear friend.

"All right, I know you wouldn't deliberately do anything to step in harm's way, but the bad guys don't take kindly to prying into their affairs."

The petite, auburn-haired young woman smiled. "Thank you, Mary; I appreciate your concern." Sarah glanced at the clock over the bed. "Oops, my time is up; they're very strict about visitors here. One last thing, I spoke with Amy and Cameron. Both plan to be here by the weekend; you'll be able to enjoy their visit in the comfort of your own home."

"It'll be good to see them. It's unfortunate this incident came so close to the death of their mother. They've had a lot to deal with."

"True, but they're both very strong, and they love you and Mac. I also heard from your daughter. She has called every day to check on you. She said to tell you she loves you, and wishes she could come, but her obstetrician won't let her travel so close to her due date."

Mary smiled. The birth of her first grandchild was imminent. She couldn't wait to hold her grandson.

"Thank you for all the information. I don't know what Mac and I would do without the two of you."

Sarah leaned down to kiss Mary's cheek. "Glad to do it; you guys have always been there for us, too."

\*\*\*

Detective Warfel and his team spent the next two weeks investigating each person involved with Cora Larkin and Rebecca Dorland. Gus Averill still had their full attention too. The detectives knew that he and Becca Dorland met outside the gym and there were several calls between their cell phones. Gus also had a criminal record for petty theft, and his juvenile record was peppered with numerous incidents. He had been involved in everything from smoking pot to stealing a car for a joyride with friends. He had lived with his grandmother most of his life until age twenty. Warfel decided to speak with the grandmother to see if she could shed some light on her grandson's activities and acquaintances.

Warfel drove across town and pulled up in front of the run-down bungalow belonging to Gus Averill's grandmother. The rusty gate of the chain link fence was hanging crookedly by one hinge, and it creaked loudly when Tom pushed it open. The yard was small, with patches of dead grass. A flowerbed by the front porch had once sported a rose garden, but now grew only weeds.

Tom ascended the three steps to the porch and reached for the doorbell. There was no sound in response to the pressure applied to the doorbell, so he decided to knock instead. His efforts were rewarded after some minutes, and a small stooped woman with white hair opened the door.

"Mrs. Averill?"

"Yes, who are you? I ain't buying nothin', so don't ask."

"Mrs. Averill, I'm not selling anything. I'd like to speak with you." Tom flashed his badge and identified himself.

"What do you want to talk to me about?"

"I'd like to come in and ask you about your grandson, Gus."

The eyes of the old woman came alive. "What's he done now? I told him the next time he got into trouble he shouldn't expect me to get him out of it. I've wasted all the money I can on that worthless boy."

"Mrs. Averill, I'm not here because he has broken the law, I just need some information, that's all. May I come in?"

The door was opened with a reluctance that was not lost on the detective. Apparently, the woman had dealt with police before and had no desire to renew the acquaintance. She shut the door behind her visitor and locked the dead bolt. She motioned Tom into a nearby sitting room and followed him with a shuffled gait.

"Sit anywhere. I don't use this room much; I watch TV in the back room."

Tom chose to sit on the worn sofa facing the large picture window. Mrs. Averill sat at a right angle to him in a matching overstuffed chair. His host offered no refreshments, and it was obvious this visit was an unwelcome interruption. Tom decided to get to the purpose of his visit quickly.

"Mrs. Averill, thank you for letting me come in to speak with you. Can you tell me about Gus as a boy? I know he had several scrapes with the law as a juvenile; can you tell me why?"

"Well, yes, he was arrested a few times in his teens, but only because he had been influenced by an older cousin who was in a gang. By the time Gus turned thirteen, I couldn't get him to stay in school. I would drop him off at the front door, and he would go right out the back. He missed more days than he attended one

160

year. It brought me a world of trouble, I'll tell you. I couldn't do anything with him, and he finally was placed in a juvenile detention center. He went into the Navy when he turned eighteen. I was relieved because I thought the Navy would be good for him. When he finished his tour of duty, he came back here, but not for long. He moved out after a few months and got his own place."

"Do you know who his friends are now, Mrs. Averill?"

"Only one I know is Jason Sutton. They grew up together here in this neighborhood. They fell out just before Gus went to detention but started hanging out together again when Gus came home from the Navy."

"Do you know where I can find Jason?"

"He lives two doors down—with his grandmother." Mrs. Averill pointed a bony finger in the direction of the house.

"Do you see Gus now, Mrs. Averill? Does he come by?"

"I haven't seen him for at least six months. He used to come around wanting money. I'd give him a little, but it was never enough. He threatened me the last time he came here wanting a handout and I refused. I told him to leave and not come back. I'm afraid of him, Detective. I'm not very strong any more, and I wouldn't be any match for him."

Warfel could see the worry behind the steel will of the stooped woman. She had done what she could for a boy who was already too far down the wrong path when he had come to her. He had repaid her kindness with hostility and threats of violence.

"Thank you, ma'am, for your time and information. Here's my card with my cell phone number on it. If you ever feel uneasy, or if Gus threatens you again, just call me."

Arthritic fingers reached for the card as her eyes met those of the detective. She could hear the sincerity in Warfel's voice and pity in his eyes. She quickly looked away, not wanting the detective to see the vulnerability in her own. She broke the silence with a return to gruffness.

"I don't like policemen, but I realize you have a job to do. Good day, Detective." Mrs. Averill led the way to the front door, unlocked, and opened it.

"Thank you, again, Mrs. Averill. Have a good day."

Tom descended the steps to the cracked sidewalk but sensed that Mrs. Averill was still at the door watching him. He glanced up as he reached for the gate latch and found that his hunch was right. The old woman was standing inside the storm door staring out at him with an expression of sadness, as if the visit had brought back old demons from her past with Gus. Tom nodded to her, but she didn't respond. She was still standing there as he made his way to Mrs. Sutton's house, a white frame home with peeling green paint on the shutters.

Tom assumed Mrs. Sutton wasn't home when she didn't answer after two knocks. He turned to walk back to his car, but an older woman pulling a folding shopping cart behind her shouted to him from the sidewalk. "You have to knock loud, mister; Lorie is nearly deaf."

Warfel raised his hand in greeting and thanked the woman. She nodded but didn't wait around to see if Tom would be successful.

The detective turned back to the door and

162

applied greater pressure to his knocking effort. Within a few seconds he heard a thin and high-pitched voice call from inside.

"Come in."

Tom hesitated, unsure if he had heard correctly. He didn't want to frighten the elderly woman.

"Come in!" The voice repeated, but with more urgency.

Tom turned the doorknob and gently pushed the door open halfway. "Hello?"

"Come in, come in. No need to stand there gawking all day."

Tom complied and pulled his badge to show the woman. He stood before the steel gray haired lady and thought to himself that he had never seen anyone who looked more like a shrunken wizard. Her eyes were a faded blue, much like an old pair of jeans, but they displayed intelligence and curiosity. Senility was certainly not this woman's problem, but arthritis was. Her back was fixed in a C-curve, her hands gnarled and drawn, and Tom could see the deformity of her feet even in her cloth house shoes. She was sitting in an electric wheelchair, controlled by a toggle switch on the right armrest. Tom wondered how she managed with cooking, bathing, and other necessary daily activities.

As if she had heard his thoughts, she explained. "You're wondering how I manage, aren't you?" The old lady flashed a smug smile. "You young'uns think you have to have everything just perfect in order to function, don't you? Well, I'm here to tell you that a person can do a whole lot more than they think they can if they just put their mind to it. This chair gets me around where I want to go, I have an aide who comes three times a week to help with bathing, cooking, and cleaning. I eat leftovers on the days she isn't here. Neighbors bring food, too. Now, sit down over there and tell me what you want."

Tom produced his credentials, and the woman reached for them so she could examine them more closely. She held it close to her eyes and squinted as she carefully read it.

"It says here you're a Detective, is that right?"

"Yes, ma'am. I've been on the force twenty years."

She nodded approval and extended a bony hand to return the badge. "So, why would a detective come to see a dried up old bean like me?"

Tom smiled in spite of himself. With a little effort, he composed himself and explained his purpose. "I understand you are Jason Sutton's grandmother, is that correct?"

"Yes, you see his mother ran off with a man who promised her the moon. I'm his grandmother, but he calls me Mama Lorie because he was too young when she left to remember her. I've had him with me since he was six months old. He's studying now and working out at a gym to pass the firemen's fitness test. He's always wanted to be a fireman, like a lot of little boys. It's all he ever wanted. After high school he worked at a few different places, but never gave up his dream of being a fireman."

"You say he works out; do you know which gym he uses?"

"Don't know the name, but it's the one on Chestnut. He showed it to me once as we were driving by. He takes me to my doctor's appointments and gets my groceries. He's such a good boy."

"Mrs. Sutton, do you know a young man named

164

Gus Averill?"

"Now, that's a curious question. A month ago, I would've said, yes, but not now. I don't know what happened, but Jason told me just two days ago that Gus Averill wasn't the person he thought he was and that he wouldn't be spending any more time with him. He was pretty upset."

"Do you know what changed his mind?"

"No, he wouldn't say, he only told me that Gus was in to something bad and he wouldn't go along with it."

"Mrs. Sutton, do you know how I can reach Jason? I'd like to ask him some questions regarding Gus Averill."

"Mrs. Sutton eyed the detective suspiciously. "I don't know. Jason is biracial. Police look at him differently than they do white boys. He gets stopped at least twice a month for nothing. Racial profiling is still a big problem, Detective, and I want my Jason treated right. He's a good boy."

"I'm sure he is, ma'am, I just want to talk with him, that's all. He's in no trouble with the police, and I'm sorry he's experienced unfair treatment. Attitudes change slowly, I'm afraid."

"Humph! You got that right! Jason still lives here with me, but he's in class right now." The woman looked at the carriage clock on the mantel above a brick fireplace. "No, wait, he finished his last class twenty minutes ago. He should be home any minute. If you want to wait, we could pass the time with some coffee and cake. My friend Alice brought some apple cake over this morning. It's really good."

"That sounds wonderful; may I go to the kitchen and fix the coffee?"

"Yes, please. I'll go with you and show you where everything is." With a practiced movement, she maneuvered her wheelchair to the spacious kitchen. It had been refitted to permit the arthritic woman accessibility. Cabinets were lower than normal and the work surface had a built-in cooktop. A built-in oven completed the changes. Tom had to bend over the low counter to prepare the coffee for brewing. The elderly lady showed Tom where to find plates, and a knife to cut the cake. Once everything was ready, the two sat at the kitchen table and enjoyed Alice's apple cake and conversed like old friends.

"This is delicious; please thank your neighbor for me. Tom started to say more, but he became aware of footsteps in the front hall.

"Mama Lorie, I'm home!"

"I'm in the kitchen, Jason. We have company."

A lanky young man with skin the color of café' au lait appeared in the kitchen doorway. He saw Tom, who had risen to greet him, and regarded him with curiosity. There was no sign of fear or distrust.

"Jason, I'm Detective Warfel, could I ask you some questions regarding Gus Averill?"

"Sure, can I cut me a slice of that cake first? I'm starved!"

Once settled with his cake and a large glass of milk, he sat across from Tom and said, "Okay, what d'ya want to know?"

Tom questioned the young man for thirty minutes but gained only one useful piece of information. Gus Averill had been running a con with some of his gym clients. He was mixing up chocolate milk, adding a few liquid vitamins, and bottling it. It was presented to unwary customers as a wonder drink with secret

166

ingredients guaranteed to bulk up muscles and provide more energy. Jason had no idea if the gym manager, Mr. Snow knew of the scheme. Jason had broken off all communication with the con artist. Jason couldn't say for sure if Gus was dealing drugs, too, but he said he wouldn't be surprised. Gus was always looking for a way to make a quick dollar.

Tom thanked the pair and left feeling as if he was finally making some progress. Gus Averill was apparently up to his neck in illegal activity.

## Sixteen

Mary had been home a week and was making good progress. A bed had been placed in Mac's study for Mary's convalescence after her hospital stay. She was sitting propped up with pillows with Mac sitting next to her. Aggie had moved in with the couple, so Mary wouldn't be alone when Mac needed to go out. The kind housekeeper walked into the study carrying a lunch tray for her employers.

Mary looked up as Aggie came through the doorway. "Ah, Aggie, you're a dear; lunch is just what I need."

Aggie beamed as she carefully placed the tray on a nearby table. "I fixed chicken salad today with walnuts and grapes, just the way you like it. What would you like to drink?"

"Thank you, Aggie, just water for us today," Mary answered.

"Okay, coming right up. When you finish your sandwiches, I have some pudding also."

"What would we do without you? You have certainly done everything you could to help my recovery. When I'm fully recovered, we want you to take some vacation time on us. You deserve it—and more."

"Thank you; I would like to see my sister. She's been rather ill lately, and a couple of days to visit her would be a blessing."

"I'm glad you'll be able to see your sister, but we'll try to convince you to take more time. You've worked day and night for us."

Aggie smiled and left to get the glasses of water.

Mary took a bite of her sandwich. Mac could

168

tell something was on her mind but refrained from asking her about it. She would tell him in her own good time. Finally, Mary swallowed and turned to him.

"Mac, have the police found the bearer bonds?"

"No, I spoke with Tom Warfel yesterday, and he said they had pretty much run out of places to look. If Cora hid them, she did a mighty good job of it."

"But why would Cora get mixed up with something like that to begin with? It doesn't make sense. She had sufficient income, and it certainly wasn't her nature to do anything dishonest."

Mac shook his head. I agree; it doesn't make sense. Maybe she was misled or didn't know what she had." Silence settled in the room as the pair tucked into their sandwiches, but both continued to pursue the mystery as they ate.

Pudding followed the sandwich, but Mary's appetite was sated, so she saved the dessert for later. She watched Mac surreptitiously as he finished off his dessert. She knew what he was about to say; it was inevitable.

Mac put the spoon in the empty dish and patted his stomach. "Aggie is a good cook, but I'm afraid I've gained a few pounds since we've been forced to be less active lately."

Mary smiled in response but knew there was more than his weight on Mac's mind.

Aggie entered the room and took away the tray of dishes. "Thank you, Aggie, it was delicious. I was too full to eat the pudding though, so please save it for later."

"Okay, is there anything else you need right now? I thought I might go to the grocery this afternoon."

169

"I believe we're fine, Aggie. Thank you."

Once they were alone again, Mac turned to Mary and uttered the words that Mary had dreaded, though expected to hear. "Mary, the investigation into Cora's murder seems to be stalling. I can't bear the thought of her murderer getting away with it. She deserves justice, and Cameron and Amy deserve closure. Amy and Cora were so close; this has been especially tough on her."

Mary waited patiently for Mac to get to what he wanted to tell her.

"I think I'll check some things out. I knew Cora as well as anyone; maybe I can discover something that might help the investigation."

Mary carefully chose her next words. She knew her husband could not leave the investigation alone. *Once a detective, always a detective*, she thought.

"Mac, I understand your need to find closure for Amy and Cameron, and to seek justice for Cora, but I want you to promise me one thing."

"Yes?"

"I want you to promise me that you'll leave the dangerous stuff to Detective Warfel and his team. The detective seems very competent, and you are recovering from a serious injury."

Mac smiled at his beautiful wife and reached for her hand. "Don't worry, sweetheart, I'll be careful. In fact, it's my middle name."

Mary laughed, but a look of concern quickly replaced the amusement. "I don't know what would become of me if I lost you, Mac. You've given me a new lease on life that I never expected. I wake up every morning looking forward to another day with you. You're my everything, you big lug!"

Mac's expression softened as he took in Mary's

words as he would the aroma of a fine perfume. His life had been changed as well. It would be impossible to tell Mary how she had transformed the crusty, divorced ex-detective. He reached for her and held her close as he whispered assurances in her ear. When they parted, Mary's eyes were brimming with unshed tears, but she was smiling.

"Okay, Mac. Do what you feel you need to do—just be careful!"

"I will, please don't worry. Now, you get some rest. I think I'll take my laptop out on the back porch and check some things out, maybe make some phone calls. You have your cell phone, so call or text me if you need anything."

"I will, thanks."

Two hours later, Mac had more questions than answers. He had researched everything he could find on bearer bonds. They would certainly make a good place to hide money. Ownership was not recorded, so they could be passed to others undetected. This also made them attractive to thieves. Was Cora a thief, or just a pawn in a very dangerous game? He had to find the answer to that question.

Tom had told Mac that the gym Cora attended was a focal point of the investigation. Mac decided to check it out for himself. After all, he needed to get into shape. What better way to do it than to join a gym? Aggie was back from shopping, and Mary was sound asleep, so Mac told his housekeeper where he was going and to tell Mary when she awoke.

Mac grabbed a jacket and the keys to his truck and left by the back door. As he walked to his vehicle, he waved to one of the men who had been hired to help with the horses while he recuperated. He missed being in the barn himself, but knew he wasn't up to wrangling horses just yet, so he left the work to others.

He slid behind the wheel of his truck and started the engine. He entered the address of the gym into his phone's navigation system and aimed his truck toward the highway. It took less than thirty minutes to cover the distance. The step-by-step directions took him directly to the gym. He found a parking place near the entrance but passed it up in favor of one near the street. He carefully backed his truck into the space, turned off the motor, and sat watching the building. He didn't know what he was looking for, but he did want to get a feel for the area. His years of detective training had taught him to always know his surroundings.

Mac's patience was rewarded as he saw a young man leave the gym through a side door, closely followed by an older man with a paunch. The older man was yelling. Mac couldn't hear what was being said, so he quietly opened the door of his truck a few inches to hear more clearly.

"What do you think you're doing? You'll never get away with it!" the older man yelled. "Michael will cut you down before you see him coming!"

The younger man turned to face his pursuer. "Why should Michael get most of the action? What are we, huh? We take all the risks, and he takes all the money. Well, I'm tired of getting the scraps, I want more!"

Then both started yelling at each other, making it difficult for Mac to sort through their words. He caught only part of what they said, but it was apparent that drugs were involved. After several minutes of heated discussion, both men returned to the gym through the side door.

172

*That's it*! Mac thought. They're running drugs through the gym. *Oh, Cora, what did you get yourself mixed up in?"*

Just then, a Lexus pulled into the parking lot and took the open space that Mac had passed up near the entrance. An attractive middle-aged blonde got out, retrieved her designer gym bag from the back seat and strutted into the gym, with hips swinging. Mac couldn't help admiring her figure; obviously the gym had done its part in sculpting the curves, but the cynic in Mac decided a plastic surgeon must have had some role as well.

He thought, *I must be crazy to do this, but if this is what it takes to find Cora's killer, then so be it.*

Emboldened by the pep talk with himself, Mac opened the truck's door. He stood looking at the front of the gym for a full minute before proceeding. BODY TRANSFORMATIONS looked innocent enough from the outside, but the secrets it held within its walls were the reason Cora and others were killed. Mac would uncover those secrets if it was the very last thing he ever did.

Mac took a deep breath and entered the gym. An attractive receptionist greeted the newcomer within seconds of his arrival. Mac approached her desk and inquired about new member registration. The receptionist produced the application from a file cabinet next to her desk. Mac set to work completing the form.

By the time Mac had completed half of the registration, a rotund, middle-aged man emerged from an inner office and greeted him. It was the same man who had been part of the argument in the parking lot earlier.

"Good morning, sir! I'm Robert Snow, the

manager."

Mac accepted the outstretched hand and returned the man's smile. He had decided against using his own name. "Herb Bailey, good to meet you."

"So, you're planning to join our gym Mr. Bailey?"

*This guy's no Sherlock Holmes,* Mac thought. "Yes, I had recent surgery and I thought your gym could help me get back to my old self."

"Excellent! I'm sure we can design a program to help you. What are you interested in? Aerobics, strength training, weight loss?"

"It all sounds good. Could I have a personal trainer to help me reach my goals?"

"Absolutely! Once you finish your form, someone will show you around and get you acquainted with the equipment."

"Sounds good, thanks."

"Not a problem at all. Well, I need to get back to my office, but it was a pleasure meeting you Mr. Bailey. Please let me know if there's anything at all we can do for you."

"Okay, I will, thank you." *Yeah, buddy, you can begin by telling me what other business is conducted here.*

Mac watched as Robert Snow walked back to his office and closed the door. His detective senses were tingling. Mr. Snow was definitely a phony. His slick, polite exterior did little to hide the real person beneath, and Mac intended to expose the secrets held so closely by the gym manager.

Mac finished the forms, being careful to list a fake name and address. Almost immediately an attractive young woman in exercise clothes appeared to

174

show him around the gym. Once she had finished the tour, she directed him to the men's locker room so he could change his clothes. She flashed him a flirty smile and bounced off to help another client. Mac wondered, not for the first time, if he was being foolish. Did he still have the skills of a detective? Or was he fooling himself? He would soon find out.

## Seventeen

Mac dressed quickly and took a moment to check his reflection in a full-length mirror. *Well, old boy, just remember this is for Cora.* Mac tried not to show his nervousness as he stepped out into the gym. He was accustomed to hard work around the farm, but this was different. His every move would be evaluated to ensure he was using the equipment properly. With this in mind, he decided to start on basic equipment and gradually work his way up to the more advanced workouts. Mac was on his second set of bicep curls when Gus Averill appeared at his side. Mac immediately recognized him as the young man who had argued with Robert Snow in the parking lot.

"Hey, man, you're doing pretty good with those curls. Not many can start with that amount of weight. Do you work out regularly?" Gus asked.

"Nah, I'm used to farm work, but I had a recent injury, so I thought I would join the gym to get back in shape," Mac explained.

"Well, this is as good a place as any. Have you signed up for any classes yet?"

"Classes?"

"Yeah, we have aerobics, spin class, yoga, Tai Chi, and several others. Classes are good motivation, and I would recommend that you join at least one. I have an aerobics class beginning in fifteen minutes if you're interested."

"Uh, well, sure. Do you think I'm ready for that?" Mac asked. "I'm a bit out of shape at the moment."

"Sure, we have all levels in the class. If something's too hard, skip it and try the next exercise."

176

"Okay, I'm in."

Mac grabbed a bottle of water, drank a third of it, and reported for class. Gus was right about one thing; there were beginners, experts, and everything in between. He marveled at how easily some in the class completed an exercise, while others struggled with the basics. He decided he was in the middle of the group, not an expert, but not a novice either. He felt he would be near the top of the class in ability before long.

The class time went by quickly, and Mac headed to the locker room for a shower before returning home. After the shower, he sat down on the bench in front of his locker to put on his shoes and socks. As he reached for his second shoe, he overheard a conversation on the other side of his locker.

"I'm telling you it's a good deal, man; you won't find it any cheaper." The voice seemed to be that of Gus, but Mac couldn't be sure. He moved closer and was able to see Gus through a gap in the lockers but the other man had his back to him.

The other voice replied, "I don't know; the last stuff you gave me was pretty strong. I couldn't go to work the next day."

"Aw, you'll get used to it. It's good stuff."

"I only have a hundred to spend today; I'll bring more next time."

"That's fine, and just to show you how much I trust you, I'm going to give you a special deal—I'll throw in extra product. It's worth thirty dollars. My treat."

"So, I don't have to pay for the extra?"

"No, as I said, my treat. Maybe I'll need you to do me a favor someday."

"Sure, but I have limits. I don't want to get into

177

trouble—I need my job."

"I understand completely," Gus assured good-naturedly as he put a hand on the other man's shoulder. "Just a favor for a friend, that's all."

Mac knew this had to be a drug deal. His initial impression of Gus had been right. Not wanting his presence to be known, Mac finished tying his shoes, silently picked up his gym bag, and made for the door. He was just approaching the doorway when he heard footsteps coming from behind just around the corner. Needing to act quickly, he turned around as if he was coming into the locker room, not leaving it. He pulled his face into a neutral expression but flashed a wide grin when he saw Gus.

Gus was obviously surprised by Mac's presence. "Oh! Where did you come from...I mean what do you need?" Gus couldn't hide his nervousness behind a fake smile. Mac noticed that the second man had not come into view behind Gus and suspected he had retreated back behind the row of lockers.

"I just forgot my sunglasses. I believe they're in my locker." Mac knew they were in a case in his gym bag and hoped Gus would not follow him to discover the lie.

"I see, well, have a good one—see you next time."

"Sure thing, Gus. I enjoyed today's class, but I might need a couple of days to recover before I come again," Mac said with a laugh. He gave a final nod and walked to his locker. He turned the combination and opened the door. Peripheral vision told Mac that Gus had gone out the door, presumably back to the gym. Mac breathed a sigh. *That was close—too close!* He thought. Vowing to be more careful, Mac closed the

178

locker, retrieved the sunglasses from his bag, put them on, and left the gym. Gus watched Mac carefully as he exited the fitness center. He *seemed* all right, but there was something familiar about him. Both men were now alerted to the other. This would be a true contest of cunning and skill.

Mac slid into his truck, threw the gym bag on the seat beside him, and started the engine. He wondered, not for the first time, what was going on in the gym. He drove a few blocks, pulled into a parking lot and killed the engine. He took out his cell phone and dialed a now familiar number. Tom had given Mac his direct cell phone number for quicker access.

"Hey, Mac, what's up?"

"Tom, I have reason to believe there's drug dealing going on at the gym where Cora went."

Tom's eyes widened at the news. "Mac, why do you think so, did you go there?" A tone of displeasure registered in his voice.

"Yes, I did. I can't stand idly by while Cora's killer goes free. Anyway, I overheard what sounded very much like a drug deal in the gym's locker room. They didn't know I was there."

Curious now in spite of his displeasure, he asked, "Did you recognize either of them?"

"It was the trainer, Gus, and some guy I couldn't see very clearly. White guy, about five feet eleven inches tall. He's slim but muscular. He must work out a lot."

Tom sighed in exasperation. "Okay, Mac, we'll take it from here. Please don't go back there again. You don't know who you're dealing with. If they are involved in Cora's murder, they won't hesitate to take you out, too."

"I understand your concern; I was a detective too, remember?" Mac pointed out. "I'll be careful. I joined the gym under a false name and the guise of needing to get stronger after an accident."

"You joined the gym? As a former detective, I know you understand how a civilian who butts into a case can foul things up rather badly." Tom was getting more impatient, verging on angry.

"Yes, I know what you're saying. All I'm saying is that I have a right to join a gym." Mac reminded himself to stay calm as nothing was achieved by getting angry. "I signed up for Gus's exercise class. He actually invited me."

"Oh, he did, did he? Well, he might have done that because he wanted to keep you close so he could keep an eye on you. He's the man who acted suspiciously at Cora's funeral and he will likely remember you from that day."

"Maybe, but I have to do something to help find Cora's killer. My kids need closure, and I do too."

Warfel knew when he was beaten. "Okay, it goes against every rule in the book and my own preference, but I'd rather have you work with us than on your own. Will you share anything you find out and clear any future visits with me first? If all hell breaks loose, I want to know if you're there."

"Understood. My next class is Wednesday at two o'clock; I want to check out our suspect a bit more"

*Our* suspect? Please remember Gus is dangerous, has possibly killed before, and is our number one suspect. I don't want you blowin' this operation, do you hear me?"

"Loud and clear. Don't you want to know what they said?"

180

Tom shook his head in frustration, but permitted Mac to continue. "Go ahead, spill it."

"Well, they were well acquainted with each other. I could tell by the conversation."

At the other end of the call, Tom nodded as if he were face-to-face with Mac.

"So, the guy I couldn't see asked for his supply, but he was short of money. Gus gave him the product he couldn't pay for, said he could just do a favor for him in the future."

"That was generous of him," Tom said with unmasked sarcasm.

Mac resumed his narrative. "He told Gus he wasn't sure about the new product, that it was too strong."

"Must've been the heroin laced with Fentanyl that we've seen around lately. We've intercepted some coming in. It's deadly stuff. We've had several overdoses and a couple of deaths related to it."

"So, do you think Cora was killed because she found out about the drugs?"

"No, I don't. I believe she was killed for the bonds, and they're still missing, so you need to stay close to Mary and keep your household safe. The bad guys are looking for them and they don't care who gets in their way. That's why you and Mary were attacked and your home ransacked."

"Makes sense, but are you sure?"

"Pretty much." Tom trusted Mac but couldn't divulge what else he knew just yet. Rebecca Dorland's life and the success of the task force depended on secrecy.

Mac sensed Tom was holding back. "I see, well I wanted to pass along the information. I'll take your

181

advice and be careful."

"You'd better be. I don't want to face Mary with bad news concerning you."

Mac grinned. "No, I wouldn't envy you that task. She is petite and demure on the outside, but inside resides a tiger. You're smart to avoid getting to know that side of her."

"I've been married a long time, Mac. I can't say I completely understand women, but I do know how angry Mary would be if anything happened to you. I don't want that on my conscience."

"Nor I, my friend." Mac agreed.

# Eighteen

Becca woke to darkness. She listened carefully for what had interrupted her dream. She heard footsteps. With heart racing, she pushed the covers back and scooted to the edge of the bed. Now fully awake, she pulled on her slippers and robe.

As Becca neared the closed and locked door of her bedroom, she heard a scraping sound. Her adrenaline kicked in, and she searched frantically for the recently purchased gun she had placed in the top drawer of her dresser. She then looked for her cell phone, but it was in her purse—in the living room. She stumbled in the dark of the unfamiliar bedroom. In an effort to hide from her pursuers, she had moved to a furnished apartment across town from her former residence. She had refused Warfel's offer of armed security for her at the hospital and had taken a leave of absence instead. *How did they find me?*

Becca tried to control her breathing as she listened at the bedroom door and wondered how long the flimsy lock would hold if tested. With trembling fingers, she managed to load the nine-millimeter and tried to remember what the salesman had taught her. She could hear the intruder searching through her kitchen cabinets. The sound of glass breaking and the clanking of pots as they hit the floor told her the intruder didn't care if Becca knew he was there. Becca continued to listen— and wait. She sat on the edge of her bed with the gun aimed at the bedroom door. Minutes passed, each seeming like an hour. Eventually, she heard heavy footsteps on the hardwood floor outside her bedroom door. The footsteps stopped momentarily before she saw the doorknob being tested. They would be in her bedroom in seconds! She lifted the gun, called out a warning that she had a weapon and fired wildly in the direction of the door. The footsteps retreated and she heard her front door slam. She heard nothing more but didn't trust that she was now alone.

Fingers of light reached into the room as dawn approached. There had been no sounds beyond her bedroom door for several minutes, but Becca remained in her bedroom. She sat on her bed, frozen in place and ready to fire her weapon again at the slightest noise.

Neighbors heard the shot and called police. A uniformed officer knocked on Becca's front door and identified himself as a policeman. Was it a ploy? Becca emerged with caution from her bedroom and approached the damaged front door. She warned the person on the other side that she had a gun and wouldn't hesitate to use it. The policeman instructed her to look through her peephole at his credentials. Becca did as instructed, was satisfied as to his identity, and opened the door to admit the policeman. He stepped inside and surveyed the chaotic scene before him. In the living room, the sofa and chair had been ripped open and stuffing pulled out. Damage was not confined to the living room, however. The kitchen cabinets had been nearly emptied. Drawers stood open and broken dishware was scattered on the floor.

The policeman asked Becca to put down her gun. The stunned woman was slow to respond so the demand was repeated. The words finally penetrated her brain and she placed the revolver on the coffee table.

The officer recognized symptoms of shock in Becca, so he gently guided her to a kitchen chair and motioned for her sit to down. "Ma'am...ma'am? Can you look at me?"

A pair of terrified eyes rose to meet the confident brown eyes of the officer.

In an effort to calm her, the officer knelt in front of her at eye level. "Ma'am, can you tell me what happened here?"

"I...uh...there was someone here." Becca waved her right hand in a sweeping motion to indicate the detritus around her. "He started to come in the bedroom, so I fired a shot to scare him away."

"Did you wound him, ma'am?"

"Wound him? No, I don't think so. After I fired the shot, he left in a hurry and I stayed in my bedroom until you came."

The policeman took a small notepad from his shirt pocket and made a few short notes. Becca sat staring straight ahead as if she were watching a replay of the incident. She reached for her purse, which the intruder had thrown to the floor, and retrieved her cell phone. Her hands shook and she found it difficult to punch in the number she wanted to call.

"Ma'am, who are you calling?"

"Detective Warfel."

The young patrolman was puzzled by her answer. "Why are you calling Detective Warfel? He works homicide, not burglary."

"It's too much to explain quickly, but this is probably related to an active murder investigation. It's time I filled him in on a few things."

It took three tries, but Rebecca finally managed to dial the detective's cell phone number. The patrolman stood by.

Tom was having toast and coffee in his kitchen when the phone buzzed. "Warfel." He listened as Rebecca Dorland related the incident. "I'll be right

185

there. Is there anyone there with you now?"

"Yes, a policeman. Someone must have heard the shot and called for him."

"Let me speak with him, please."

Becca handed her phone over to the perplexed officer. He listened as the detective tried to make sense of what Becca had just told him. "No, sir, she doesn't appear to be hurt—just frightened. She has a gun and scared the intruders off by firing a single round from inside her bedroom. The place is completely tossed; they were looking for something, that's for sure. Yes, I'll stay with her until you get here. Yes, sir—goodbye."

Twenty minutes later Tom and Drew arrived at Becca's apartment. Drew took the patrolman's statement before letting him leave. Once he filed his report, his shift, which had been relatively quiet until he got this call, would be over.

Tom approached an obviously distraught Becca, now with a blanket around her shoulders. "Ms. Dorland...Ms. Dorland?"

Becca raised her head slowly and stared at the detective with vacant eyes. The terror was still there, unmitigated by the presence of law enforcement. Warfel had seen many victims and witnesses in shock and knew the emotional trauma must be dealt with before anything else.

Detective Warfel pulled another chair over and sat down next to Becca. Keeping his voice low he said, "Ms. Dorland, look at me."

The shaken woman slowly turned her head to look at the detective. The vacant look was replaced slowly by the dawn of recognition. She blinked several times and shook her head, as if to shake off the physical threat.

Ms. Dorland, I know you already told the patrolman what happened, but I need you to go over it again with me—okay? Let's start at the beginning. Where were you when the intruder broke in?"

"In my bedroom. I've been sleeping with the door closed and locked. I heard a noise and woke up. It was terrible; I just knew he would break through the door and hurt me."

"So, you didn't see who did this?"

"No, I didn't leave my bedroom and the intruders didn't break in. They could have—easily. The lock is not sturdy at all. I could hear them searching all through the living room and kitchen cabinets. As you can see, they were pretty thorough. When they finished looking in here, they came to the bedroom door and tried to turn the doorknob. That's when I shot at the door to frighten them off. It must have worked because they left after I fired."

Warfel looked closely at the woman. "Ms. Dorland, do you feel you need to be seen by a doctor?"

"No, I'm better now; I'm starting to think more clearly. It's funny, I thought I would know how to protect myself from an intruder, but when it actually happened, I froze. I had foolishly left my cell phone in my purse in the living room. It should have been on the bedside table. Before you ask, yes, I have a permit for the gun, and I know how to use it."

At that moment, Drew Samuels walked in. Warfel rose and stepped aside to speak privately with his partner.

"She knows who's behind all of this; I'm sure of it, Drew. She's keeping quiet for reasons of her own, apparently," Warfel said.

"Maybe she's in too deep to get out—afraid of recrimination if she talks. This might have been a warning."

"I'm sure it was, but they were looking for something, the bonds probably. They still think she either has them or knows where they are."

"Sir, if she admits to taking the bonds, she risks prosecution. Maybe that's why she isn't talking to us."

"I believe you're right, Drew. I think the bonds are at the heart of this case. All we have to go on is a torn edge of a bearer bond, but it was found where it shouldn't be, so it is an anomaly, and those scream for attention. I think I need to talk with the Commonwealth's Attorney and see if there could be a deal for Ms. Dorland in exchange for giving us the identities of the men who are after her."

\*\*\*

An hour later, Becca was sitting in an interview room of the Braxton Police Department. Her violent shaking had stopped, but her mind was still far from settled. Various scenarios played out in her mind as she waited. Would she soon be under arrest? Her anxiety level rose as she sat in the dreary, beige painted room. There were marks on the wall where others had placed a foot as they stood and leaned backward. How many others had sat where she sat now? Had their lives been as messed up as hers? Would she be able to hold it all together, or fall apart completely? She knew she was only a step away from a complete breakdown. Cora's dead eyes haunted her. Everywhere Becca looked, she could see the corpse fall out of the car and land on the sidewalk below, and each time she saw those eyes she felt haunted by the dead woman.

188

Drew and Tom watched Becca from an adjoining room through the observation window. They could see the increasing tension in her. The once in-control hospital executive was now spinning out of control. Both felt now, while she felt vulnerable, was a good time to get the information they needed.

As the door to the interview room opened, Becca appeared startled. "Oh, sorry, Detectives, my nerves are just a little raw at the moment." Her voice betrayed her deep-seated fear. The detectives were hoping to use that fear to get her to cooperate.

Both men sat across from Becca. Drew clicked a button in the middle of the table and positioned a small, cordless microphone so that it would pick up their conversation. Tom placed a manila folder in front of him and held a gold and silver tone Cross pen in his right hand. Becca was curious to know what was in the folder but restrained from asking.

Tom sat looking at the woman sitting across from him. He had already decided upon his approach, and he had an amnesty offer for her from the Commonwealth Attorney's office in exchange for what she knew about Cora Larkin's murder. He would have to time the offer at just the right moment, once she was thoroughly convinced of her vulnerability.

Becca's deep brown eyes rose to meet Warfel's crystal blue ones. She could read the resolve in his countenance and realized she was probably no match for the experienced detective.

Warfel cleared his throat and opened the folder. He pulled out the torn edge of the bearer bond which had been found in Mac's shed. Without speaking, he slid it across the table to Becca. At first, she was puzzled by his action, but as she took a closer look at the torn paper, her eyes widened, and she took in an involuntary breath.

The reaction was all Warfel had hoped for. She recognized it for what it was. Now, maybe the case could gain some traction.

"Ms. Dorland, I'm sure you know what this is, or at least what it came from. I can tell by your reaction to seeing it that you recognize it."

"I don't know what you mean, I..."

Warfel cut her off. "Ms. Dorland, it's our belief that you somehow came to have in your possession bearer bonds worth several million dollars, and that these same bonds are what got Cora Larkin killed. Is that getting pretty close to the truth?"

The question hung in the air like the smell of spoiled fish. Becca didn't know what to do or say to plausibly deny the accusation. How much did they know, or did they only suspect her involvement?

The time had come to make her decision. She could open up to the police and risk jail time or continue to deny any knowledge of the bonds and risk her fate to the men who had killed Cora. She looked from one man to the other. Yes, they would not hesitate to prosecute her for what she had done, but the alternative was too dreadful to consider. Cora's dead body, with her vacant eyes staring up at her from the sidewalk, came into her mind's view. She shuddered, lowered her head, and began to sob.

The detectives gave her time to become more composed before continuing their questions. Finally, when the crying had stopped, Warfel asked her again about the paper in front of her.

"Yes, I know what that is. It's a torn corner from a bearer bond."

190

"Have you had any bearer bonds in your possession recently, Ms. Dorland?"

There it was. Her answer to the question would determine her future. She sat back in her chair and took a deep breath. Her hands were shaking, so she moved them from the table in front of her to her lap. She decided it was time to come clean.

"I have a confession to make."

She paused, but the detectives remained silent and allowed her to proceed at her own pace.

"I stole the bonds, four million dollars."

"I see. And, where are these bonds now?" Warfel asked.

"That's just it; I don't know. When I came under suspicion, I handed them off to Cora Larkin. I don't know where she put them. They must be well hidden because the original owners want them back and think I know where they are. That's why I was kidnapped. Apparently, my captors planned to torture me to get the information. It wouldn't have done any good; I don't know where they are."

"Who are the men? I need names."

"I only know the first name of the guy who kidnapped me. One of the other men at the cabin called him Murray."

"Who is their boss? Whose bonds did you steal?"

Becca hesitated. "I can't tell you that. He would kill me!"

The seasoned detective took a paper from the folder in front of him. "I have an offer for you, Ms. Dorland. You tell us the name of the person responsible for the death of Cora Larkin and you won't be charged with the theft of the bonds. You will have to testify in court if it comes to trial as well. We'll provide

191

protection for you to ensure your safety."

Becca's eyes were wild. "Safety? You can't protect me from him!" Her voice was rising to near hysteria. "If he found me last night, he'll find me anywhere!"

"Ms. Dorland, you have admitted you have no idea where the bonds are. Your life is in danger whether you testify or not. Even if you produced the bonds and returned them, an example would be made of you. Your only chance to go on with your life is by cooperating with us."

Tom decided to give Rebecca some time to consider the offer of immunity. "Let's take a break; would you care for some water or a soda?"

Rebecca Dorland stared at the detective, nodded, and asked for water. Her reserves were spent. She wrung her hands in her lap and her shoulders slumped. She was trapped and she knew it. She accepted the bottle of water that Drew got for her. Her mind raced as she unscrewed the bottle top and took a sip. Warfel could see her inner struggle, but again chose to remain silent. He was rewarded for his patience.

"Okay, I'll tell you what you want to know. The leader's name is Michael. I don't know his last name. It's my fault Cora was murdered, and I'll be punished for that for the rest of my life every time I remember her lying at my feet on the sidewalk."

Tom nodded encouragement, but he was definitely surprised when Rebecca Dorland, with her next words, added a twist to the case he had not expected.

Rebecca took a sip of her water and cleared her throat. She hesitated a moment before continuing. Once she revealed what she was about to say, her destiny was in the hands of the police. She took a deep breath, straightened her shoulders, and began her narrative.

"Detective, there's a part of all of this you don't know about, at least how it fits into this investigation." Warfel made no comment, as he didn't want to hurry her statement.

Rebecca took another sip of water. "I'm sure you've discovered by now that the gym is a front for a large drug operation—and that the bonds were part of the money laundering scheme. What you might not know is that human trafficking is also part of the operation. A gym is a perfect place to recruit young women and teenage girls into prostitution. That age group is really into fitness and appearance, so there is always a good supply to choose from. If you can extend my immunity to cover my involvement with the human trafficking activity, I'll give you all the details you want to shut this operation down for good."

The two detectives looked at each other in surprise. They were certainly aware of the human trafficking activity in their area, but it was not part of their jobs as homicide detectives to investigate it, so they had not made the connection to their murder investigation. The case had just gotten a lot bigger. If what Rebecca Dorland was saying was true, "Michael" was a kingpin of crime. Nabbing him would solve several ongoing investigations at once.

Tom addressed Becca, "Ms. Dorland, just to clarify, you are saying that human trafficking is part of the same crime organization as the drug dealing and money laundering—correct?"

"That's exactly what I'm saying, detective. Now, can we make a deal?"

The next two hours passed in a flurry of activity

as calls between the Commonwealth's Attorney, Warfel, and Becca Dorland's newly hired attorney worked out an arrangement for Becca. She would be the key witness in a case that had become bigger than any ever handled in the Central Kentucky area. Once her immunity had been assured, Becca's attorney permitted his client to provide the details that would literally dismantle the crime organization headed by the mysterious Michael. Tom and Drew listened to Ms. Dorland with increasing excitement. Here it was! They had an eyewitness to the inner workings of the criminal organization. When Becca finished she sat back in her seat, retrieved her purse from the floor next to her and pulled out a key. There was one more surprise in store for the detectives.

"There's one more thing you might need. This key opens a storage locker. You'll find the bonds there."

Warfel accepted the key, but couldn't believe what he was hearing. "Ms. Dorland, you just told us you didn't know where the bonds were."

"I know. I guess I was afraid to let go of them. They were my escape plan—from Michael."

"How did you come by the bonds? Did you give them to Cora Larkin?"

"Yes, that part is true, and when I was kidnapped I still had no idea where they were. I only discovered them last week."

Okay, let's get this straight. You stole the bonds, gave them to Cora Larkin when you came under suspicion by this Michael person, then what happened to them?"

Becca paused; there was no turning back now. "Gus Averill had them. I recently came to the

194

conclusion he must have been the one who killed Cora in order to get the bonds back. You see, we stole the bonds together. Gus worried that he would be suspected, so he gave them to me. When Michael suspected me as well, I handed them off to Cora for safekeeping. She had no idea what I had given to her. I learned that Gus had the bonds last week when he called me after you questioned him. He was afraid you would discover the bonds with a search warrant, so he asked me to hold onto them again. That's when I realized he must have killed Cora."

"I see," Detective Warfel responded. The pieces were falling into place. "Did Gus Averill tell you where he found the bonds?

"He said they were hidden at some guy's farm in a shed. He broke in and stole the bonds," Rebecca explained. "Gus and I were planning to leave town the day after tomorrow and disappear. The money was our ticket away from Michael. I've been afraid Gus would leave town and leave me to take the fall for all of this by myself, so when he gave me the bonds to hold the second time, I felt relieved."

At this point, Warfel asked Becca about the human trafficking, and for the next thirty minutes, she told him everything she knew about the operation.

The case was coming together. Now they had Gus for theft, burglary, the assault on Sam, and the murder of Cora Larkin. The scope of the investigation was now beyond one department. Warfel knew he needed to take this information to his boss and request a joint task force. Together, they would bring down this crime syndicate headed by the ruthless and mysterious man named Michael, and it was Ms. Rebecca Dorland who had connected the dots.

The next morning, eight representative members of the newly formed task force, including two FBI agents, met to hear testimony from Rebecca Dorland. They gathered in a conference room at KSP headquarters. Becca sat at a table in front of the room with her attorney on her right side and Detective Warfel on her left. The stakes were high, and her heart was pounding in her ears as she realized the enormity of what she was about to do. Becca had been assured she could have a new identity and be relocated as part of her immunity agreement. She wasn't sure she would accept this part of the agreement, but was comforted by the possibility. If Michael were never found, she could live with a new name far away from the cruel and vindictive crime leader.

Tom Warfel quieted the members of the joint task force and presented background information on the case. Each participant had a written summary of the investigation to date except for the testimony they were about to hear. Tom filled in some detail and assured the group that questions could be asked at the end of Ms. Dorland's statement. Becca and her attorney had crafted her narrative and Becca clutched her notes tightly in her lap. Copies would not be distributed until after her she finished speaking. She had insisted on that as she wanted to reveal what she knew about the criminal organization in her own words, and in her own voice before the team in front of her judged her simply by reading the words on the paper.

Becca remained seated as Tom introduced her and reviewed for the group the provisions of her immunity in exchange for her testimony. Once Tom finished his statement, he resumed his seat beside Becca and nodded for her to take over.

Becca sat up a bit straighter and cleared her throat. "Good morning ladies and gentlemen. My name is Rebecca Dorland and I am making this statement of my own volition, without any coercion from law enforcement. It will actually be a great relief to tell you what I am about to say as I have lived in fear for months. I have been kidnapped, threatened, and endured the terror of seeing an innocent woman fall dead from my car. I pulled her into a situation over which she had no control and she paid a dear price for doing what she thought was a simple favor."

"What I'm about to tell you will shock you, but I pray it leads to the arrest and conviction of the members of this criminal organization. It is a cancer on our community and it needs to be eliminated."

Becca paused to get a sip of water before continuing. She glanced at her attorney and was given a sympathetic pat on her arm. "I first got involved with this horrible group of people in a very innocent way. I joined a gym to lose a few pounds and as an outlet for the stress of my job as Chief Nursing Officer for Braxton's hospital. I met Gus Averill there when he became my physical training coach. He was very amiable and encouraged me at every visit. I lost weight due to his guidance and formed a casual friendship with him. We had coffee a couple of times after my workouts. One of these times, I told him I was having trouble keeping up with the demands of my job and the related stress. He said he had an all-natural product that would help me with my energy level and concentration. I was hesitant at first, but Gus assured me it was safe and all natural. So, I tried it. It actually did help, but I seemed to need more and more of it to get the same result. So, he switched me to another product, and

197

another until I was hooked."

The entire task force was transfixed by Becca's testimony. A few took notes, but most just listened to the gripping narrative.

"I make a good salary as a CNO, but the products eventually became too expensive even for my budget. Gus told me there was a way I could earn extra money to pay for the 'product'. I realized by this time that I was probably taking illegal drugs but, like I said, I was hooked. I asked Gus what he proposed. He said that I could earn a lot of money if I helped recruit teen girls and young women to the gym. I didn't really understand how that could earn a lot of money for me, but I knew quite a few women who might like a free membership, so I provided them with coupons as an inducement to join the gym. For several weeks, I thought that was all there was to the scheme. I had no idea how tangled I would become in a web of human trafficking and pornography."

Becca took a few moments to take a sip of water and gather her thoughts. What she said next would shock the room. "I soon realized that some of the girls were being singled out and offered money for photo shoots. The women I had recruited were very pretty, so I didn't think much of it until one of them called me screaming about her experience. The photographer had wanted her to model in the nude. He had assured her she would have a drape to cover her body, so she reluctantly agreed. The first few photos were done just as he had told her—with a drape and nothing much exposed. Then he pulled the drape a little to show more skin, then a little more, then he pulled it away entirely and directed her to pose in provocative ways. She grabbed the drape and ran from the studio with nothing

198

but the cloth around her. She was too embarrassed to go to the police for fear her family would find out, so she called me."

"I went to Gus and reported the incident. He pretended to be shocked and said he would take care of it. Before long I noticed that none of the women and girls I had recruited were coming to the gym. Again, I didn't think too much about it. I simply thought they had decided not to join the gym once their free visits ended. Then, notices about missing women and girls started making the news. In my job I don't often have much time for television, so I catch only the national news, and even that only sporadically. The local news was full of the disappearances but I had no idea they were happening. I guess I recruited about twenty women and girls in all before my assistant at work told me about the missing women and girls and I made the connection. I was horrified as I realized I had contributed to their disappearance by recruiting them."

"Once I suspected what was going on, I confronted Gus. He tried to downplay it, but I pressed him for the truth. When he finally confessed what was really happening, I was sick to my stomach—literally ill. I couldn't sleep, I couldn't eat, and my work was being affected. What's more, I was told I couldn't stop recruiting. If I did, I would be set up to take the fall for the disappearances. That's when I realized I was in trouble and needed to find a way out of my predicament. I needed money, lots of it, to effect an escape."

"About this time, Gus was also coming under intense scrutiny. The manager of the gym, Robert Snow, was a go-between for the leader of the organization and the employees of the gym who helped with the schemes of drug dealing and human trafficking.

Gus, however, was selling illegal drugs on his own without turning over the money to the organization. He was warned by Mr. Snow that the leader, a man named Michael, was suspicious of Gus's sideline business, and he had better watch his back. So, Gus also began looking for a way out. I don't remember just when we decided to steal the bonds. Eventually, we both had become aware of an additional purpose of the gym in addition to drug dealing and recruitment of females. It was also an effective tool for money laundering. Fake memberships flooded the client roles and accounted for some of the income from drug trafficking, as well as the bearer bonds. These were delivered to the gym late one afternoon and placed in the safe at the gym until Mr. Snow could take them to Michael the next day. Gus said this was our chance to get the money we needed to escape."

"I was desperate, so I went along with his plan. He said he needed an accomplice to distract the night watchman while he got the bonds from the safe. He had watched as Mr. Snow opened the safe a week before. Gus noticed that Mr. Snow kept the written combination in his desk. My part was relatively easy; I told the night watchman I needed to access the gym so I could look for my billfold. I told him I thought it was probably on the floor near where I had worked out just before closing. I didn't have to turn on a lot of charm. The watchman responded to the flirting and let me into the gym. He even helped me look for it. As he searched the area near the elliptical machines, I dropped the billfold on the other side of the gym and pretended to find it. I made sure Gus had time to access the safe and leave the office before I pretended to discover my billfold."

"I was terrified when I came under suspicion for

the theft right away. The night watchman had logged my entry into his nightly report. That's when I asked Cora, whom I had met at the gym, to take the tote bag with the bonds and keep them safe for me. Gus asked about the bonds and I told him I gave them to Cora. He was irate. I tried to reassure him. I told him Cora was reliable and had no idea what was in the locked bag. I didn't know until recently that Gus went to Cora's apartment and demanded she turn over the tote bag to him. Cora was too loyal for that and refused to meet his demands, so he threatened her. She finally gave in, likely too afraid not to do what he said. She led him to somebody's farm and told him where to find the bonds. Once he had the information, he killed her. I only pieced this together very recently. I confronted Gus with my suspicions. I thought he would deny killing Cora, but he didn't. In fact, he bragged about it. He told me he had the bonds and we could leave our problems behind once he finished a business deal he was working on. The business deal was selling drugs. He was greedy—his half of the four million wasn't enough."

Becca paused again, took a deep breath and continued. "I suspected that Gus planned to take all the bonds and set me up to take the blame for the theft and for the human trafficking, so I made sure he couldn't. Gus is not very imaginative, so it wasn't hard to find where he had hidden the stolen bonds. He told me before we took them that he had a storage unit near the gym where he kept the things he had collected from clients at the gym. What he hadn't stolen, he had traded for drugs. At any rate, he had amassed quite a few items. He showed it to me just before we took the bonds. He also was careless enough to let me see that he kept the key to the unit on a chain around his neck—

except when he showered."

There wasn't a sound from the room as Becca continued. "I knew he showered at the gym after his last session of the day. He told me the shower in his apartment had terrible water pressure, so he preferred to shower at work. Now, normally I wouldn't even think of entering the men's locker room, but nothing was exactly normal about the situation."

"I waited until Gus was the only person in the locker room. The last male client had left the gym only moments before. Once he was in the shower, it wasn't difficult to find the key tucked into one of his shoes. I pocketed it and replaced it with another key of the same type. He didn't realize the key was not the one to his storage unit for a full forty-eight hours. By then, I had accessed the unit and taken the bonds. I actually rented a storage unit only three away from the unit Gus had rented. Once he discovered the theft, I knew he wouldn't leave town without them. I'm not sure if Michael knows or only guesses that I have the bonds, but I knew he would keep looking for me. I decided my best course of action was to cooperate with Detective Warfel and tell him everything I know about this criminal organization. I only hope it's enough."

"Well, that's pretty much all of it. I deeply regret my actions—all of them—and I am very grateful for this chance to start a new life."

The ensuing question and answer session lasted nearly an hour, and Becca left the meeting exhausted. Drew escorted her from the room and personally drove her to a location known only to Tom and him. The other members of the task force went to work immediately to sort out the details and to work out a plan to end the criminal activity that had plagued their community.

# Nineteen

Mary woke from her nap and was immediately aware of voices from the hall. Sarah had come to visit, but upon hearing that Mary was napping, had decided to leave. Mary called out to let her know she was awake and wanted to see Sarah.

Sarah entered the room and leaned over Mary's bed to hug her friend and mentor. "I hope I didn't wake you; I know you need your rest."

"No, I needed to wake up. I won't sleep tonight if I sleep too long. The pain meds keep me so drowsy. I'll be glad when I can give them up, but I tried to cut back yesterday and couldn't quite manage the pain."

"Don't rush it, Mary. You need time to heal."

"I know; I'm just so impatient. I feel useless just lying here."

"Well, I have something I need help with, and you are just the person to do it."

Mary brightened. "Oh? What is it, some research, or do you want me to edit something you've written?"

"None of the above. I need some insight and wisdom."

"Now, you have me curious." Mary pushed herself more upright in bed, threw back the covers and asked, "Help me to my chair, will you?"

Once settled in her chair, she looked at Sarah with an excited look. "Okay, what can I do for you?"

"I was thinking about Cora and this whole situation. So, we know she went to the same fitness center as Rebecca Dorland, and she had something in her possession that someone else wanted badly enough to kill her for. That something was probably bearer

204

bonds, correct?"

"So far, so good," Mary agreed.

"Okay, so first of all, why did Mary have the bearer bonds? Where did she get them?"

"Mac and I were wondering the same thing. Cora was a very honest person. She once returned to the grocery to pay for a can of tuna that had been missed by the checkout clerk. She could have easily let it slide or paid for it at her next visit, but she was afraid the clerk would get into trouble if her drawer didn't tally at the end of the day. Now, that's an honest person!"

"Yes, it doesn't sound like someone who would steal bearer bonds. Was she the type of person who did favors for others?" Sarah asked.

"Absolutely. She never said, 'No'. Mac told me she fell for every sob story she heard. She would give money to people on the street—you know the ones who hold up signs saying they're hungry?"

"Yes."

"Well, she fell for that every time. She said she would rather be guilty of helping someone who didn't need it than withhold assistance from someone who was truly in need."

"So, it seems unlikely that she stole the bonds. That brings me to my second question. Do you think she got them from Rebecca Dorland?"

"She seems a likely candidate. Tom's depiction of her was of someone who was out for number one: ambitious, dismissive, evasive, and greedy. Someone like that is a definite candidate for taking the bonds."

At that very moment, Rebecca was reading her statement before the task force, but Sarah and Mary had no knowledge of that. In spite of this, the two women were coming very close to the truth without any assistance.

Sarah was thoughtful. Mary allowed Sarah the quiet she needed. Mary was accustomed to Sarah's brainstorms. They had produced amazing results in the past. It had brought near disastrous consequences as well.

Finally, Sarah spoke. "Okay, if the gym is the only common factor, then it must play a role in this somehow."

"Right you are, Sarah," Mac stated from the doorway. "It seems there is a rather active drug ring operating out of there. I heard a drug deal going down in the men's locker room when I was there a couple of days ago."

"Mac! They didn't see you, did they?" Mary asked with fear evident in her voice.

"No, that is not until their business was concluded. I pretended to be just coming into the locker room because they caught up with me at the doorway as I was leaving."

"Please be careful, darling. These people play for keeps!"

"You're right about that! Money is such a strong driving force for some people. Nothing gets in the way of getting more of it."

"Mac, do you know if Rebecca Dorland was involved in the theft of the bonds?"

"Tom is sure of it."

"Then let's assume that Rebecca Dorland gave Cora the bonds for safekeeping. Where would Cora be likely to hide them?" Sarah asked.

"That's a good question," Mac replied, "but not one we can answer at the moment. The gym must be the money laundering connection. Some of the drug money probably bought the bonds."

"So, where does Ms. Dorland come in? Do you think she's part of the money laundering operation?" Sarah asked.

"Maybe, but I think it more likely that she became aware of the bonds, saw an opportunity to take them, hoping she wouldn't be suspected. She may have fallen under suspicion, so she handed them off to Cora. Poor Cora, I doubt she even understood what she had. The bonds have not been found and the bad guys are still searching. That's why there has been so much violence; we were simply in the way of their searching for the bonds."

"I have no idea why they think Cora would have given them to us," Mary offered.

"They are probably grasping at straws right now. The bonds could be anywhere. Perhaps Cora's family connection to us was discovered," Mac suggested

"Or, someone followed her here," Mary added. "This has to end. None of us will be safe until the bonds are found and/or the bad guys are caught." Neither Mac nor Sarah disagreed.

"Mac, do you think it was Cora who hid the bonds in our shed?" Mary asked.

Mac nodded. "I've been thinking about that. I think it likely it was Cora who hid them here. That's the only thing that makes sense. Where they went from there, I don't know."

The conversation was interrupted by the arrival of Tom Warfel. Aggie directed him to Mac's study.

"Tom, we are discussing the case. We can't understand how or why Cora got involved in something that got her killed," Mac explained.

Tom considered his response. What he needed

to say was for Mac's ears only, but he knew the women were waiting for an answer.

"I know you want answers, and I don't have all of them yet. We are, however, making progress on the case. Please be patient; I think we're close to a breakthrough." Tom hoped this would be enough to satisfy Mary and Sarah. Before either could ask another question, he turned to Mac.

"Mac, I need to ask a favor; could we step outside for a few moments?"

Mac appeared surprised at the request, but agreed. "Uh, sure. Excuse us, ladies." Mac directed Tom to the back porch. "Have a seat, Tom." Both men sat in rockers on the sunny porch. The day was warm for October and the horses in the pasture were taking full advantage of the sunshine.

Tom looked out at the peaceful view and remarked, "You have a beautiful place, Mac."

"We're very happy here; it suits us," Mac answered, though he could tell there was something else on Tom's mind. "Okay, Tom, why did you come all the way out here? I'm sure it wasn't to admire the view."

"No, but being here helps me put this case in perspective—shows me what really matters." Tom paused, took a breath and got to the reason for his visit. "What I just told the ladies is true. We're very close to wrapping the case up. What I'm about to tell you now is confidential. I'm only telling you because I need a favor. Once I tell you what we've just learned, you'll see why I need that favor."

"Okay, you have my full attention."

Tom stood and faced Mac. "Rebecca Dorland decided to come clean with us. She finally became more frightened of the mastermind behind this case than she

208

was of us. She gave a full account of the criminal organization, as much as she knows anyway. It seems there is a lot more going on there than we realized. In addition to the drug dealing, it seems the gym is a recruiting ground for human trafficking. Ms. Dorland got caught up in their dirty business without intending to, and couldn't get out of it. She really fears for her life. Long story, short, she and Gus Averill stole the bonds—four million dollars worth—and were planning to use the money to escape the clutches of the crime boss. Cora got involved when Gus and Ms. Dorland came under suspicion. Dorland asked her to hold onto a locked bag for her. It's not clear whether or not Mrs. Larkin ever discovered the contents of the bag, but apparently she did become fearful for some reason because she brought them here and hid them in your shed."

Mac listened with a growing sense of alarm as he pictured Cora in a situation over which she had no control.

"Ms. Dorland told Gus Averill that she had passed the bonds off to Cora to prevent their discovery in her possession. Gus apparently forced Cora to tell him where the bonds were hidden. Once he had the information, he killed her, presumably to prevent her from telling anyone about the bonds and his involvement with them."

Mac was furious as he pictured how badly Cora had been used. Tears formed in his eyes as he pictured how frightened she must have been. "I can't believe this; it all seems so pointless. Gus killed her just to keep her quiet? If he had known her better, he would have realized that all he had to do was ask—or have Ms. Dorland get the case back."

Tom could see how deeply moved Mac was. The woman who had been his first love and the mother of his children was killed for nothing more than greed. "I know; money is a powerful motivator for some people. It makes them do things they might not otherwise even consider. Gus only recently told Ms. Dorland what he had done and that he had the bonds. Through a rather clever ploy, she took the bonds back from Gus."

"Where are they now?" Mac asked.

Tom smiled. "We have them. As proceeds related to a crime, the bonds will become police property. I'm sure we'll find a good purpose for them. It's been a long held dream to provide more for fallen officers' families, including firemen and EMT's. We also have a camp for underprivileged children where we try to establish a good rapport between the kids and our officers. They fish, hike, learn archery, and a lot of other things with the officers. It gives them a chance to see the police as people who want to help them and their community, not just as men and women with guns who show up to make arrests. We can do a lot of good with that money."

Mac nodded, "I'm glad something good will come from the bonds. Goodness knows a lot of bad things have been done to possess them."

Tom didn't reply, sensing that Mac was trying to make sense of what he had just heard.

Mac finally looked up at Tom and asked, "So, what is the favor you need?"

"Mac, I want you to know that what I'm about to ask is strictly a request; you can refuse and I'll not ask again. Understood?"

Mac nodded. "Sure."

210

"I want you to make one last visit to the gym. We have enough information to arrest Gus Averill for Cora's murder, but this would tip off the head of this organization. We have a mole in our department feeding information to this crime boss. We thought the mole had been identified and dealt with, but we now believe there is more than one. Aside from my partner, I don't know who I can trust in my department to do what I'm asking of you. You're a gifted investigator and you have good instincts. You're the only one I can trust to do this." Tom paused to give Mac time to consider his request. A minute passed, then two, before Mac responded.

"I'll be honored to do this, Tom. I owe it to Cora. I can't bring her back, but maybe I can help bring her killer to justice. I don't understand how Gus can simply carry on without some remorse for his actions."

"I think Gus is likely to become unhinged very soon. He doesn't know where the bonds are, or where Rebecca Dorland is. For all he knows, she has taken off without him. This must be weighing pretty heavily on him. He has to be wondering who will come after him first—us, or Michael, the crime boss. We could serve a warrant on him and the gym, but we're not ready to show our hand just yet. We're after Michael."

"Just Michael, no last name?"

"Not yet; we're working on it."

"I see. So all I need to do is go to the gym and keep my eyes and ears open?"

"That's it; watch Gus closely. Let us know if he makes any phone calls or if he meets with anyone. I know you want to help, but I can't put you in danger by getting you more involved than that. You are now a civilian and I won't risk your safety. Will you do this for us?"

"Absolutely! When do you want me to go?"

"Tomorrow morning around ten o'clock. Gus is usually there by then."

"Okay, no problem. I want to get this guy Michael as much as anyone. If arresting Gus will get us there, I'm all in. I'd like to see his face when you arrest him for Cora's murder. I'm sure he'll fold like an accordion. He might be able to give you more information that will help you find Michael."

"Let's hope. Thanks, Mac."

"Don't mention it. Now, we'd better go in and see the ladies. I'm sure they're wondering what we're up to."

"Yes, we are!" Mary's voice from the door behind the men startled them.

"Who's Michael?" Sarah asked.

The men looked at each other looking for an answer the ladies would believe. "He's a key witness in our case. We need to find him, that's all," Tom explained. Sarah didn't comment, but she had heard enough of the men's conversation to know that his answer was not exactly a lie, but far from the truth as well. She let it go for now, but the name stuck with her.

Mary invited the men to come into the kitchen for an afternoon snack. Tom explained he would love to, but he needed to get back to work. The friends watched as the detective got in his car and drove away. Mac turned around to re-enter the house, but Sarah had other ideas.

"Mac, we need to talk."

Mac sighed. "Tom asked me to keep our conversation confidential. He said they're close to solving the case and he wanted to run something by me."

"Mac Osborne, you're holding something back. Of all people, you ought to know Sarah and I can keep secrets," Mary challenged.

"That's right," Sarah agreed. "Now, who is this Michael? Does he have a last name?"

Mac realized he was defeated and responded. "Okay, okay, you know it's no fair to double up on me." The ladies smiled, but made no comment as they expected answers, not deliberately misleading information. "Let's sit down in the kitchen, and I'll fill you in."

With a fresh glass of cold sweet tea in hand, Mac decided to tell Mary and Sarah just enough to satisfy them, but not mention Tom's request for Mac to visit the gym, or the identity of Cora's killer. "To start with, no, this guy Michael doesn't have a last name. He's the kingpin of a rather large criminal organization based here in Central Kentucky. In addition to drug dealing, human trafficking is also an ugly activity part of what goes on in the gym."

Hearing this, both women gasped. It was not what they had expected to hear. Sarah asked, "Are you saying that human trafficking is taking place at the gym where you went a few days ago?"

"Yes, that's what I'm saying. They recruit the girls to the gym and some are snared into the prostitution trade. They are exported the same as one exports other goods for sell. The girls may end up in Asia, Russia, or other parts of the world. It's a top bidder situation."

"How horrible!" Mary exclaimed. "Where do the bearer bonds come in?"

"The bonds were part of the money laundering

scheme," Mac explained.

"Okay," Sarah began, "so we're back to where we were an hour ago—how and why did Cora have the bonds?"

"Tom told me that is something he isn't ready to tell me yet, but he did say that Cora was innocent in the situation. She only thought she was holding something valuable for a friend."

"And Michael?" Sarah persisted.

"He's still a mystery," Mac explained. Tom doesn't want to proceed with what he has without proof of who Michael is. If he starts arresting the little guys in the organization, Michael will simply pack up and leave. Tom would prefer to hold off arresting anyone until he can catch the organization's leader. That's about it."

"Hmm...I think you're still holdings something back, but that's a start. Well, I had better get going. Mrs. Hoskins is taking Anna with her to run errands, and I want to see her before they leave and Sam will expect me to provide dinner. It's been so long since I cooked an entire meal, they might be better off if I buy take out on the way home," Sarah explained.

Mac and Mary laughed as they walked with their guest to her car. "Give Sam and Anna our love," Mary instructed.

Sarah nodded, put her SUV into gear, and returned home.

# Twenty

Sarah arrived home from her visit and related to Sam what she had just learned. Sam listened attentively until she had finished.

"It sounds like some progress; let's hope the police find these men. There's been enough violence connected with this investigation to last all of us a lifetime. Thank you for leaving the sleuthing to the detectives, Sarah."

Sarah returned a rueful smile. She knew how much she had put Sam through with past situations as she had searched for clues. It was probably no small miracle that both of them were still alive. She reached for Sam's hand as she considered Sam's comment. "I guess marrying you, having little Anna, and settling down to life on a farm has performed its magic. I'm definitely more aware now of the consequences of inserting myself into an investigation. But that doesn't mean I can't do a little research and provide insight. From what I've seen, a case can hinge on the smallest detail. The entire mystery can be solved once a key piece is provided for the puzzle."

"Is this what motivates you to try to solve the mystery—to be able to supply the missing piece that pulls it all together?" Sam asked, already knowing the answer. His wife was endowed with a natural curiosity, but she also had an uncanny ability to see a crucial clue differently. Her perspective was not that of a trained detective. It was purer than that. She was able to assemble facts, see the missing pieces and present the result in a cogent fashion. It was a trait that could not be taught; it was just part of her DNA. Sam reached for his auburn-haired bride and held her close to him as she

215

answered.

"I suppose so. I've always loved to solve puzzles, but it's more than that. I seem to be able to read people. I can usually tell if they're not telling the truth or holding something back. Maybe I developed that trait as a result of the hundreds of interviews I've conducted for my articles."

"Well, Miss Investigator, what am I thinking right now?" Sam asked, with a twinkle in his eyes.

"That's easy; with Mrs. Hoskins and Anna in town shopping, we have the house all to ourselves." Sarah rose on tiptoes to kiss her handsome husband, taking in the love he wanted to give. Theirs had always been an easy relationship with each completing the other.

Sam smiled his lopsided grin and the two lost themselves in each other, and for the moment, set aside the heavy burden they had carried in recent weeks.

\*\*\*

Tom Warfel spent the balance of his day in less romantic pursuits. He realized that he needed to revisit his conclusions to date, and compare them to what Becca Dorland had told him. He tried to make sense of the pieces he had, but they just wouldn't come into focus. After sitting alone in his office for over an hour, he realized with a start that it was getting late. His wife would worry. He pulled out his cell phone, made a quick call to let her know he was on his way and suggested they go out to dinner. Recalling how tenderly Mac spoke of Mary, he had feelings of guilt for the many hours his wife spent alone as he pursued a suspect. Resolving to make that up to her, he put the case away, and considered where he would take his lovely wife for dinner.

216

Tom's wife Katie was pleased, although somewhat surprised, when her husband called and suggested dinner out—just the two of them. She always knew when Tom was deep into a case. His distracted answers to her questions, the long hours he worked, and the look of intensity he wore like a mask told her when he was struggling to find a breakthrough. She left him alone at these times and assumed more of the household and parenting duties. She knew he loved her, and this gave Tom the freedom to be the best detective he could be. She knew the case he was currently working was particularly troublesome. He had not been sleeping well and he had been keeping even later hours than usual. So, this evening was definitely something out of the ordinary.

Tom showered and dressed carefully in gray slacks and the sweater Katie had given him last Christmas. The couple decided to try a new seafood restaurant in town.

Over dinner, Katie noticed the effort Tom was making to listen attentively to the narrative of her day. She worked part-time at the local library and was telling him about an author's book signing event she was arranging. Tom proved he had paid attention by asking pertinent questions and praising her for being able to snag such a well-known author. Mary beamed with pleasure at his compliment. She sensed he was trying hard to please her. Finally, she asked him about his day, curious as to what had prompted this sudden departure from his normal routine.

"Tom, how is the case going? I know it has become quite complicated. The newspaper has been full of the violence associated with this one."

Tom's smile faded as he was pulled back into the

dark corners of the case at hand. "Katie, you're right, it's very complicated. It's like a maze that I can't seem to navigate. It's amazing, though; I've met some very unique individuals in the course of this investigation. They've taught even this old dog some new tricks." He reached across the table for Katie's hand. "They've taught me that no matter how tough a case can be, my joy, my sustenance comes from you. I know I've neglected you many times as I've chased down the bad guys—often giving the dead more attention than I've given you. I'm sorry for that, I really am. Forgive me?"

Katie squeezed Tom's hand. "I know you love me; I've never doubted it, but it is good to hear it every now and then. I think I like your new acquaintances. If they can bring about this transformation, they must be pretty special people."

"I know you'd like them. After this case is over, I'd like you to meet them."

"I think I would. Now, let's finish our delicious meal. It isn't every day we get to eat together and have a conversation just to ourselves."

Tom took a bite of salmon and realized that food seemed to taste better when he wasn't totally absorbed by his work. He decided he should step aside from a case and take time for his marriage more often.

After dinner, Tom and Katie walked the five blocks to their home. It was getting late, but once he walked into his front door a thought suddenly came to him. He kissed Katie and told her he needed to work for a while. Katie smiled her understanding and went upstairs to check on their teen daughters.

Tom went into his study, turned on the desk lamp, and sat behind the battered oak desk. The desk had been his father's, and for many years resided in the

218

home where Tom was raised. Tom ran his hand over the scratched surface and recalled the many hours his father, an attorney, had spent working behind it. He could see him now with his head bent over papers as he prepared for a trial. He had been a successful prosecutor and had passed away only the year before. As part of his inheritance, Tom had received the desk and all the memories it held.

Tom smiled at the recollection before returning to the case at hand. A theory was taking shape in his mind. The time he had spent with Katie had cleared his mind and wiped away his preconceived notions of the case. It had allowed him to see it from another perspective. He picked up a pencil and began writing on a yellow legal pad. He listed all the names he knew that were related to the case. Included were Mr. Snow from the gym and all the employees he had interviewed there. Cora, Dr. Larkin, Mac and his family, Sam, Sarah—they all made the list.

Rebecca Dorland came next, as well as the mysterious Michael. He wasn't sure he could believe all Dorland had told him, but for now he assumed her story was true. Her recent brushes with death had frightened her sufficiently to choose the potential consequences of the legal system over the ruthless revenge of the men who had brought horrible misery to so many.

From these names he made a grid of their association—what was in common, when events had occurred, such as the brutal attacks on Sam, Mac, and Mary. Finally, he listed the discovery of the torn corner of the bearer bond at Mac's farm. He had eliminated Mac as a suspect early into the investigation. He pondered that decision and concluded the assumption was true. He had found nothing to indicate that Mac had lied. It was possible, he supposed, that Cora Larkin had come to Mac to hide the bonds for her. That would implicate him as an accomplice in the theft of the bonds. Yes, the injuries he and Mary had suffered could have been retribution for his part in such a scheme, but he saw nothing in Mac's history to indicate duplicity of any kind. He had been a decorated detective and now rescued unwanted foals and trained them for adoption, or to be used in Sam and Sarah's horse ministry for foster kids. The man was a Boy Scout. No, Tom decided to waste no more time on hunting for skeletons in Mac's closet.

The one thing that was nagging him, however, was the gym connection. That was where he needed to focus his team's attention. The gym was where Cora Larkin and Rebecca Dorland met and where Becca had first started using drugs. The human trafficking angle was shocking, and he wondered if the organization's kingpin was someone he had already met in the course of the investigation. The head of this organization obviously craved power and control. The gym was also one of the ways women and girls were found. The trail started there. He studied the notes he had just made, but couldn't make the critical connection he needed to put it all together. *What have I missed? I know we're close, but why can't I make the connections?*

He was about to call it a night when his cell phone rang. It was Sarah Richards.

"Sarah? What can I do for you?"

Sarah gave a quick chuckle. "Tom, it isn't what you can do for me; it's what I'm about to do for you and this wretched case."

"What are you talking about? I don't understand."

220

"When you were at Mac's earlier you said the name of the crime boss was Michael—right?"

Tom let out a frustrated breath. "That wasn't for your ears; anyway, what about him?"

"I think I know who Michael is!" Sarah exclaimed.

Tom was stunned. How could she know the identity of the most notorious criminal the area had seen in quite some time? "Now, Sarah, it's late. Maybe you should get some rest. This might all look different in the morning."

"Don't patronize me; I've figured it out. I believe I know his identity!"

"Okay, I'll bite; who is he?"

"I think he's Dr. Michael Larkin!"

Tom was speechless for several moments. His first impulse was to reject Sarah's theory outright, but when he considered the possibility, he realized she could be right."

"Uh, Sarah, how did you come to this conclusion?"

"Don't you remember what he said at Cora's funeral?"

"I'm not sure; refresh my memory."

Sarah was warming to her argument. "After the service, Mac went up to him and shook his hand. He said, 'It shouldn't have been Cora.' None of us thought anything of it at the time, but Mac told me that Ms. Dorland told you she thought Cora was mistaken for her. Maybe Ms. Dorland was supposed to be murdered, not Cora. How would he know that if he wasn't THE Michael?"

Tom was beginning to see the merit of Sarah's argument. The more he thought about it, the more plausible it seemed.

To Sarah, though, he said, "Mrs. Richards, Sarah, what you are saying is possible, but unlikely. I will check it out, but in the meantime, I beg you to keep this to yourself. The crime boss, whether he is Dr. Larkin or another man by the same first name, is very dangerous. If he feels his identity has been discovered, he will react with violence. We are dealing with a sociopath; he won't think twice about adding you to his growing list of victims."

The lecture hit its mark; Sarah realized what she had told the detective could lead to additional harm to her family.

"You're absolutely right, Tom. I'll keep this to myself—I promise. I don't intend to do anything that could potentially harm my family. I felt you should at least hear me out."

In a softer tone, he said, "I appreciate that you called me with this. I'll check it out first thing in the morning. Good night, Sarah."

"Good night, Tom."

Tom ended the call and sat at his desk for several more minutes as he considered Sarah's call. He shook his head and laughed. "Mac's right, she does have a head for solving puzzles. She'd make a fine detective," he thought as he turned out the light on his desk and made his way upstairs.

He performed a quick check on his daughters; they were sleeping soundly. Katie had also succumbed to sleep, and Tom was soon snoring softly beside her.

# Twenty-One

Michael swore under his breath. "We should've taken care of that little pip squeak before now. He's sure to ask that detective for a deal to save his own skin. I still think he's the one who stole the bonds!"

The four other men in the room remained silent; it wasn't a good idea to attract Michael's notice when he was angry. Rebecca Dorland's escape had enraged him, but the thought that Gus Averill might escape his grasp had taken Michael's anger to a new level—nearly equal to how he had reacted when he heard of Cora Larkin's death. Everyone present knew that Michael wouldn't hesitate to kill someone he thought had failed him, like Murray. No one asked about Murray. It was assumed he wouldn't be joining the group any longer, but no one dared to voice the question. The two men standing behind Michael had most probably eliminated him. They always appeared when Michael needed the really dirty stuff done. No one knew the goons' names, nor did anyone want to know. It was best to stay clear of the two over-muscled thugs.

Michael turned his attention to the other men in the room. "Someone knows where the bonds are, and I expect you misfits to find them! Is that clear?"

As one, the men nodded. Stanley, the smaller of the two, swallowed hard and opened his mouth to ask a question, but Michael's glare killed the words before they were spoken. Michael was a demanding boss and all their lives were in jeopardy if they failed again.

Michael's rant continued. "I've never seen such a bunch of screw-ups in my life! You can't get anything right!" He paced back and forth across the room as his mind considered different options. His men were almost afraid to breathe for fear they would meet the same fate as Murray. Finally, the pacing stopped.

"Stanley, I need you to take care of something."

Stanley jumped at the sound of his name, but managed to utter, "Yes sir!" The little man stood up to receive his orders.

"You know your way around the jail; who do we have there on our payroll?"

Stanley thought for a few seconds before listing the men on his fingers. "Well, there's Patrick, Simms, Greg Reynolds, and Richard Madsen at the local jail. Do you want to know the ones at the regional jail, too?"

"Not now. Find out from one of those guys if Gus Averill is cooperating with the police. I want to know as soon as you do—got it?"

"Yes sir!"

"And, one other thing, you and Kyle find Rebecca Dorland!"

Stanley nodded, pulled Kyle's sleeve and almost ran from the room. Once safely outside, Kyle caught his breath and considered the mess they were in. He hadn't signed on for kidnapping and murder. No, his talents were breaking and entering, petty theft, and a few con games. He was out of his league with this bunch.

"Stanley, why did you talk me into joining this operation? You said that all we had to do was scare some people so they would hand over what they stole. Those two guys of Michael's have killed people. Randy got killed, too. He was only supposed to scare the people at that farm so they would leave and he could search their house. He ended up in a shootout with an armed guard!"

Stanley turned to face his long-time friend and partner in crime. "Kyle, you've gotta get a grip! We

224

can't back out now; Michael will have us killed!"

"That's what I'm trying to tell you, Stanley! We're gonna end up dead anyway, just like Murray."

Stanley resumed walking toward his truck. "All we hafta to do is find out if Gus caved in to the police to save his own skin, and find that bitch Dorland."

"Is that all?" Kyle answered incredulously. She's been one step ahead of us this entire time."

"We'll find her."

"Oh, you think so, do you? Surely you can't forget how angry Michael was when he found out Mrs. Larkin was killed? He wanted the Dorland dame snuffed out instead. If he finds out who did that, he'll kill them with his bare hands!"

A shiver went down Stanley's spine. He knew Kyle was right, and they should run for it now while there might be enough time to get far away from their boss. He stood by his truck weighing the possibility. Kyle was standing on the other side of the truck waiting for Stanley to unlock the door. Stanley turned his key in the lock, opened the door and got into the large truck. Kyle slid in beside him.

"Look, all I'm sayin' is we've got a chance if we hightail it outta here now, but if we wait we could end up at the bottom of some river! This guy's playin' for keeps. I don't know about you, but I'm done with this whole mess!" Kyle shouted above the sound of the truck's faulty muffler.

Stanley didn't answer. He put the truck in gear and drove away. He had an idea and it just might save them—both from the police and Michael. If he was really lucky, there might be some cash in it as well. That would certainly help them disappear long enough to avoid Michael's wrath.

"Okay Kyle, I've gotta plan. Let's take care of the stuff Michael wanted so he doesn't get suspicious, then I will tell you what I have in mind. I'm still working out the details, though; this has to be perfect."

Kyle was mollified for the moment but didn't like the part about the plan needing to be perfect. Nothing was perfect, at least not in his world. He had partnered with Stanley a long time, though, so he decided to go along with him, at least for a little longer. "Okay, but we need to leave soon or it'll be too late."

"I know, trust me." The pair rode along in silence as Stanley's mind was actively pursuing his plan. With each passing mile, it came more clearly into focus until, after thirty minutes, he smiled, looked at Kyle and said, "I've got it!"

## Twenty-Two

Mac walked into the gym the next day as nonchalantly as he could. The environment still felt foreign to him, and he fought back the urge to turn around and go home. As he entered, he noticed Robert Snow having a heated conversation with Gus. He couldn't hear what they were saying but decided the younger man was getting the worst end of the conversation. Gus seemed to be making a plea of some sort, and the older man threw up his hands and walked away.

Gus turned around and noticed Mac looking at him. Was Mac a little too interested in the conversation that had just taken place? Gus weighed the possibility that Mac was working with the cops but dismissed it almost immediately. *I have to calm down; I'm seeing enemies everywhere.*

Mac pushed the knowledge that Gus had killed Cora as far back in his mind as he could. He flashed a friendly grin and waved at Gus before heading to the locker room to change. Gus dismissed his paranoia and made preparations for his next class. He had to keep his routine normal so he wouldn't attract attention—from Michael or the police. He would cooperate with the cops up to a point, but he didn't plan on getting himself killed for it. If only he could take the bonds now and escape. He would be a free man. The thought made him smile until he realized he needed Rebecca Dorland to make it happen, and she was nowhere to be found. He resisted the thought that Becca had double-crossed him. She had told him she was holding the bonds so he wouldn't get any ideas about leaving without her. Could he trust her?

Mac emerged from the locker room and went straight for the free weights. There was something pure and simple about using the weights compared to the various pieces of equipment, and he preferred simplicity. As he worked out, he kept watch for Mr. Snow, but the manager didn't leave his office. Mac could tell that Gus was in a foul mood, and he gave the young trainer a wide berth. He didn't want to be pushy and tip his hand.

After an hour, Mac ended his workout and headed to the shower. He realized after he was already wet that he had forgotten to get his soap out of his gym bag. He leaned his torso out of the shower, and reached for the soap. With his head out of the shower, he could hear angry voices. They were coming through the air vent on the wall next to the shower. He recognized Robert Snow's voice but couldn't place the other one. The second man was yelling at the gym manager. Mac couldn't hear everything that was said because Mr. Snow's responses were little more than a loud whisper. Someone was shouting, obviously very angry. Mac reached for a towel, wrapped it around his waist, and stepped out. He left the water running to give the appearance he was still showering, and crept closer to the air vent.

"Are you out of your mind? If Michael finds out what you're up to, he'll take care of you for good!"

Robert Snow hissed, "Take care of your business and I'll take care of mine; I know what I'm doing!"

"Do you? Are you so sure of that? Michael knows the police questioned Gus. Did he make a deal to save his own skin?"

The gym manager replied, "He said he didn't, that he told very convincing lies and half-truths and they were too stupid to know the difference. Would he have come back here if he had made a deal? No, if he had cooperated with the police, he would be hidden somewhere and protected as a witness."

"You give Gus too much credit, Robert. His type is only out for himself. That makes him mighty dangerous now that the police are snooping around. How did they get onto this place anyhow?"

"Through Rebecca Dorland and Cora Larkin. I don't know if Ms. Dorland made the connection for them after Mrs. Larkin's body was found in her car, or if both were traced to the gym. The connection would be easy to find with only a minimum of effort."

"I knew it was a mistake pulling Dorland into our drug and prostitution operations. Now she's missing and has presumably cooperated with the police. That idiot Murray couldn't even hold onto her in a locked shed!"

Robert Snow assumed a conciliatory tone. "Look, Stanley, I'll speak to Gus again, tell him to lay low, stay away from the gym for a while. He understands what's at stake here; we could all go to prison for this."

"You do that, but if he doesn't cooperate with us, he'll be eliminated. Michael has no tolerance for mistakes."

"Yes, I know," replied Mr. Snow. "I found that out a long time ago." Robert looked down at his right hand and stared at the stump that had been his pinkie finger. It had been the price for only a minor mistake. He shuddered to think what Michael would do to him if that snoopy detective Warfel stumbled onto what was really going on in the fitness center.

The voices faded away as the two men made for the exit. Mac quickly slipped back into the shower and remained there another ten minutes to avoid the two men. He supposed they thought the storage area next to the locker room was a good place for a private conversation. If they had discovered that he could hear their conversation he would be toast.

Mac dried off, dressed quickly, and left the gym with as much nonchalance as he could manage. He didn't pull out his cell phone until he was several blocks away from the gym in case he was being observed. He turned his truck into a McDonald's, got a soda from the drive-thru, and parked in the back of the restaurant. Warfel answered on the second ring.

"What can I do for you, Mac?"

Mac proceeded to repeat the conversation he had overheard. Warfel gave a low whistle.

"It looks like we have stirred things up a bit. Mac, I don't want you going back to the gym; it's too dangerous. Mary would never forgive me if I let you walk into a trap. These people play for keeps. The number of bodies associated with this case is rising steadily. The leader, this Michael fella, even has a reputation for eliminating some of his own men. He's ruthless."

"Yeah, I got that impression from Robert Snow's conversation in the locker room. That's all the more reason to get the evidence we need to arrest him. I'll do as you say, you're in charge of this investigation and I'm just a civilian, but I want to help get this scumbag. I owe it to Cora and to the kids."

"Mac, you're making this too personal and you know what happens when even good detectives do that. They take unnecessary risks and get themselves and others hurt."

"I hear you Tom; I do, but I can't just sit around

*because* it's so close to home."

"Okay, Mac, you need to know there's some new developments I can't share with you yet, but we're getting close to an arrest. You'll have to trust me on this one and let us do our job."

"Developments? Hard evidence?"

"Let's just say we pretty much know what this gang is up to, and maybe the identity of their leader, but we need a bit more to arrest them and make it stick in court."

Mac was thoughtful. "I see. I know you can't share everything about the case with me. I'd handle it the same way. It's best to keep as much as possible a secret until you're ready to make your move. All I ask is for you to keep me in the loop when you can, okay?"

"Absolutely. I respect you and the fine reputation you built as a detective. I have no intention of insulting your intelligence."

"Thank you. That means a lot to me, and I agree with staying away from the gym." Mac smiled ruefully. "Besides, Mary needs my attention now that she's home. I can't leave it all for Aggie."

"Give Mary my best wishes, Mac. I'll come by to visit again soon. I'll catch you up on what I can when I see you."

The men said good-bye, and Mac turned the ignition on his truck. He knew Tom was right. If Mac had been in charge of the case, he might not have been as forthcoming as Tom had been. Besides, Mary needed him. He would leave the investigation to Warfel and his team. Mac pulled out into traffic but failed to notice the dark sedan that followed. He might have intended to step back from the investigation, but the occupants of the dark sedan planned to pull him right back into it.

## Twenty-Three

Mac was preoccupied with his thoughts and failed to notice the car following him. It wasn't until he paused at a stop sign that he became aware of the trailing car. Mac glanced into his rearview mirror out of habit but quickly looked again when he recognized one of the men. He had just seen him at the gym and was probably the one he overhead talking with Robert Snow. Mac pulled away from the stop sign and slowly accelerated. As he sped up, the car behind him kept pace. Mac had been heading to his farm, but he changed direction and drove back toward town. He needed people around him for safety. He also didn't want to lead the men to his farm—and Mary.

Mac said a quick prayer and picked up speed, but his old truck was no match for the sleek Mercedes behind him. Before Mac was able to reach a more populated area, the Mercedes picked up speed and passed him. Mac braked as the Mercedes darted in front of him and stopped. The old truck came to a stop just shy of the sedan. Mac's instincts took over, and he reached for the gun he kept in his glove box. But, before he could retrieve his weapon, a man was already standing beside his truck with a gun pointed at his head.

"Put the gun down and get out!" The man's inflection and body language indicated he meant business.

Mac took his hand off the gun and reached for the door handle. He had no choice, as now there was another man with a gun standing on the passenger side of the truck. *Where did he come from?* Mac had seen only two men in the car from his rearview mirror at the stop sign, and the second man was still in the car. The

233

question was answered as he noticed a second car parked behind him. Two cars had been following him. He was now outnumbered three to one. With a sigh he emerged from the truck with his hands in the air.

"What's this all about? If you want money, there's about a hundred dollars in my wallet." Mac didn't really believe they were after money, but he needed a few seconds to consider his next move.

Mac looked around; there was no one for miles. Traffic was light even on a busy day, and Mac realized he was on his own. He tried again.

"Look, guys. I don't know what this is all about, but I'm sure we can work something out. What do you want?"

Neither man answered him as they grabbed Mac by his arms and led him to the Mercedes. The back door was opened, and Mac was shoved into the back seat. He landed beside the last person on earth he expected to see.

"Hello, Mac. I thought we should have a little talk."

Mac righted himself in the leather seat. He was at a loss for words as he regarded the man beside him. The Mercedes pulled quickly away, and Mac was thrown back against the seat. *None of this makes any sense,* he thought. Mac decided he would get the answers to his questions, but he wasn't sure he would live to tell anyone. He thought of Mary, his children, his peaceful farm, and wondered if he would ever see them again.

&#42;&#42;&#42;

Rebecca Dorland paced the floor of the tiny apartment. For the second time in less than a month she was living in a different place. Her clothing told her she had lost weight, and she thought she might be getting an

234

ulcer. Uninterrupted sleep was only a memory as she lived in fear of the men pursuing her. Detective Warfel had taken her gun. He had told her he was afraid she would accidentally shoot the officer stationed outside her apartment.

The apartment had only one door. That was good and bad. The apartment was on the sixth floor so no one was about to come through a window—that was good, but that also meant she had only one means of escape if an intruder broke in.

She thought of her job that she had all but abandoned. She had taken a leave of absence after the break-in of her last apartment. She hoped she had a job to return to when this was all over. Her deal with Warfel had meant no jail time, but her situation was creating quite a stir at the hospital. Her conservative work place had made it clear that she must be guilty of *something.*

She was looking for a way out, and one day Gus provided it. Gus had entrusted the bonds to Becca for safekeeping until they could plan their escape. It was enough money to live a comfortable lifestyle on an island somewhere. The young trainer had convinced the middle-aged woman that they had a future together— that he loved her. *What a laugh,* she thought bitterly. She understood now that Gus had planned to take the bonds and abandon her. He had only given her the bonds in the first place because he knew he would be suspected, and he didn't want to be found with them.

Deep down, Becca had not believed that Gus loved her, but she did feel they could work together, split the money, and then go their separate ways. When Michael showed up on her doorstep demanding the bonds, she knew who had given her name to him—Gus.

Michael and his two goons searched her apartment top to bottom but found nothing because Becca had given them to Cora. She had only told the older woman that the tote bag had some very important items that she didn't want to have her ex-husband find. Cora had believed the sob story Becca had related. She had said that her ex-husband cheated on her, hid money from her, and lied in order to get custody of their son. None of the story was true, but that didn't matter as long as Cora believed it.

Cora. Her dead face haunted Becca day and night. Becca had told no one except Gus that Cora had the tote bag with the bonds. Poor Cora, poor helpful Cora. She had admired Becca's clothing; especially the outfit Becca gave her. It was a designer original and looked stunning on the petite older woman. It was the outfit she was wearing when she was killed.

Becca's recurring nightmare had been that Cora was killed instead of her. Now, she knew it wasn't true. Gus had killed Cora, but it was still Becca's fault. She had given the bonds to Cora. She should not have involved the timid woman. The gnawing pain in her mid-section became more acute as fear and guilt were taking a heavy toll. *How will this all end? Will I ever be able to find peace with what I've done?* Becca shook her head as if she could dispel the worry that had overcome her.

She felt like a prisoner in the small space, so she decided to go out, even for a little while. She put on her coat, grabbed her keys, and stepped into the hallway to inform the patrolman of her intention, but he wasn't there. Becca waited a few minutes, thinking he might have taken a restroom break, but he did not appear. She took the elevator to the first floor and peered out the front door of the apartment building. The patrolman's car was parked across the street, as it had been all morning. She walked over to the squad car and found it empty. Panic gripped her. The patrolman's absence could only mean one thing: Michael had found her!

Before she could return to the relative safety of her apartment, a strong arm reached around her and covered her mouth. She struggled with her assailant and recognized the tattoo on his right arm. He had been one of the men with Murray at the cabin where she was taken after her kidnapping. She continued to struggle, but was no match for her attacker's strength. *Think, Rebecca, think!* The image of Cora, as she fell dead out of her car flashed in Becca's mind. She was about to meet the same fate.

The man's hand shifted on her face as he began to drag her backwards toward his car. Becca bit down on his hand as hard as she could while simultaneously kicking her heel into his left shin. The man recoiled in pain, allowing her to escape his grasp. Once free, she turned and poked an index finger in each of his eyes, temporarily blinding him. Then she ran.

Becca ran for three blocks and hid behind a privacy fence that surrounded a large back yard. Becca fought to catch her breath. She knew that what she did next could mean life or death. She was under no delusion that she was now safe. She had been given police protection in a safe house, and Michael had still found her. He must have informants within the police department. There was no other way he could have found her. *So, who do I trust now?* Becca crept across the backyard to an alley and walked in the shadows as she searched for a place to feel safe.

***

The Mercedes stopped outside an old building. Mac was pulled out of the backseat and half-dragged through the entrance. It was very dark inside, with only a single light bulb shining overhead. The only furniture was a table with three unmatched chairs. He was shoved into one, and one of the men zip tied his hands behind his back. The air was cool but smelled of rotting wood and dead vermin. Moments passed as Mac tried to make sense of his situation. The sound of a chair being dragged across the floor alerted Mac that the time for whatever was about to happen had arrived.

Michael turned the chair backwards and straddled it as he leaned forward on his elbows. "Now, Mr. Osborne, let's get started, shall we?" A smile creased his face. "Yes, you thought you were fooling everyone by giving a false name at the gym, but as you see you are well known to me."

Mac didn't reply. His mind was still trying to make sense of what was happening.

"So, you're probably wondering why we brought you here. Well, let's start with a little story, shall we?" Not waiting for a reply, Michael began his narrative. "This all started with a couple of people who decided to steal from me. Those people were Rebecca Dorland and Gus Averill. My associates approached both of them to recover my property but were unable to do so. Since then, it seems that Mr. Averill and Ms. Dorland have lost the bonds. These two," Michael waved to indicate his two goons present in the room, "were supposed to grab Ms. Dorland and make her talk. Instead, I awoke to discover that my ex-wife was dead, something I truly regret. I thought my associates here had killed the wrong woman, but apparently someone else killed her.

Tears fell from Mac's eyes at the mention of

238

Cora and how senseless her murder had been. He lifted his head to meet Michael's gaze. "Cora was a good woman; how could she have married scum like you?"

"That story is for another day; now, that brings us to our current dilemma. I think you know where your ex-wife hid the bonds. We have discovered that she had them in her possession before she...uh, before she died. Where did she put them, Mr. Osborne?"

Mac knew the answer to Michael's question, but knew if he revealed what Lieutenant Warfel had shared with him, he would be signing his own death warrant. He decided to play along with Michael's theory. "I have no idea. We didn't talk much, and she certainly never told me about having your bonds. I only know of the bonds because a torn corner of one of them was found in a shed on my farm."

"I don't believe you."

"I have no reason to lie to you; my life is comfortable and I'm a happy man. I don't need your bonds!"

"Four million dollars is a lot of money, Mr. Osborne. Now, let's be honest with each other. I believe you know where the bonds are. All you have to do is tell me, and you're free to go."

Mac looked directly at his captor. "You said to be honest, so let's be honest. There's no way you'll let me go whether I tell you what you want to know or not. I can identify you."

Michael smiled, "Yes, you can, but there is another reason for you to tell me where the bonds are. It's true, I can't let you go, but if you don't give me what I want, your wife will be taken, tortured, and killed. Do you want that, Mac? Even if you can't save your own life, it's in your power to save hers."

Mac's mouth went dry and he strained against his restraint. "You're an animal!"

Michael laughed. "That may be true, but I'm a rich and powerful one. You would do well to give me what I want."

Mac felt helpless as his mind struggled with the threat to Mary. He had to prevent Michael's goons from hurting his sweet wife. His mind considered possibilities and discarded them until he came up with a plan that might buy him, and Mary, some time.

"Okay, you win. I'm not sure, but I think I know where Cora could have hidden the bonds."

"Now, we're getting somewhere. "Spill it. We don't have all day."

Mac pretended he was giving the information reluctantly. He thought Michael would see through his ploy if he gave the information too easily.

"When Cora and I were married she had the habit of hiding her valuables—some jewelry, a little cash, that sort of thing. It was like a game with her. She might have done the same with the bonds."

"Oh, yeah? Where did she hide her so-called valuables?"

"In the return air vent in our bedroom. I had to admit it was a good hiding place. As a detective, I always told my men to check the air vents when we searched a residence. That paid off a couple of times."

"Why haven't you gone after the bonds?"

"I told you, I don't need them, and I don't want them. They cost Cora her life. I don't need that kind of trouble. You're welcome to them."

Michael nodded to his minions and stood up. "Mac, this is what we're going to do. We'll check out Cora's apartment. I know it hasn't been rented out

240

again, so that will give us free access and plenty of time to search. You get to stay here and ponder what will happen to your wife's pretty face if you're wrong. You had better be right or I won't be very happy. You won't like me when I'm not happy."

Michael turned and led the way outside to the waiting Mercedes. Mac heard the engine turn over and gradually fade away. He looked around at his surroundings more carefully than before as he searched for anything to cut the zip ties. The room's darkness surrounded the small circle of light in the center of the room. He would have to scoot his chair to explore the dark recesses.

Mac picked the corner directly behind him to explore first. He planted his feet, leaned forward in the chair, and pushed backward. The chair scraped across the cement floor, a few inches at a time. He repeated the process several more times before he reached the wall. He allowed his eyes to adjust to the lower light and looked around him. Nothing. Mac repositioned himself so he could push to the left into the next corner. After fifteen more minutes, he reached the second corner and achieved the same result. Nearly exhausted from his effort so far, he decided he had only one more try in him. Even if he could make it to the fourth corner, Michael and his goons would be back soon. The choice to continue in the same direction he had been heading was both practical and logical. He would reach it sooner and he had a better chance of reaching it before his strength gave out completely.

*Dear God, let there be something there to help me,* he prayed. Mac took a deep breath and began the painstaking trek. As he neared the wall he could see the outline of a piece of equipment. It was probably something left from the original purpose for the building. The object was large, with a lot of jutting pieces. It was still a long shot, but it was a chance, and it was more than he had going for him just moments before. It was difficult to see clearly in the nearly dark room, and Mac couldn't use his hands to explore the machine. From the darkness, he could see several moving parts, but nothing sharp to cut the zip ties. He did, however, see a loose screw sticking out of a long protruding arm. He pulled the chair closer and used his mouth to remove the screw. *Now what?* He thought. *What can I do with this?*

An idea began to form in his mind. He spit out the screw and realized he still had his cell phone in his jacket pocket. Mac pulled at his bound hands but couldn't free them. He decided to tip the chair in an attempt to free his phone. He knew the fall could also render him unconscious, but he had little choice. Mac ensured he would not fall against the piece of equipment and began to rock the chair sideways. The impact stunned him, but he remained conscious. He searched for the phone and found it a few inches from his right side. *So far, so good, I hope this works.* Mac attempted to press the home button with his nose, but couldn't create enough pressure. He picked up the screw with his teeth and used it to press the home button of the phone. Mac breathed a sigh of relief; he only hoped help would come in time. He dropped the screw, leaned forward over the phone and used his nose to dial 9-1-1. It took three tries, but he was rewarded finally with the sound of a female dispatcher. He quickly explained his situation and gave directions to his location. *Thank goodness I wasn't blindfolded on the way here.* Mac stayed on the phone with the dispatcher, praying each moment that help would come before Michael returned. Minutes seemed like hours as Mac lay on the cold floor, but soon he heard the wonderful sound of a siren and hoped it was coming for him. Mac expected a patrolman or two but was surprised to see the face of Tom Warfel instead.

"I was nearby and heard the call on my radio. How in the world did you manage to call for help?"

"I used a loose screw from that machine over there, and my nose to work the phone. I'm not sure I could do it again, but I'm grateful that it worked this time," Mac explained.

Tom cut the zip ties holding Mac's hands and helped him to his feet. "Come on, let's get out of here."

"Fine by me."

As the pair emerged from the warehouse, two patrol cars arrived with their lights and sirens. At the end of the block Michael's car made the turn onto the street. At the sight of law enforcement, the driver threw the car into reverse, and sped away from the scene. Detective Warfel directed the patrolmen to pursue the fleeing car. The two cars give chase, but Michael and his associates were long gone.

Mac, visibly shaken, turned to face the detective. "Thanks, Tom. I really thought I was a goner."

"It was a bold move from Larkin; he must be getting desperate. Did he say why he kidnapped you?"

"He thought I had the stolen bonds. I tried to tell him I didn't have them and didn't know where they were, but he didn't believe me. He threatened to hurt Mary if I didn't tell them where the bonds are. You have to protect her!"

Tom dispatched two patrol cars to Mac's farm while Mac called Mary to warn her.

He left out the part about his kidnapping until he

could break the news to her in person. They had been through so much already. "Mary, I have reason to believe that Michael Larkin is coming out to the farm; get Howard and any men helping out to come into the house. Lock up tight; police are on their way." He turned to Tom, his eyes wide with terror.

"Mac, she'll be safe. Larkin won't go after her now; he knows we're onto him so he'll probably make a run for it."

"Do you really think he'll leave all that money behind?"

"Yes, I do. He may be motivated by money, but even four million dollars in bearer bonds doesn't compare to getting caught and convicted. His life here is over. C'mon, I'll give you a ride home and you can tell me how you managed to call us with your hands tied behind your back," Tom chuckled

As Tom drove, Mac explained how he made the call.

"Wow! That was really quick thinking!"

"When faced with certain death, I can get a little creative," Mac replied ironically.

Warfel sensed that the retired detective was calming down. When they were almost to the farm, they received word that four officers were at Mac's, and all was well. Mac visibly relaxed after that, although it would take some time to recover from the ordeal.

"Mac, there's one thing I want to know. How did you manage to be alone in the warehouse so you could work out an escape?"

"I decided to buy some time by telling them that Cora might have hidden the bonds in the return air vent in her bedroom. So, Larkin and his goons left to check it out. Larkin is very motivated by greed."

"That was fast thinking, Mac. If you had told him the bonds have already been found, they would have killed you outright. What made you think of the air vents? Was Cora in the habit of using air vents to hide valuables?"

Mac chuckled. "Nah, I made that up, and thank goodness they fell for it." Mac paused before continuing. "Tom, how did you know it was Larkin who kidnapped me?"

"Believe it or not, it was your protégé, Sarah Richards who figured it out."

"I can believe it; I've seen her in action before. She makes connections very few others can."

"She's very astute, that's for sure," the detective agreed.

Mac assumed a serious look. "I had no idea Larkin was like this. Poor Cora, she didn't have a chance."

The detective didn't answer. He didn't have all the answers Mac wanted, at least not yet.

## Twenty-Four

Becca was cold, hungry, and scared. Several hours had passed since her attempted kidnapping. She had walked most of the night, mostly to keep warm. She wasn't certain where she was but felt it might be safe to find shelter. She came upon a gas station with a diner and went inside. Several big rig trucks lined the highway nearby, so Becca decided the food must be pretty good.

She was shown to a booth in the back of the diner, and Becca chose to sit facing the door. If the waitress noticed Becca's disheveled appearance, she didn't let on. She took the order of eggs, toast, and coffee with practiced precision. Before long, Becca was warmed by the coffee and felt she might be out of danger—for now. She had no idea where she was going from the diner.

She suspected Michael had policemen on his payroll, so she reached for her phone and dialed the only other person she felt she could trust.

*** 

That afternoon Warfel met with the other members of the investigation. Drugs, human trafficking, corruption, and murder had been linked to the group led by Michael. There were few illegal activities in the Braxton area that he didn't control. Until recently, Michael had been a shadowy figure with no last name. That had now changed thanks to the testimony of Rebecca Dorland and Mac Osborne. They had the proof they needed; now, they needed to find him.

The death of the police officer stationed outside Becca's safe house apartment shook the entire police force. Warfel knew this meant he had a leak on his team. The team meeting's purpose was to discover the

246

identity of that person or persons. With the cooperation of the tactical unit leader, Warfel planned to disclose false information as to the whereabouts of Becca Dorland. The person who showed up to silence Ms. Dorland would be the culprit. There was no guarantee of success, but he hoped the temptation of silencing Becca would draw out the leak in his department.

Team members filed in and took their seats. "Okay, everyone, settle down. There have been some developments in our investigation. As you know, we lost one of our own last night. Patrolman Brandon Miles was killed while on protection duty. He was surprised by his assailant and strangled with a rope. He didn't have time to draw his weapon, apparently. Now, Ms. Dorland is missing. We haven't heard from her, so we fear the assailant took her."

A low rumble went around the room. Warfel silenced the group. "Another person pertinent to our investigation was also snatched yesterday. Mac Osborne was a victim of carjacking and kidnapping. He was taken to a downtown warehouse but managed to get to his cell phone and call for help." Warfel observed each face carefully. Was there anyone with a surprised look? The astute detective thought he saw an unguarded expression cross the face of Lt. Simms. Was he part of Michael's organization, or was Warfel finding corruption where there was none? One thing was for sure—the investigation was heating up and Michael was getting bolder and more careless. It was only a matter of time before Larkin was caught, and it couldn't come soon enough for Warfel. The bodies were piling up.

Samuels entered the room, whispered a message to Warfel and took a seat near the back of the room.

Tom turned his attention back to the combined task force. "Now, we need to make assignments. Metcalfe, take your team and follow up on the drug suppliers. We need to make sure the pipeline to this part of the country is cut off. We now have some names, so let's find them and get them in here for questioning. Worley, I want you and Randall to track down the location where the girls are held until they can be sold or traded. We're close to shutting that operation down. Members of my squad will be assigned three ways. Two of you will provide around the clock protection for Mac Osborne and his family, three of you will be assigned surveillance duty on the gym, and two of you will guard Ms. Dorland. Yes, I've just been told that she is safe and is now under our protection." Again, a stir went through the group. "Hank, you and Walters do that."

Warfel continued. "Ms. Dorland's present location is Valley View hospital. She's being checked out as we speak, and should be discharged later today. She'll be taken to a new safe house. We'll use the one on Clinton Street. Any questions?"

With assignments in hand, the team members dispersed. Samuels approached his partner. Warfel turned to face him.

"Drew, Simms and Reynolds might be our leak. They exchanged looks when I announced Ms. Dorland had been found and was safe. I'd be willing to bet a month's pay they are our culprits, but they may not be the only ones. Is everything in place on Clinton Street?"

Samuels nodded. "We're ready, Tom."

"Good, now let's go get us a couple of bad cops. Did Gus Averill tell you why she called him?" Warfel asked.

248

"Yes, she told him she didn't trust the police because her so-called safe location had been found twice. She didn't want to risk calling you," Samuels replied.

"Did Gus say why he called us? Why not hide Ms. Dorland from us?" Tom asked.

"He didn't say, but my guess is he doesn't want to jeopardize his deal with us. As part of his agreement, he promised to keep us in the loop with new developments." Drew laughed. "The brave Mr. Averill folds pretty quickly it seems. The machismo he shows is just an act."

"Does Ms. Dorland know Gus called us?"

Gus said he hadn't told her yet because she was really spooked, and he was afraid she would run again."

"For good reason, I'd say."

Gus told me that Ms. Dorland fought off an assailant then ran for her life. She ended up at a gas station outside of town. Gus picked her up there."

"Where is she now?"

"He took her to a friend's house in Owenton. She'll be safe there for a while."

"Good. Now let's go catch a crooked cop," Tom said with steely determination in his voice.

Drew smiled; he had seen that look before. It meant nothing less than full success with the operation would satisfy his partner. He picked up his jacket and followed Tom out of the building. Everyone was in danger until the department leak was eliminated.

They drove to Clinton Street and Drew parked the car in a used car lot a few houses down and across the street from the safe house. The autumn sun was setting, and streetlights along Clinton Street came to life. The corner streetlight at the edge of the car lot was burned out, and gave the detectives cover in the shadows.

"Do you think they'll chance it tonight?" Samuels asked.

Warfel was thoughtful. "Yes, I do. Ms. Dorland has slipped through their fingers more than once, and I think they're getting desperate. This is also the most vulnerable time. They might want to hit it quick before we can get full protection in place."

"It sounds like he might try to make a run for it—close up shop here and open a new operation in another town or state."

"That's a definite possibility, but he might still try to get the bonds back. He doesn't know we already have them," Warfel said. "How we've kept that a secret from the leak in our department, I don't know."

"That fact will help us eliminate some of our team from suspicion," Drew offered.

"Absolutely! You were with me when we found the bonds, and you signed them into the evidence log. Who logged them in?"

Drew thought some moments before answering. "It was Sargent Maggard. I told him to log them by number, not by contents, so we could keep their discovery a secret. Obviously, he kept that to himself."

"Good thinking, Drew."

"Okay, that leaves our team. Only the two of us were present when we retrieved the bonds. Did you mention finding them to anyone?"

"No, but Hanklin and Presley were bringing items to the evidence room when I was leaving. They could have guessed what I had logged in," Drew explained.

"Yes, that's possible, but it isn't definitive. So, that leaves almost all of the team. What about...okay, here we go."

Both men went on high alert as they watched a dark Mercedes slow down in front of the false safe house for Ms. Dorland. The house had its shades drawn, but lights were on inside to give the impression that someone was there. The Mercedes sped up, but reappeared two minutes later, presumably after circling the block. Again, the sleek car slowed, but didn't stop. Warfel saw only one person, the driver, and swore under his breath. Michael wasn't in the car. Warfel and Drew waited, but the car left and didn't return.

"The car matches the description Mac gave us, so we can assume the department leak was in the briefing room today," Drew concluded.

Warfel nodded. "That leaves us with eight possibilities."

"My money is on Simms and Reynolds," Drew surmised.

"That's a good bet, I'd say."

Darkness began to claim the street, and the meager illumination provided by the streetlights did little to dispel the long shadows covering most of the block. Another thirty minutes went by before an older brown sedan drove slowly past the safe house. Both men watched as the car continued on down the street.

"I counted two men, Drew. Is that what you saw?"

"Yeah, two."

Warfel contacted his team members hidden nearby. He used his cell phone, because he didn't want to alert anyone listening to the radio frequency. He wanted it to appear as if only a lone patrolman guarded the location.

The sedan passed again and pulled into the alley two doors down from the safe house. Two men emerged, and one had drawn his gun. Two officers covered the back of the house. They were well hidden behind a patio screen of the house next door. They notified Warfel by text of the development. He and Samuels drew their weapons and left their car.

"Drew, cover the front. I'll circle around to the back," Tom whispered. Drew nodded.

Warfel crept around the far side of the house from where the two men were approaching. In the near darkness it was difficult to make out the silhouettes of the assailants, but Tom could hear them talking in low voices as they approached the back door. The men climbed the three steps to the back porch and peered into the door's window. Lace curtains covered the space but offered little in the way of a shade. In the distance, the men could see the flickering screen of a television and assumed Rebecca Dorland was in the front room watching a show. One of the men stepped back and slammed his foot into the door, shattering the wood frame. Without wasting any time, both men charged into the space and headed for the living room. It was empty. They looked at each other to decide their next move. Before either could speak, however, the two uniformed officers stormed the house, followed by Warfel.

"Stop right there! You're under arrest," one of the officers commanded.

The man closest to the officers put his hands in the air, but the other man—the one with the gun—made a break for the front door. He had only gotten to the front porch when he encountered Detective Samuels, who had his gun drawn and pointed at the intruder.

"You're not going anywhere; put the gun down," Drew commanded.

The next few moments were difficult to recall exactly as they happened. The man made a break for it and fired his weapon at Drew. The detective fell backward onto the sidewalk and one of the officers immediately went in pursuit. Warfel ran out the front door as well but was halted in his tracks when he saw Drew lying on the ground. The patrolman who had been assigned to guard the safe house had emerged from his car to assist Drew, but Warfel directed him to pursue the suspect instead.

Warfel was deaf to the activity around him as he knelt beside his partner. "Drew! Where are you hit?"

Drew struggled to speak, but his breathing was erratic and in short gasps. Tom pulled out his radio and requested an ambulance, and then he searched for the entry wound. Blood was soaking Drew's shirt near his left shoulder. Warfel frantically ripped open his partner's shirt and searched for the bullet wound. Seconds seemed like an eternity as he wiped blood away. There it was! Just above the protective vest. Tom pressed into the wound as he gently turned Drew on his side. He knew there would be an exit wound, as there was a pool of blood forming under his partner. As he cradled Drew on his lap with his hands pressed into the wounded man's chest and back, he kept up a constant dialog.

"You can make it, Drew. You're gonna make it. Hold on, just a little longer. I hear the sirens coming. You'll be in the hospital before you know it. Hang in there, Drew."

The EMT's took over as soon as they arrived on the scene. Warfel stood aside and watched as the crew worked on his partner. He felt helpless as he watched Drew's blood seep into the cracks in the sidewalk. "Is he going to be okay? He has to be okay!"

Neither EMT responded to Warfel's pleas, but the look between them indicated how seriously Drew was hurt. Their thoughts weren't verbalized but it was apparent that neither thought Drew would make it.

As the detective was loaded into the ambulance, Tom turned to observe the scene around him. More patrol cars had joined the scene and the man captured in the living room was loaded into the back of one of them. Tom recognized him as Greg Reynolds. For the first time since seeing Drew lying on the ground, Tom thought of the suspect who had shot Drew and fled. He was told that the man had gotten away in spite of a hastily established perimeter for several blocks around the scene.

Tom turned to another detective. "The man who ran away is most likely Patrick Simms, one of our own. He wore a mask, but I recognized the tattoo on his right hand. He'll go home eventually, so it shouldn't be hard to find him. Get someone out there to pick him up."

Warfel approached another members of his team, and put him in charge. "I'm going to the hospital with Drew. Let me know when Simms is in custody."

"You got it, Tom. Keep us posted on Drew—okay?"

"Sure thing," Warfel responded, as he attempted unsuccessfully to keep the emotion he was feeling out of his voice.

## Twenty-Five

Michael was in another rage. "All I have are screw ups! Mac Osborne managed to slip through our fingers even though he was zip tied to a chair in an empty room! Rebecca Dorland should be dead by now, and I still don't have my bonds!"

Patrick Simms stood before the crime boss not daring to speak. He regretted leaving the safe house without his partner. They were cousins and had grown up together. But people didn't matter to Michael who was pacing the floor cursing and throwing any item within his reach. Kyle and Stanley stood in a far corner, barely daring to breathe lest their irate boss notice them and direct his anger their way.

"I should have handled this myself. Get out—all of you!"

The three men quickly complied. They were relieved to be away from the angry tirade. No one spoke as they exited the building. Kyle and Stanley turned left and walked together to their waiting truck parked down the street. Simms turned right and disappeared around the side of the house. Kyle and Stanley assumed he had a car in that direction.

Once in their truck Kyle turned to his friend. "Stanley, I told you, we have to get out of town! Michael's a maniac! He would kill us and not think twice. He's crazy!"

Stanley sat behind the wheel of the ten-year-old Chevy and nodded his head. "I know. I was hoping we'd get paid for this job before we left. It's a lot of money, Kyle."

"Are you kidding? How can we spend money if
255

we're dead? I'm telling you, we need to get out of here now!"

Stanley turned the key in the ignition, put the truck in gear and pulled out. He didn't say anything for several minutes as he drove toward the southern city limits. When they passed into the next county, Kyle asked, "Where are we going?"

"Does it matter? You're right; we need to cut our losses and get out of town. If we don't we'll end up dead or arrested."

Kyle breathed a long sigh and rested against the seat. This job had been a nightmare from the beginning. A little breaking and entering was more his style. He, too, would have preferred to get paid before leaving town, but he was content to get away from this situation with his life. At least they had enough money put back to last a few weeks. Florida sounded like a nice destination, maybe the Keys. It was warm there, and more importantly, it was far from Michael. He closed his eyes and dreamed of being on the beach as the rhythmic motion of the truck rocked him to sleep.

Stanley smiled as he glanced over at his sleeping partner. He hadn't shared with him yet that his plan had been successful. Stanley had intercepted two drug payments totaling almost one hundred thousand dollars. He had simply robbed the men on their way to give the money to Michael. He had worn a mask to prevent detection, so he was reasonably sure no one knew who had taken the money. He realized that Michael would be irate, but he sensed that the crime boss would soon be arrested or dead. Either suited Stanley just fine. He decided to let his friend sleep for now. He would tell him about the money when he woke up. For now, Stanley was content to drive into the night.

\*\*\*

Warfel parked his car outside the hospital's emergency room and rushed through the double doors. He tried to follow Drew as the EMT's hurried him down the hall but was stopped by a security guard.

"Hold on there, fella; you can't go in there."

Warfel tried to pull rank. "I'm a police detective, and that's my partner. He's been shot!"

The security guard didn't back down. "Then let the doctors take care of him. You would just be in the way. Now, come over here and take a seat. I'll let someone know you're here; you'll be updated soon."

Warfel had no choice but to comply. The guard was right. He could do nothing for Drew now. He turned and found a seat in the waiting area and dreaded what he had to do next. He pulled out his phone and dialed a familiar number. It was answered on the third ring.

"Julie? This is Tom Warfel. I'm afraid I have some bad news. Drew was shot this evening and is at the hospital." He paused as the woman on the other end of the call absorbed the blow.

"How bad is he hurt?" Julie asked as she fought back panic. The call she had always dreaded was now a reality.

"He, uh, lost a lot of blood, but I'm sure the doctors will replace it right away. Do you have someone to stay with the children?"

"Yes, my neighbor next door babysits a lot for them. I'll be there in ten minutes," Julie replied as she looked around her for her keys and purse.

"I already have a squad car coming to pick you up, Julie. It should be there any minute."

"Oh, okay, sure. Thanks."

Tom hung up his phone and returned it to his pocket. He sat in the hard plastic and metal chair staring at the wall opposite where he was sitting. There was a poster on it that warned of the symptoms of the flu and cautioned everyone to wash their hands frequently. Tom looked down at his own hands and became aware of the dried blood, Drew's blood. His sleeves were painted reddish brown as well. There had been so much blood. *Can Drew survive losing this much blood?* A deep sigh escaped him as a strong hand rested on his shoulder. He looked up to see six fellow officers standing before him. The men in blue always stood together. Their presence comforted him and, somehow, he felt it would strengthen Drew as well. Each man found a seat nearby and kept a silent vigil for their brother.

\*\*\*

Sam handed Mac a bourbon and Coke, then sipped his bourbon on the rocks as he and Sarah listened to Mac recount his experience with Michael.

"I can't believe it, I just can't believe it!" Sam exclaimed. "I didn't notice anything off about him."

"Neither did I," Sarah added. "I guess we assumed respectability because of his profession."

Mary nodded. "Yes, at least I'm sure I did. One doesn't expect an orthopedic surgeon to be a mastermind of crime. Poor Cora, I wonder if she saw the monster beneath the white coat."

"It's a definite possibility," Mac added. "It would be hard to keep up the façade in the intimacy of marriage."

Sam took a sip of his bourbon and savored the warmth as he swallowed. "So, what's next? Does Detective Warfel have any leads on how to find Michael and shut down his organization?"

"I think he has some leads, but..."

Aggie came rushing into the room. Turn on the TV; a policeman's been shot! I'm not sure who it was but I did see Detective Warfel standing behind an ambulance, and he had blood all over him."

Mac reached for the remote control. The news was running a loop of the incident. The wounded officer had not been identified. There were few real facts in the reporting, mostly on-the-scene footage and a broad statement from the Chief of Police. The lack of news was maddening. Mac couldn't help but wonder if Warfel was also wounded, or if the blood on him was from the downed officer. There was only one way to find out.

Mac sent a text on his cell phone to Tom. *Saw the shooting on TV. Are you okay?*

Several anxious minutes passed before Warfel sent a reply. *I wasn't hurt; it was Drew. He's in surgery. Say prayers.*

Mac relayed the message to the group and led them in a prayer for Drew's recovery. Mac was transported back to a painful memory from his time on the force. He had lost a partner in much the same way and still carried the guilt of his partner's death. If only he had stepped forward at that awful moment instead of his partner.

Mac shook his head to dispel the memory. He knew it did no good to dwell on the past; he couldn't change it. Mary sensed a sorrow in Mac and reached over to hold his hand. Her touch brought him back to the present and how he had narrowly escaped death in the warehouse only hours before. He would never give Mary all the details of his ordeal. A sanitized version of the incident would be all she would hear. He squeezed her hand in recognition and smiled. He knew he was a lucky man in many ways. The future was the important thing now; the past was gone.

Sam and Sarah left for home with assurances that Mac would let them know of any news of Drew. Mac then helped Mary settle in for the night.

"Thank you, sweetheart. I appreciate everything you do for me," Mary said.

"It's my pleasure; I would do anything for you. You're getting stronger every day, and before long you'll be up and around like before."

"I hope so; it seems like I've been like this forever, and yet I know I've come a long way."

Mac sat on the side of the bed next to Mary and leaned over to kiss her goodnight. "Sweet dreams!"

"Aren't you coming to bed?"

"Not yet, I'll stay up a bit to see if there is any news from Tom about Detective Samuels."

Mary smiled at her husband. "You always act so strong, Mac, but I see the old softie beneath the tough ex-cop exterior—and I love you for it."

Mac smiled back. "Guilty as charged, my lady. Now, get some sleep; I'll be to bed soon."

It would be several hours, however, before Mac succumbed to sleep. He replayed the details of his kidnapping over and over. There was something important he couldn't remember. He gave up after two hours and decided to fix a snack. He was spreading peanut butter on crackers as his mind formed an image. That was it! He remembered the elusive detail.

His snack forgotten, Mac pulled out his cell phone and punched in Tom's number. It was answered on the first ring.

"Tom, any news of Drew?"

"Hey, Mac, yeah he just got out of surgery. The bullet nicked an artery, but it looks like he'll make it." Mac could hear the fatigue in his friend's voice.

"Thank goodness! We prayed for him and will continue to do so."

"Thank you, he can use all the prayers he can get. It was a close call," Tom replied.

"Please give our best wishes to him and his family. Listen, I just remembered something. It might help, might not."

"Okay, Mac, what is it?"

"Well, before Michael and his henchmen left me alone in the warehouse, I heard one of the men say something that might help you find Michael, that is Dr. Larkin."

"You've got my attention, go ahead."

"One of the men whispered to the other, but loud enough for me to hear him say something about 'girls on a houseboat' and 'Lake Cumberland,' Does that help?"

Tom's tired mind struggled to put together this information. Suddenly, he realized the significance of what Mac had heard. The missing girls! It was some seconds before he answered, and Mac thought he had lost the connection

"Tom, are you still there?"

"Yes, and that definitely could help!"

"Why would he say, 'girls'?"

"Mac, I'll explain later—thanks!"

The line went dead and Mac suddenly felt the fatigue he had resisted all evening. He climbed into bed next to Mary, closed his eyes, and was asleep in seconds.

# Twenty-Six

Warfel ended the call with Mac and immediately dialed Captain Lewis of the tactical unit. His next calls were to his team members and the Kentucky State Police. He needed to get the team to Jamestown as soon as possible. *This could be the break we need. I only hope we are in time,* he thought as he began to put a plan into place. There would be no sleep for him tonight.

Jamestown, Kentucky is home to one of the most beautiful lakes in America—Lake Cumberland. Fishing, water skiing, swimming, and hiking are but a few of the activities available. The park also permits camping, and houseboats can be rented. However, the heavily wooded park is an ideal location to conceal illegal activities such as human trafficking.

\*\*\*

Warfel arrived at Lake Cumberland's lodge within two hours after receiving Mac's call. Local members of the Kentucky State Police had established a command center there. Warfel strode into the command center and approached a table where Lieutenant Ron Wallace was seated.

"Are you Tom Warfel?" the lieutenant asked.

Tom nodded. "I appreciate your assistance in this. We've been after this guy for a long time but didn't know his identity until recently. He's involved in some pretty bad stuff."

"So I hear. We're glad to be of assistance."

"The rest of my team should be here shortly. In the meantime, can you help me map out the area for our search teams?"

"Sure, but it will be difficult to begin a search before dawn. The lake covers more than sixty-five thousand acres and there's one thousand two hundred fifty-five miles of shoreline."

Warfel whistled. "Yes, I see the difficulty. We think the kidnapped women and girls are being held on a houseboat. Are there many docks?"

"Let me see. The lake covers six counties, so there are quite a few docks, but the boat could unload along a bank. Some shorelines have high stonewalls, but there are literally thousands of other places where the boat could be unloaded. Also, keep in mind that in summer as many as fifteen hundred houseboats could be on the water. Luckily, this time of year there won't be more than a few dozen; the rest are docked until spring."

"We have helicopters ready to go at dawn, right?"

"Yes, we diverted them from marijuana field surveillance."

"Crime never takes a holiday," Tom said ruefully.

"You've got that right," agreed Wallace.

Within an hour, the rest of the team had assembled and logistics were being worked out. Dawn was fast approaching and their window to find the girls would close quickly. Tom had no doubt that Larkin would move the girls soon.

After Mac's phone call, Warfel contacted the missing persons division of the Kentucky State Police and spoke with Captain Dominick Meyers. Meyers had been investigating the disappearance of two-dozen girls and women in the past six months. Most had lived in the Central Kentucky area, and Dominick believed the disappearances to be related.

Captain Meyers arrived just as the organizational meeting started. He introduced himself to Warfel and was invited to speak first to the group. A fifteen-year veteran of the KSP, Meyers had been with the Missing Persons Division from the start of his career. His favorite outcome was the successful reuniting of missing persons with their loved ones. His least favorite times were when the missing persons were found dead. Even fifteen years on the job had not hardened him to the shock and grief he witnessed in those left behind. He cleared his throat and addressed the group.

"Many people believe that human trafficking exists primarily in foreign countries and not in the United States. Nothing could be further from the truth. Nearly every community in America is at risk. Runaways, girls lured by offers of fame and money, and outright kidnapping supply the never-ending demand for illicit sex. Some girls, and boys, are even sold into slavery by their parents. It's a terrible blight on the children of a country known for freedom and opportunity." He paused to gather his thoughts and continued. "For several months my team has been working on the uptick of missing females ranging in age from fourteen to forty-one. We've come close to finding them a couple of times, but they were moved before we got there. I want this group—bad. I have a daughter myself, and I don't know what I would do if something like this happened to her. We're told to keep a professional distance in our jobs, but every evening when I see my beautiful twelve-year-old, I'm reminded that every one of those who've been kidnapped belong to someone. Personal? You bet it's personal. Let's get this guy!"

Warfel listened to Dominick's statement and thought of his own daughters. Yes, it was personal. There was too much at stake to fail.

As dawn arrived, assignments were handed out and the team was informed that the choppers were in the air. It was time to initiate their plan. Troopers, dressed in plain clothes, checked campsites and cabins. Helicopters began their air surveillance, and Tom's team began to visit docks. What couldn't be predicted was where the unloading of the human cargo would take place. In spite of more than one hundred men and women working on the operation, the girls could slip right past them under the cover of the deeply wooded area. The lack of leaves on the trees would help, but only if those searching happened to be in just the right place in the vast forest. Warfel tried not to think of how daunting their task was; he only knew there were two-dozen women and girls counting on someone to find them and free them from their living hell.

By ten o'clock the team had been searching for three hours. No one wanted to admit defeat, but hope was dwindling by the minute. There was just so much area to cover. It appeared that the wilderness had aided in smuggling the human cargo away from the area.

By noon, even Warfel had serious doubts about the successful outcome he so desperately sought. Throughout the rest of the day the team searched as many possible locations where the girls could be as was humanly possible, but the girls, as well as Michael Larkin, were most likely gone. Even Warfel was having serious doubts, but then he remembered Drew battling for his life and was more determined that ever to succeed.

As each group checked in with the command center throughout the day, the situation became progressively grimmer. A few offered little tidbits that initially held promise, but didn't pan out in the end. No one had found anything to advance the investigation until one young state trooper called into the command center.

"I haven't found the girls, but I just spoke to a fisherman who told me he saw three girls slipping along a bank near dawn this morning. He might not have thought too much of it except the girls weren't dressed for the weather or for their location. Instead of jeans, a jacket, and hiking boots, they were wearing light cotton tops and shorts. One of the girls didn't have shoes. He thought it odd, but he fishes here a lot and has seen some strange sights over the years. He probably wouldn't have reported it if I hadn't specifically asked him about anything he had seen recently that was unusual. I'm checking out the area now where he said he saw them."

As the trooper relayed the information, a new spark of hope was ignited. "Give us your location; we'll send a team there to help you look," Meyers responded. The trooper gave his coordinates and Captain Meyers relayed the information to the entire team.

"Now, I know you've been at this nearly twelve hours and you're all tired, but we're very close to finding these girls before they are shipped all over the world. Once they leave the U.S. their lives are over. We need to find them. With this new information, we can focus our search to a targeted area. Let's divide again into teams of three to four and assign areas to search."

A few men moaned under their breaths at the thought of returning to the rough terrain. One of the men close by turned to face them. "What if these were your sisters or daughters? Would you complain then?" The point was taken and no one else offered comment. The park's kitchen staff had set up a sandwich bar and each officer grabbed a quick meal before heading back out.

Warfel then turned to Captain Meyers. "Dominick, the girls may have already been transferred to a land vehicle by now. We have no way of knowing how many we're talking about, but I would think at least fifteen or twenty. If the three girls spotted by your trooper have managed to escape without being recaptured, they could be a good source of information for us. They can tell us how many others are being held, how many guards, and if they know their destination."

"Yes," the captain agreed, "we need to find them, both for their own sake and for that of the others. As for ground transportation, I've set up roadblocks in a thirty-mile radius. County and city law enforcement in twelve counties are helping with this. The roadblocks have been manned since early this morning, so if they plan to make a break for it and drive the girls out of here, we'll catch 'em."

"Good, there's nothing to do now but wait. I need to check on my partner who was shot last night by this same group. He made it through surgery but is still in pretty rough shape."

"I'm sorry to hear that. Go ahead, I'll monitor the radio while you check on him," Meyers offered.

"Thanks." Warfel excused himself and found a quiet corner of the reception area. The wall of glass faced the lake and provided a stunning view. Geese flew in a V-formation overhead as Warfel pulled out his phone. He hesitated before punching in the number for the Braxton Hospital. So much had happened related to this case, and it wasn't close to being concluded. Michael Larkin's crime organization had reached its tentacles of destruction throughout the area. The cancer on the community had to be stopped. Failure was not an option. With renewed determination, Tom dialed the hospital. Once connected, he asked for the nursing station where Drew was a patient.

When a voice answered, "ICU, this is Madeline, how can I help you," Warfel's hopes were dashed. He had hoped Drew would be out of intensive care by now. Tom asked for the nurse taking care of Drew and was soon connected with Drew's nurse, Janet.

"How is he today?"

"Well, we're having some difficulty keeping his blood pressure where we want it to be, but his pain is under control, and he responds to verbal stimulation. We're keeping him pretty well sedated to protect the arterial graft and incision. The more he rests for the next several days, the faster he will heal," Janet explained.

"How much longer will he be in ICU?" Warfel asked.

"Probably a couple more days. The step-down unit is currently at capacity, so there'll be no hurry to move him to a lower level of care. Be assured, Detective, your partner is being well cared for and monitored very carefully."

"I'm sure he is. Thank you."

"You are very welcome, call anytime."

Warfel ended the call and returned to the command center to check in with Lt. Wallace and Captain Meyers. "What have I missed?"

The lieutenant flashed a sly smile. "Oh, not much—just that we found the three girls."

"You're kidding!"

"Nope. They are cold, hungry, and more than a little scared, but they will be fine. They should arrive here any minute. They're really hungry, so they can eat while they tell us everything they know. After that, as a precaution, we'll get them to the local hospital to be checked out.

"That's amazing, and more than a little lucky. Maybe things will turn our way today after all."

At that moment, the front doors of the lodge opened and the three girls were brought to the command center. They eyed the sandwich bar but didn't move. Each had spent more than a month as a captive and had been programmed to do nothing without permission. Various bruises on their bodies attested to the brutal treatment they had endured.

A female officer who had accompanied the teenagers to the lodge stepped forward and quietly assured them they could eat anything they wanted. They could also wait for a hot meal to be prepared if they preferred. Hunger won and the girls quickly chose sandwiches, fruit, and cookies. The female officer stayed with them to provide comfort and assurance.

Tom conferred with Dominick Meyers, and both men agreed that the female trooper should remain with the girls during questioning. It was apparent that the girls were comfortable with her present.

Once the trio had eaten all they wanted, Tom and Dominick approached the table where they were sitting.

269

The female officer stood up to leave but was waved back into her chair by Meyers.

"Good evening. Ladies. I'm Captain Dominick Meyers, and this is Lieutenant Warfel. Did everyone get enough to eat?" The girls nodded. "Good." Dominick looked at the female trooper and asked her first name.

"Michelle, sir."

The captain nodded his thanks. "So, I'm sure Michelle has told you that you'll be taken to the local hospital to be checked out. We want to make sure each of you receives any needed medical care before we return you to your families. Michelle gave us a list of your full names and family contacts, and we are taking care of notifying your relatives now. You will be able to speak with them on the way to the hospital. First, however, I'd like to get some information from you. I'm sure you can appreciate how vital it is to find the other girls as soon as possible. Anything you can tell us might help us to do that. Is it okay if we talk for a few minutes about what you have experienced since you were taken?"

Each girl nodded shyly.

"Okay, first of all, how many girls were with you?"

At first, no one spoke, but finally a thin girl with light blonde hair said, "There were seventeen of us in all. I heard the men say they wanted at least twenty before they moved us though."

"Where were you being held?"

The same girl spoke up, apparently the spokesman for the group. "On a houseboat. It was really crowded. They fed us only once a day and would hit us if we asked for anything."

"How many men were there?"

"Three stayed with us all the time, but a couple more would come and go."

"Do you know where the other girls are being taken?"

"I'm not sure, but I did hear one of the men talking about Miami. "

"I see. Do you know how the girls were being transported to Miami?"

"All I know is that it was a truck of some kind. We were told that we had to be quiet and not talk to each other when riding in the truck."

"Do you have any idea where the other ladies are now?" Warfel asked.

The girls looked at each other, but no one spoke up. Finally, one girl hung her head and very quietly uttered one word: "No. " Tom could tell she was crying.

"Okay, that's enough for now," Dominick stated. "We'll get complete statements from each of you after you're checked out at the hospital. Unless you need to stay at the hospital for some reason, you will return here to stay the night. By morning, your families should all be here to take you home." Warfel and Meyers shook hands with each girl and thanked them for their cooperation.

Warfel hoped the girls received counseling once they returned home. He made a mental note to follow up with the girls. The trauma they had experienced could affect them for the rest of their lives.

Michelle accompanied the girls to the hospital and made sure each one spoke with family on the way. Warfel passed along the new information by radio to his team, and Meyers did the same. Each of them felt an excitement building in response to finding the girls. They finally had solid evidence of the human trafficking operation. Until now, it was surmised, rather than known. This was proof that could get a conviction in court. Now, they needed to find Dr. Michael Larkin, the chameleon that had fooled so many people for so long. Warfel found it difficult to understand why a successful orthopedic surgeon would turn to a life of crime. He had not simply overbilled insurance for his services; no that would have been too obvious and simple. Michael Larkin had created a criminal organization to rival those in large cities such as Chicago, Miami, or Detroit, and he had done it while appearing to be a respectable surgeon. By all reports, he was a talented and respected clinician, with a healthy income. Why would he risk so much? Warfel would make that the first question he asked the crime kingpin once he was apprehended.

Tom's cell phone interrupted his musings. He listened to the voice on the other end with increasing agitation. Once the call was completed, he slammed his fist into the seat cushion of his chair. He swore loudly, catching the attention of Lt. Wallace.

"What is it, Tom?" Wallace asked with obvious concern.

Tom exhaled loudly and took several moments to answer. "One of my witnesses in this case was found murdered this morning. He eluded his protection detail and put himself directly into the path of his killers."

Wallace understood the implication. Cases were won or lost based on witnesses. "You have the three kidnapped girls," he offered.

"Yes, that will make our case on the human trafficking charge, but that is just the tip of the iceberg. This guy is into major drug dealing and money launderings as well. He has a number of businesses he launders money through. He has left a trail of destruction in his wake. That witness could have testified to all of that and more."

"Will you still be able to make your case?" Wallace asked.

"I'm sure we will. We have another witness who has been very cooperative. Her testimony will be compelling, but it would have had more weight with two witnesses. We do have a great deal of physical evidence and the sworn statement of the deceased. It should be enough to convince a jury," Tom explained. As he pondered the effect the loss of Gus Averill would have on his case, a sudden thought gripped him. Mac!

Tom pulled out his phone and nervously tapped a pencil against the table until the call was answered. "This is Warfel; do we still have two men at Mac Osborne's farm?"

"Yeah, that's what you said you wanted, sir."

"Okay, get four more men out there—now! Larkin won't hesitate to go after Mac after killing Averill. Get him out of there, and his whole family and farm staff."

"Yes, sir!"

Warfel hung up and dialed Mac's cell phone. The call went to voice mail. "Where are you, Mac?" Tom hung up and redialed the number, but with the same result. "Damn!" Tom scrolled through his contacts and found the number for Sam Richards. "Come on, Sam, answer!"

"Hello?"

"Sam, this is Tom Warfel. Do you have another number for Mac? He's not answering his cell."

"Sure, Mary has a cell phone and there's a landline."

"Give me both numbers." Warfel wrote them

down.

"Is something wrong?" Sam asked.

"I'll have to explain later; thanks, Sam." Tom tried the landline first and was greeted by Aggie's friendly voice. "Aggie, this is Detective Warfel; is Mac there?"

"Yes, but I believe he's in the shower. Is there anything I can help you with?"

"This is really important, Aggie; can you get him for me, please?"

"Uh, sure, just a minute." Aggie heard the urgency in the detective's voice and hurried down the hall. Aggie knocked on the closed door.

Mac opened the door dressed in jeans and a tee shirt. "What is it, Aggie?"

"Sorry to bother you, but Detective Warfel's on the phone, and he says it's really important. He's on the house phone"

"Okay, I'll pick it up in here. Thanks, Aggie."

Mac closed the door, walked over to the bedside table and picked up the phone. He heard a 'click' as Aggie hung up in the kitchen. "Tom, what is it?"

"Mac, where's Mary?"

"She's sitting on the back porch talking with Sarah. What's up?"

"Mac, I've sent four more officers to your place. Gus Averill was found dead this morning. I'm afraid they'll make a move on you next."

"I appreciate that, Tom, but your two officers are here and seem to be doing a good job patrolling the area around the house."

"I can't take any chances with you or Mary. Is there somewhere else you can go—and take Aggie with you?"

"Well, sure. Sam and Sarah would take us in, I'm sure, but do you really think that's necessary?"

"I do, Mac. I'll place officers in your house. If someone comes there after you, they'll get a surprise."

"Okay, I'll go talk with Mary. Will there be any protection provided for us at Sam's place?"

"Sure, the two officers already there will go with you, but in plain clothes. I don't want to draw attention to your presence there."

Mac laughed. "This is a lot of cloak and dagger for me, Tom. I can protect Mary and me. We won't be surprised again."

"I know you're very capable, Mac, but it's my job to protect you. You've been put in danger twice now. Humor me, I'll sleep better."

"All right, all right, I give up! We're going...and Tom?"

"Yeah?"

"Get this guy!"

"You got it!"

Mac hung up, finished dressing, and walked out to the porch to talk with Mary and Sarah. The conversation ran along the same lines as the one with Tom.

"Why do we need to go anywhere? We're well aware of the danger; we've faced it personally," Mary protested.

"I know, I assured Tom of that, but he insists. Apparently, he thinks Michael Larkin will try to eliminate me as a witness."

"I see. Okay, we'll leave. So, where do we go?" Mary asked.

"That's easy," Sarah interrupted, "stay with us."

Mac laughed. I told Tom that's where we'd end

275

up. What about Aggie? She's been staying here with us while Mary recuperates. She's taken this opportunity to have her house painted inside."

"No problem, we have room for everyone. Mrs. Hoskins will be thrilled to have us all under one roof."

"Okay, ladies, let's break the news to Aggie, pack a few things—I said few, and hurry. It's already getting late."

Forty-five minutes later, Serendipity Farm was full to the brim. Every bedroom was claimed. Anna had been asleep for some time, so everyone quietly settled in before regrouping in the kitchen. Mrs. Hoskins had fresh banana bread ready. The two plainclothes officers were stationed by the front and back doors, alert for any trouble.

By midnight, everyone's nervous tension was spent and the group decided it was time to turn in. Mary closed their bedroom door and turned to Mac. She put her arms around his neck and her head on his chest. "Oh, Mac, I'll be so glad when all of this is over."

"I know, sweetheart, I know." Mac held her close. "From what Tom said, the case seems to be coming to an end. Let's hope so. You just concentrate on getting stronger. Now, let's get some rest."

Within minutes, the house grew quiet, as everyone, except for the two officers on duty, was asleep.

# Twenty-Seven

No one in the command center in the lodge at Lake Cumberland was asleep. A large paneled van had been spotted as it pulled onto a gravel road near one of the roadblocks. The road led only to a handful of houses before it ended.

"This could be it!" Warfel exclaimed.

Ron Wallace was directing his men to close in on the van, but to keep some distance until the safety of the girls could be established. A patrol car pulled into the opening of the road, essentially cutting off the van's escape. With protective gear on, troopers crept toward the van, being careful to avoid a floodlight shining from one of the houses. Long shadows were cast across the lawn by bushes and trees in the path of the light. The officers struggled to separate shapes in the near darkness as they approached the vehicle. Officers reached the doors on either side of the van's cab and counted down silently before suddenly opening the doors. Four guns were drawn on either side of the vehicle, but the effort was in vain. The cab was empty!

The message was conveyed back to the command center. The men were instructed to open the van's back doors. Officers again took a stance outside the van, guns ready, as two men unlocked the doors and slowly swung them open. Two men were pointing rifles at the officers but lowered them when it was obvious they were outnumbered. Behind them huddled fourteen girls and young women. Too frightened to move, they watched as the two men were taken into custody. The officers assured the group they were safe now, but the pronouncement did little to reduce the rapid heartbeats of the girls. Since each girl's abduction, fear had been the primary response. The only comfort they had experienced was in each other's presence. They remained huddled together, drawing strength from their collective presence.

Finally, it was decided to bring a female officer to the scene to enter the van and speak with the girls. Trust would have to be earned a little at a time.

Officers began searching the area for the men who had escaped from the cab of the van. It didn't take long to find two of them hiding in a shed behind a home only a short distance from the van, and the third man was discovered hiding under a porch. Barking dogs had led the officers to the fugitives, which caused most of the homes' occupants to wander outside to see what all the fuss was about. Everyone was shocked to discover the manhunt underway. The homeowners were instructed to stay inside, but the temptation to be in on the excitement was too great. Several people watched as the men were cuffed and led away. It was more excitement than the sleepy rural community had ever seen. In spite of the spectators, the remaining three men were apprehended without incident. The stories of the manhunt and capture grew with each telling in the days ahead as the neighbors tried to outdo one another.

Warfel and Meyers breathed a deep sigh of relief when told of the girls' discovery and the capture of the five men. Now, all their efforts would be focused on finding and arresting Michael Larkin.

\*\*\*

In a nondescript apartment building on the outskirts of Braxton, Larkin opened a wall safe and began throwing papers and money into a duffle bag. The name on the apartment lease was James Sullivan, one of several aliases used by him. In a few hours, if all went well, he would use one of his other aliases and be on his way to a sunny Caribbean island. It was time to let go of the dynasty he had created in sleepy Central Kentucky. Within twenty-four hours the girls would be taken to Miami and sent from there to places all over the world. The drug business could be transferred to wherever he liked. There was no shortage of people with expensive habits willing to pay anything for their next fix. He would have to set up new businesses to launder the money, but he would be more careful in the future if he invested in bearer bonds. The stolen bonds would be a total write-off. He no longer believed that his ex-wife's murder was a case of mistaken identity. No, it was a deliberate act, most likely tied in somehow with the stolen bonds.

Thoughts of Cora saddened him; he had not meant for her to die. Rebecca Dorland should have paid that price. With some difficulty, he brushed Cora's memory aside and resumed stuffing the duffle bag.

Michael zipped the nearly full bag, looked around the room for anything he might have missed, and headed for the door. His cell phone rang before he reached his car.

"Yeah? Are you sure? Finally; something went as planned." A rare smile covered his face at the message he had just received. Gus Averill had been eliminated. The fool had stolen the bonds and, in so doing, had signed his own death warrant. Michael punished disloyalty.

Michael slipped into the back seat of the Mercedes. He was leaving Braxton for good; his business in the town was all wrapped up, and most, but not all, witnesses had been silenced. *It won't matter who knows what now. I'll be out of the reach of the law*

279

*in only a few hours.* Michael rested against the fine leather of his Mercedes as it barreled down the highway.

"Take me to the airfield."

The man driving merely nodded his acknowledgment, picked up speed, and headed to the Somerset, Kentucky airport. Michael had a private plane waiting there that would take him to the Dominican Republic. It was one of his favorite places and now would become his home. He leaned back into the soft leather seat and congratulated himself on his sagacity. He had more than enough in offshore accounts to keep him in a nice lifestyle for many years. He could start a new operation and continue as he had for the past five years. While it was true that his days as a respected orthopedic surgeon were over, he would find new ways to occupy his time. It was a good thing he had no wife to consider, although he deeply regretted Cora's death. She had been the only decent thing left in his life and didn't deserve to die. He had lost a great deal of late.

He forced himself to put that entire episode aside and he savored the thought of living a Caribbean lifestyle, his phone rang again. Michael swore after hearing what the caller had to say and threw the phone to the floor of the luxury car. The news he just received sent a shiver through him. *How did they know about the girls? I was so careful to keep all my operations separate.* The lost shipment of girls would cost him a million or more. Michael hated to lose—at anything. He could afford the financial hit, but was enraged at being beaten by the likes of Warfel.

As Michael's car sped toward the airfield, Warfel met with the other leaders of the joint task force. "The girls are on their way to the hospital to get checked out, and the men who were holding them are in custody.

Perhaps one of them has knowledge of Michael Larkin's whereabouts and would be willing to make a deal."

Lt. Ron Wallace agreed. "Larkin could be anywhere by now. Our best chance to catch him is with inside information. The question is which one of these reprobates actually has anything we can use?"

"Let's question them all at the same time—let them know about the deal," Warfel began, "then we'll tell them that the first one to give us information leading to the arrest of Larkin will get the deal."

Wallace nodded and picked up his cell phone. We'll need to wake up the Commonwealth Attorney for that. I spoke with him earlier, and I think he'll agree to the plan."

Forty-five minutes later, the captured men were hauled into KSP Post 15 and placed in separate interrogation rooms. Most of the men had numerous prior arrests, and now kidnapping and human trafficking charges would be added to their rap sheets. Each man knew he would be lucky to ever see the outside of a jail cell. This made it all the easier to dangle a carrot in front of them.

Lt. Wallace chose to interrogate the driver of the van, and Warfel chose one of the two men found in the back of the vehicle. Other team leaders interrogated the rest. Each officer had the same document in front of him in a manila folder. If anyone provided information leading to the arrest of Michael Larkin, he would receive consideration in his sentencing. He would get a better prison assignment, with more privileges, and possibly a shorter sentence.

Interrogations yielded little information as every one of the men claimed to have no knowledge of Michael's likely whereabouts. Indeed, he was even considered a man of mystery by the men, with no one knowing very much about their boss.

Warfel didn't buy the story of the man he was interrogating. "I'm telling you, Mr. Brown, one of you is going to tell us what we need to know, and that person will get this sweet deal."

"Yeah, but not live to enjoy it! You don't know how ruthless Michael is. I'd be dead before a month passed once I was in prison."

Warfel shook his head. "You've got that wrong; Michael's comfy crime syndicate is history. We've busted it up—the drugs, the human trafficking, and the money laundering. It's only a matter of time before we catch the person responsible for all this human suffering, so you might as well tell me what I want to know. Just remember, this deal is only good if you're the first one to speak up. Once one of you accepts the deal and gives us meaningful information, the deal is rescinded for the rest. Now, what's it gonna be?"

The man sitting handcuffed to the table in front of Warfel was clearly struggling with a decision. His hands were sweating, his face was flushed, and he couldn't stop fidgeting. Finally, he looked up at Warfel, but averted his eyes.

"Okay, I'll tell you what I know. It might help you, it might not, but it's all I got."

Warfel suppressed a smile and leaned forward in his chair. "Now, that's better. What can you tell me?"

"Wait a minute, I want a signed paper saying I get the deal you promised."

Warfel opened the folder, removed the document and passed it across the table. "Fine, here's a pen."

Brown quickly grabbed the pen and signed his name.

"Just remember, this deal is only good if we find Michael Larkin as a result of your help. Is that understood?"

Brown didn't look up as he nodded understanding. "If Michael is aware of all that has happened to his various enterprises, he might be considering a permanent vacation in the Caribbean. He goes to a place he owns in the Dominican Republic every few months in his private plane, a Gulfstream G 150. I've taken him up a few times myself."

"You're a licensed pilot?" Warfel asked.

"Yeah, I learned to fly in the U.S. Air Force. I flew missions in the Middle East for more than a year. When I returned home, I earned my domestic pilot's license. I thought I could make money as a pilot. I was making a pretty good living when Michael made me an offer I couldn't refuse. The only problem was once I had worked for him, I couldn't get away. The very first time I flew for him he planted drugs on the plane and told me he would turn me in if I tried to walk away. He plays dirty and doesn't care who gets hurt. He would sell his own mother if he thought he could get a few bucks."

"Where does he keep this plane?"

"That's the question. He moves it around so it's always strategically placed near where he's operating. There are a lot of small airports in Kentucky, and some who run them will look the other way for a few hundred dollars in their pocket."

Warfel thought about Brown's statement. Michael's plane could be anywhere. If he needed it for a getaway once the women and girls were sold, he would want it nearby. Suddenly, he had a thought. "Do you know the call signs for the plane?"

The man's eyes lit up. For the first time, he could sense a glimmer of hope for his future. "Sure do; I recited them enough when I flew for Michael."

Brown gave the information to Warfel and watched as the detective left the room. It shouldn't be hard to find the plane if it was in the area.

The sergeant at the desk of KSP Post 15 quickly supplied the most likely airport. Somerset had an airfield and it often served the fishermen and other vacationers who came to Lake Cumberland. Warfel called the airfield and relayed the call numbers of Larkin's plane. KSP troopers were dispatched to the scene within minutes. Tom soon had confirmation that Michael Larkin's jet was at the airport. Instructions had been received only a few minutes before to gas up the craft, arrange for a pilot, and move it out of its hanger. The airport official told Tom that Larkin had not arrived yet, but was expected within the hour.

Realizing there was no time to lose, Tom directed the troopers already at the airport to conceal their vehicles. He didn't want Larkin to get spooked before the trap for him could be set. He hung up his phone. He knew the troopers could handle the situation, but he wished he could be there to see Larkin's face when he was arrested. He consoled himself with the thought of conducting the interrogation at the KSP post. With a sigh, Warfel reached for a nearby coffee pot to pour a cup of coffee. He hadn't slept for thirty-six hours.

Lieutenant Wallace approached the detective. "Tom, we brought one of the choppers back here. It's ready to take us to the airfield."

Tom grinned; he wasn't going to miss Larkin's capture after all.

# Twenty-Eight

Michael Larkin and his driver arrived at the Somerset, Kentucky airfield only minutes after Warfel called the facility and asked that Larkin's departure be delayed as much as possible. The black Mercedes made its way slowly to the hanger where Larkin's jet awaited. Both occupants in the luxury car drew their weapons and were on alert for anything suspicious. They were surprised to find the Gulfstream still in the hanger. A tow bar had been connected to the nose landing gear, but the tug had not arrived.

"See what's holding things up! Make it clear we need to leave now!"

"Yes, sir!" The driver returned his weapon to its shoulder holster, exited the car, and walked over to a ground crewman. "What's holding things up? We called ahead to have the jet ready when we arrived."

"Yes, sir, I understand, but we're shorthanded this evening, and we've had several departures to get ready. We'll have you hooked up and onto the tarmac before you know it," the man said with a cheerful smile.

The driver returned to the car to report back to Larkin.

"I don't like this. I think they're stalling; we may need to *encourage* cooperation.

Larkin motioned for the driver to get out of the car, and he did the same. They approached the ground crewman with their guns drawn.

The man looked up as they approached and his eyes widened at the sight of the guns. He immediately raised his hands. "What do you want? I don't have any money on me, but take anything you want. There's some expensive tools over there on the bench; they would bring a fair price."

"You fool! I don't want any tools! I want this plane towed out of the hanger. Where's the pilot? I was told there would be one here when I arrived."

"He's here; I saw him. I think he went to file the flight plan."

"That's a lie; he doesn't know the flight plan. Now, tell me what's going on or you won't be going home to the missus!"

The frightened crewman couldn't think what to say next. He really didn't know what was going on. He had only been told to take his time preparing the jet. "I don't know, honest I don't. All I was told was to get this jet ready. I called for the tug, but it hasn't arrived yet. I'm tellin' ya, that's all I know!"

In the background, the usual airport noises could be heard. Prop planes and small jets taxied along the runway, arriving and departing intermittently. The sound of a chopper's blades broke through the morning air, but the significance of its arrival went unnoticed by Larkin and his driver.

"Get on the radio and hurry that tug, or it's the last thing you'll ever do!"

"Y-yes, sir!"

Larkin watched the crewman carefully as he complied with the demand, so he was unaware of the approaching men. It was his driver who noticed the threat. Warfel and Meyers had met up with the troopers and were moving into position for the arrest. The driver swirled around and fired at the approaching men. One of the troopers went down. The three remaining lawmen had weapons drawn, but were aware of the crewman in the line of fire.

The hesitation gave Larkin the opening he needed to grab the crewman and drag him toward the plane. "Get back! I want the pilot now! I'm leaving here, and you can't stop me!" Michael Larkin crept closer to the plane, forcing the frightened crewman to walk sideways with him.

The driver, sensing he was being left behind to fight it out, fired again and moved toward the plane. The second trooper returned fire and his bullet hit the man's chest. The driver fell backward onto the concrete and his gun slid away from him. He was no longer a threat.

Larkin raised his gun and fired at Warfel. A sharp pain went through the detective's right shoulder, and his gun fell from his hand. Larkin continued to back up onto the plane with a firm grip on his hostage.

Captain Meyers ran to Detective Warfel. The wound in Tom's shoulder was seeping blood, but slowly, a good sign that no blood vessel had been nicked. "Tom, do you think you can keep pressure on your shoulder until help arrives?"

"Don't worry about me; I'm not about to let this scumbag take me out. Just go get him!"

Meyers smiled. "Roger that!"

An ambulance had already been summoned when the KSP trooper was shot, so Meyers directed his one remaining trooper to go around the jet and approach from the back. Meyers would proceed from the nose.

Meyers made an attempt to reason with Larkin. "Dr. Larkin, you can't escape. Let the crewman go, and come out with your hands up!"

Larkin didn't answer from inside the aircraft.

Wallace tried again. Larkin! Give it up!"

From inside the jet, Larkin made his demands.

"I want a pilot here now, and make sure the gas tank is full! You have twenty minutes to get a pilot here and have us ready to take off or this guy will come back to you with a few extra holes in him!"

Meyers was about to answer when, from behind him, additional law enforcement officers arrived on the scene. Luke Brown, one of the men arrested in connection with the human trafficking, had been brought to the scene, too. Meyers didn't have long to wait to find out why the prisoner was there.

"Captain, I know you have no reason to trust me, but I think I can help out in this situation."

"Help? How?" Wallace asked.

"I'm a licensed pilot. I've flown this aircraft for Dr. Larkin several times. I could board and tell him that I eluded capture when you intercepted the van carrying the girls. It would be a perfectly natural thing for me to come here. It would be my means of escape too. I could pretend I didn't know Larkin and simply be the pilot you found for this assignment."

Meyers considered the offer. "He won't buy it, and what makes you think I trust you?"

"Look, I want to help. I didn't want to work for Michael Larkin. I was just an independent pilot hiring out for private flights. This would give me a chance to do something to bring this guy down."

"It's too dangerous; I can't risk the life of a civilian. Besides, I need an officer in there to disarm and arrest Larkin."

"I understand, and I know how we can do that. I always fly with a co-pilot, and Larkin knows that. One of your guys can come on board with me."

"I'll think about it," Wallace replied. He turned to one of the officers standing nearby. "Where are we

289

on finding another pilot?"

"No one so far. It's been a busy day here. There was some kind of business retreat at the lake, and all the bigwigs have been flying home today. The airport manager told me he probably couldn't get a pilot here until tomorrow morning, at the earliest."

The conversation was interrupted as ambulances arrived to transport the state trooper and Warfel to the hospital. Both men were conscious and alert. Meyers walked over to the stretchers and stood between them. "Fellas, I'm sorry you both took a bullet. You'll be taken to the hospital in London, and I'll catch up with you there. Try not to be too hard on the nurses," he added with a twinkle in his eye.

The trooper gave a faint smile just before closing his eyes. He had been given morphine to ease his pain.

Warfel, fighting his own battle with pain, looked up at Meyers. "You got it, now go get Larkin!"

The short interlude had given Meyers a chance to consider Brown's offer. He didn't see that he had any choice, but this had to be orchestrated down to the second. He turned to the officers gathered behind him. "Do any of you have any experience piloting an aircraft—any aircraft?"

One man spoke up, "my brother has a single engine prop plane. I'm not licensed or anything, but I've gone with him on many fishing trips to Canada in his plane. I know the controls and the general idea of how to pilot. Of course, this is no prop plane."

"No, it isn't, but that might be good enough to carry this off. Are you willing to accompany Mr. Brown onto this aircraft? I needn't tell you that this is a dangerous assignment."

"Sir, I have three daughters and a wife I hold

290

dearer than anything in this world. I don't know how I would feel if one of them had been kidnapped and sold to the highest bidder for prostitution. I'm willing to do whatever we can to arrest this guy."

"Well said. Okay, let's put together a plan—quickly. We'll only get one chance at this. Go ahead and let the tug pull the jet out of the hanger; it'll show Larkin good faith on our part."

Fifteen minutes later, the fueling had been completed, and Luke Brown, followed by trooper Danny Broughton, boarded the jet. Larkin met them at the door. "Brown! What are you doing here?"

Luke kept his voice low. "Michael, I managed to get away. Jake and Bob weren't as lucky. I hitched a ride here thinking you might need me to fly you out of here. It gets me clear of this mess, too."

Larkin narrowed his eyes and glared at Brown. Luke's military training helped him keep a calm demeanor although his heart was racing.

"Who's this?" Larkin asked as he tilted his head toward Officer Broughton. Danny had changed into a set of overalls provided by the airport.

"Name is Broughton, sir, Danny Broughton. I'm the co-pilot today. Luke told me this might be a long flight and said he could use some help."

Larkin accepted the explanation but insisted on patting Danny down. Satisfied that Danny had no weapon, he waved his own weapon and barked orders. "Close that door and let's get out of here!"

Luke nodded and led the way to the cockpit. He donned his headset as Danny assumed the co-pilot's seat and picked up the pre-flight checklist. As he read the items, Luke checked out each system, preparing for takeoff, attempting to make the pre-flight tasks as routine as possible. The result was all Brown could have hoped for; Larkin seemed to be relaxing.

Finally, Danny addressed his passenger. "Doc, it's time for you take your seat and buckle in—same for your, uh, guest. We'll take off as soon as we get clearance from the tower. I'm just going to taxi out on the runway and get in position."

Larkin nodded without comment and followed the directions. From his seat he could see the two men at the controls. The next move would be critical. Meyers had anticipated that his trooper would be searched for a weapon, so Brown had carried Broughton's weapon on board in a leg holster. It was a calculated risk, given the fact that Brown was under arrest for a felony, but Meyers knew it could save the trooper's life.

Brown flipped a switch, causing an alarm to sound on the control panel.

"What's that?" Larkin demanded.

"It's just the door sensor; Broughton's going to check it out. I'm sure it's nothing; we probably just didn't get it shut properly."

Larkin didn't reply, but he pulled out his gun. He wasn't taking any chances.

Broughton released his seatbelt and stood. He leaned over Brown and pointed at the control panel as he asked a question. Brown pulled the revolver out of the leg holster and handed it to the trooper. The next moments would either result in Larkin's arrest, or Broughton's death.

Danny Broughton stood up straight, but kept his body slightly turned with the gun held behind him. He refrained from making eye contact with Larkin as he made his way to the door. With his left hand, he

292

checked the door's locking mechanism. As he re-engaged the door's lock, Brown turned off the alarm. To anyone watching, it would appear that Broughton had fixed the problem.

Larkin, satisfied that the co-pilot was heading back to his seat, lowered his weapon. In that instant, Danny turned and aimed his gun at Larkin. The kidnapped crewman sitting next to Larkin drew in a breath, but quickly realized what was happening. As Larkin reached for his weapon, the crewman knocked it from his hand and got in a punch to his kidnapper's jaw.

Danny instructed the crewman to kick Larkin's gun away. Brown shut down the jet's engines and rushed to open the door. He signaled to Meyers that Larkin was contained.

Within minutes, the notorious Dr. Larkin was handcuffed and placed in a state trooper's car. It was over.

## Twenty-Nine

Six weeks later, Tom Warfel parked his car outside Mac's farmhouse. Festive Christmas lights were hung along the large front porch and a holly wreath adorned the door. Tom walked to the passenger side of his car and opened the door for Katie.

"I'm looking forward to meeting all your new friends, Tom."

Tom smiled. "I know you'll like them; they are terrific people." Before Tom could knock on the front door, Mac opened it and welcomed the couple.

"Hi, Tom, I'm glad you guys could make it! This must be Katie."

"Yes, this is my lovely wife. She has heard so much about your guys that she had to come meet you to see if all the stories are true," Tom joked.

"Welcome, Katie! Come in so I can introduce you to everyone."

Katie and Tom were led into the family room where a large blue spruce tree stood in a corner. It had been decorated with gold and cream-colored ornaments. A garland of matching ribbon threaded its way through the branches. Twinkling lights set off the decorations and were reflected in the shiny ornaments.

Sam and Sarah stepped forward with Mary to greet the new arrivals. Sarah stowed their coats in the hall closet, and Sam took drink orders. Twenty minutes later, Aggie emerged from the kitchen to announce that dinner was ready, and the couples made their way to the dining room.

Katie felt at home almost immediately. Conversation during dinner was light as she and Tom learned about Sam and Sarah's equine therapy program for foster children. Mary spoke up, "Sarah is also an accomplished author. I have a strong suspicion she will write a book about Dr. Larkin and his criminal organization."

"It would make one heck of a story, that's for sure," Mac agreed.

Sarah smiled. "I agree; it could be a riveting novel, but what I don't understand is why he did it. He was a very successful and reasonably well-to-do surgeon. Why would he risk all he had worked for by engaging in such heinous behavior? I shudder every time I think of those poor women and girls, not to mention how close we came to being killed by his goons."

Tom laid his dessert fork aside and swallowed his last bite of cake. "Sarah, I've asked myself the same question over and over. I guess because it was so inconceivable, I didn't consider him a likely suspect for a long time. His attorney plans to use a defense of diminished capacity at trial. While that may seem far-fetched, it isn't too much of a stretch to believe that only someone mentally ill could do all the things he did."

"Will he have psychological testing?" Mary asked.

"Yes," Tom answered, "as a matter of fact, he was examined by two independent psychiatrists just this week. Both agree that he exhibits a strong sociopathic personality. He has no compassion, no empathy. Added to that, he also has an overdeveloped ego. In his mind, he is smarter than everyone else. His criminal pursuits gave him power over others, and he congratulated himself on how clever he was to avoid detection while he led a double life."

Mac shook his head. "Poor Cora, she didn't have a chance, did she?"

"Cora found herself caught between Rebecca Dorland's greed and Michael Larkin's insatiable desire for power. Few people could escape unscathed," Tom replied.

The table went silent as memory of Cora permeated the room. Mac broke the silence as he proposed a toast. "To Cora, may she now rest in peace."

"To Cora!" was the response from everyone.

"How is Detective Samuels progressing, Tom?" Mary asked.

"He's doing very well. He should be back to work after the first of the year," Tom explained. His face took on a darker countenance. "I have regrets about how that night went down. I should have set it up differently."

Katie placed her hand over Tom's as it rested in his lap. He gave a squeeze in response. Mac spoke up, "Tom, we all have perfect vision in the rear-view mirror. We handle situations as they come, the best way we can."

"I know; you're right. My brain says the same thing, but my gut usually wins out," Tom said ruefully.

"You wouldn't be human otherwise," Mac agreed. "Why don't we move to the family room?"

Mary took orders for tea and coffee. Sarah joined her in the kitchen and acknowledged Aggie who had started washing dishes at the sink. Sarah turned to Mary and quietly asked, "Did it bother you when Mac proposed the toast to Cora?"

"Sarah, I could be one of those wives who find fault and take offense easily. I think I did that in my first marriage. Time and the experience of living have taught me that there is enough love to go around. I know Mac loves me, and that's enough for me. I think his feelings for Cora have a lot to do with feelings of guilt. Mac is the type of man who takes responsibility for everything. He takes it personally when something doesn't go right. So, I allow him his memories of Cora, but I know the love he has to give now is mine. I have never doubted it."

"That is so beautiful, Mary. We've all been through so much with this tragedy. I suppose you're right; we need to move forward and find the good each day and not be overwhelmed by the past. Thanks, I believe I've just had a life lesson."

The two women joined the group in the family room. Sarah put her arm around Sam and gave a gentle squeeze. Sam turned to her.

"What?"

Sarah looked into Sam's brown eyes and smiled. "I guess this is as good a time as any to tell you that we need to move Anna to the larger bedroom across the hall."

Sam's eyes widened. "And, why do we need to do that?"

"Well, because we'll be needing the nursery again next summer!"

Sam pulled Sarah into his arms and held her close. The group around them fell silent as they watched the display with curiosity.

Sam turned to his friends. "I'd like to make another toast. Sarah just informed me that our little family will have a new member soon. So, let's make a toast to Sarah and our new baby!"

Everyone surrounded the couple to congratulate them. It was a perfect end to the evening. All feelings of guilt and regret were put aside as they now had a new life to celebrate. The past had taught them lessons, but the future held new promise. It was time to move on.